This is a work of fiction.
Names, characters, places, and incidents either
are the product of the author's imagination or
are used fictitiously. Any resemblance to
actual persons, living or dead, events or locales
is entirely coincidental.

Saddlebrook

Saddlebrook

The time has come for a change of pace, thoughts mixed with emotions have developed a need for immediate attention to make a change. Jack has concluded that the segment of his life that he is in is now over and it is time to start living as Matthew McConaughey would say. The place that was once his home no longer exists as for the heart is no longer there. Home is where the heart is and currently Jack has no ties to his current community anymore. Young entrepreneur Jack who has been self-employed since he was 19 years old running a small blue collar trash company that he started in the back of his pickup truck and after a dramatic break up with his ex-fiancé famous equestrian Isabella, he has decided to make a life of his own. The city life of waking up, taking the elevator to the bottom floor of the skyscraper apartment in downtown New York City to the garage to start up his Porsche Boxster, drive it through traffic 3 miles away to his industrial storage yard to check in on his employees before they start up the four trash trucks for their 4 am shifts was a never-ending cycle. Each day, every day. Wake up press the coffee button on the Keurig, take coffee with him as he goes to work, drink it on the way to work hold it in his left hand while driving because the Boxster has no cup holders. Get to work, finish coffee, throw coffee in the trash can. Sit laugh with the staff members of Jack's trash company about whatever shop talk is for the day. His staff goes out for the day dumping all the residential trash for the citizens who signed up for their service, once his staff leaves the yard for the day, Jack answers the company's business phone line till about 5pm, clocks out of work for the day, then goes home and there is nothing left to do. Usually, Jack when he was in a relationship with Isabella, he would duck out of work early at 3pm, switch the company calls to his cell phone and zip the Porsche up to North Salem, NY to where Isabella takes her horse lessons to go watch. The peacefulness of being out of the city and around the animals is soothing even if it was only for an hour or two being there and filled with Isabella gossiping about how her main competitor Georgina is so much worse than she is. Jack's ex-fiancé would always talk about how Georgina, how she gets all the publicity because her father is a rich successful businessman. Now that Isabella has left Jack and their future marriage behind, there is so much free time in Jack's schedule after work! It is time to focus on new beginnings and moving forward. Developing a new life and figuring out what the meaning of life is! There is only going to be one chance at this. After watching the history channel and TV on how to live off the grid, how to live without electricity. How to make a homestead, how to make a cabin, what equipment is needed, how to cook and how to heat a homemade cabin during the cold winter months and how to make it happen! It is now time to put it to the test after Jack spent most of his whole life watching this on TV, he is excited to try it out to see if he can accomplish this task! Jack was searching online for properties for sale and found a 100-acre parcel for sale in Upstate New York just 25 minutes west of Saratoga Springs for only $300,000, which is a great deal for the area. The property consists of a 500' elevation difference between the bottom to the top of it! Jack considered this a perfect starter homestead property for him, because if it fails, he can hang out in Saratoga Springs or up at Lake George and get a hotel or rent an apartment there! Also, it is far enough from North Salem, NY so he can get away from his ex-fiancé, the evil Isabella.

Later that day, Jack called the listing agent and asked if it was still available. The real estate agent said it was and Jack asked if he would be okay with meeting with Jack's real estate agent, and if he liked it can show the realtor proof of funds that it would be a cash purchase that week as the money is sitting in his bank account as we speak. The agent was interested, Jack and the Realtor made a deal, and the property was purchased. Jack is coming into this new homestead cabin build, with no real plan just to play it by ear and who knows what is going to be built, just more of a hobby project for Jack. However, Jack has no real hands-on construction experience under his belt. A few laboring jobs and a few household projects around previous properties he has owned. So, this is going to be exciting, let's do this! Logistics are now to be planned, the business Jack owns that brings in almost 100% of his income, is located 3.5 hours away from where this new project is at! Jack has been going into his business every morning for years! Seeing the same guys every morning, every day. Jack has been very consistent in his work! Jack talked to his main guy who can handle a lot of responsibility in his business and before starting the new project, Jack made sure to ask if he was able to step up to be a manager as Jack is going to be running his company remotely from his new property that he purchased. Main guy (Foreman) at work takes the extra responsibility as well as an extra pay raise to compensate for the more work and the Foreman at work is appreciative of the raise at work!

Jack proceeds North to the new property he purchased near Saratoga Springs. The property sale closed and the following week on Monday, Jack will go North to evaluate for the next step, where should he build the cabin on the site, he will have to find a water source, where do they use the bathroom? All the things you must think about when you're not in the city and your way out in the country! Jack wakes up early in the morning for his regular routine, presses the coffee maker button, but instead of going into work in the morning to check in on his staff, he calls his manager on his way to the West Saratoga

Springs property to check in to make sure the Foreman (Jack's manager of the trash company) doesn't need anything for their daily operations.

The Porsche Boxster is running great today with the coffee in the left hand due to no cup holders. The Boxster is hitting its revs perfectly, yearning to hit its 6,000 rpms sweet spot that it loves to be at every gear where the exhaust will open-up. The tight winding roads that are paved nicely, the Porsche Boxster has new tires that can grip the road well and excels in the corner. As you approach the two laned highway coming into the next slight corner you can see the car ahead slowing down for the corner. However, going into fourth gear cruising low RPMs approaching the turn, confidence dwells in the driver of this machine and as the person in the slow lane is slowing down for the corner to come into, the Porsche Boxster opens-up, the confidence in the Boxster is in the cornering, it is not a top speed animal, it is not an acceleration monster. But it is a cornering lover. As Jack is coming up to a corner in his Porsche Boxster, he sees a car in front in the slow lane in the right lane, the cars rear brake lights are coming on, Jack puts the Porsche's left hand turn signal on as he merges into left lane going into the corner at 50 mph (caution sign suggested slow to 35 mph) , Jack and the Porsche are sitting around 4,000 rpm in 4th gear at 50mph now in the fast lane just approaching the back of the left bumper of the car in slow lane. The Porsche Boxster cruising coming into the corner at the 50 mph, with the RPMs sitting low in 4th gear, just passing the car moving slow in the left lane, Jack drops the Boxster into third gear and as he moves the shifter down a gear, before he releases the clutch lever, Jack revs high by putting the gas pedal down in between gears to hit the engine at a high rev at the top of 3rd gear, this opens up the exhaust, bringing the engine out revving it high, the Porsche accelerates to be tip toeing the line to almost loosing traction in the corner. With one gentle movement of the gas pedal, Jack can spin the rear wheels just enough to feel where the traction grip is at to see the limit of this corner in how the type of asphalt on the road is lining up with the type of tire that is on the Boxster. In between the gears, switching from bottom of 4th to the top of 3rd

the car's RPM Gauge moved from 3,500 RPMs to 6,000 RPMs, which makes the Porsche just hug the corner beautifully and the car pushing out of this nice flowy corner exiting it now looking down at the speedometer and tach traveling at 70 mph with rpms at 6,500 just below recommended shift for that car at 7,000 rpm. It hugs the turn, on the edge of traction and can feel it. Just passing 70mph, the car that Jack passed in the corner is long gone in the rear-view mirror as they took the 35-mph recommended speed limit for that corner. And hugging, hugging, holding, holding 6,500 RPM smooth throttle cruising, the corner is coming to an end. Jack revs it up to the max 7,000 RPM the car should be at, then he shifts the Porsche Boxster into 4th gear and then keeps the car in the low rev bottom-middle of 4th gear which puts him back to highway cruising speed gas mileage saving and at a 70 mile per hour cruising speed. It doesn't make sense to push the Boxster too hard on this 3.5-hour drive to this unknown living site that Jack is driving too that he just bought. Jack must keep the adrenaline down for the time being as energy conservation may be very important coming up. The drive from

NYC to West Saratoga Springs is just utterly beautiful, it is around April time, the trees are just starting to blossom and turning green. The energy is in the air as the economy improves and people are willing to spend money again, because the cold winter months are coming to an end. The landscaping is starting to turn green again, the mulch and the buildings are all being spruced up from the landscapers. Time is great, time is happy, times are good. Jack is enjoying life, focusing on the next step, embracing the changes that are going to be happening in his life. He is going into this next stage of his life very humble, with an open mind. Driving a Porsche of course! He is getting close to the property he has bought maybe about an hour away; the gauge is starting to get low for fuel. Keeping an eye out for an exit to pull over, sit down, fill up on 93 fuel and get a coffee. Check his phone to see if the manager needs anything for the day. Perhaps his manager needs supplies or something he must order for the business. Jack exits off the main highway, to a beautiful gas station! Dunkin donuts and gas all at the same spot! Yay perfect, $75 fills the Boxster's tank full, after filling the car's gas tank with fuel, he pulls it up to the parking area and walks inside of the Dunkin donuts at the gas station to order the ice caramel coffee medium with three cream three sugars. Once Jack ordered his coffee, he walked over to the lounge section, and it looked like very similar people to Jack here! Other New Yorkers basically from the city who come up here to get away from the city. Very cool! Observation noted.

So anyways, Jack proceeds to check his business email and for any missed voicemails. Few voicemails were followed up by emails, he opens his email app on his phone to type back to the emails that came in along his drive and quickly, he was all caught up on his work emails. The emails that came in when he was on the road were from a few customers wondering what their service days were for their curbside trash pick-up. Jack sits there feeling a feel of peace that he hasn't felt in a while, sitting at Dunkin Donuts with a nice, iced caramel coffee in his hand, a few other gentlemen there looking like there doing the same thing, either reading the news or checking on their stocks or businesses. Jack receives a phone call. He picks up the phone from the table and sees on the screen the picture of Isabella from her last horse show when she came in second place as it comes up on the screen with her name appearing Isabella <3! After Jack's Fiancé left him, he went through a real rough period, he is starting to get over her and this new project of his has really helped him move on. Jack hasn't thought of her in a while and this is the first time receiving any communications from Isabella in quite some time, kind of curious why she is calling. Also, feeling a little bit of guilt / pressure in having to answer as they did date for almost 5 years and as the phone rang a few times, he finally gave in to answer the phone as his Ex is calling.

Isabella says: (Over the phone) Jack, I'm sorry. Can we work things out, could you come here after work like you used to always do to see me.

Jack didn't respond at first because he is still very surprised that his ex is even calling him. He held there, in aw, a rush of feelings and emotions flooded his brain, he was torn between what to do.

Time passed without a response still spell bound by just everything that is going on. Is this a dream? Did Jack really buy a large property, just pass a car in the fast lane in a corner and really is sitting here at the gas station drinking a coffee randomly because he felt like it on a WEEKDAY?

Isabella goes: Jack are you there? I'm talking to you.

That tone she said and just talked in sent Jack deeper into some relationship flashbacks, where his clear head in this new environment can pick up every negative thing that the relationship, he used to be in consisted of.

Out of nowhere, Jack felt like a new person. This hold Isabella had on his life in the past has been broken, freedom has incurred, peace, tranquility exists now and without thinking twice Jack turned into an animal. Sweet, seductive, charismatic.

Jack responds to Isabella: Yeah, Hun I want to see you too, you want to come up to Saratoga

Springs when you get a chance? I'm going to be up here for a bit, I'm starting a fun new project I've always wanted to try since I was a kid and you're welcome to come say hi whenever you'd like! I'd love to see you, Isabella!

Jack knows two things! Isabella almost never leaves home – she has always lived off her parents or someone else – Jack. And that Isabella most likely will not want to see him build a cabin off the grid. Jack has an odd view after this relationship. He feels as there are two types of women, one who helps you build and one who comes around after you have built something. This Isabella, Jack's Ex-Fiancé is not a builder, she comes around after something has been created.

Jack on the other hand, he started a trash company in college with his pickup truck, very humble beginnings. He knew that you start small, keep going and every day just put a little bit more back into the company and over time it grows. Isabella for some reason just can't see how a company can start like that and grow over time. She is just the type that seeks a nice, finished product when it's already done and wants to join then. Very smart of

Jack's thinking, it puts the relationship to rekindle in a good position as it will show her true colors as if she really likes Jack for who he is as a man. Instead of for what assets and properties he currently owns as of now. Things are things, they come and go, they mostly depreciate as they get older. But who you are as an individual your values are very important. Anyways, Isabella responds to Jack's suggestion of her coming to visit him. Here is what she said.

Isabella: Urgh you're always so difficult, blah blah blah blah.

Jack zones out. He has a lot to going on in his head at this time, He is 90% sure that this conversation and answering the phone to his Ex-Fiancé was a horrible idea as the relationship was over when she left Jack for another man.

Isabella is getting impatient she says:

Isabella: Well Jack? Are you coming to see me tonight at 5pm or should I move onto another guy again? What will it be?

Jack still in awe about what is going on. In his head, Jack is like what is going on, this girl crazy.

Jack says to Isabella: I mean I don't really know what you're talking about but yeah let me know we can meet up!

Isabella says in response: blah blah blah blah (more nagging, fortunate to Jack is not his responsibility anymore, whatever she was saying, the conversation was not going to go in the right direction, and he zoned it out) Jack hangs up the phone call, not mad, not angry, just kind of humored, like, nice dodged a bullet on that one. Maybe she'll come around loosen up a little bit down the road! But right now, its coffee time and planning this cabin. Let's go!

There is a gentleman at the Dunkin donuts he is at, an older man dressed in all black, well dressed, one of those fancy velvet looking all black cowboy hats on with $200 line dancing cowboy boots on his feet. This man says to Jack after overhearing the conversation on the phone Jack just had. The old man couldn't really hear the words of Jack's Ex-Fiancé, but he knew exactly how the conversation was going as the old man could hear the high-pitched nagging tone of her voice.

The old man says to Jack: What do you have going on in Saratoga Springs up there, I got some connections there from the past might be able help you.

Jack responds to the old man saying, "I kind of had my realtor buy a 100-acre parcel there that I want to just build a little cabin at for fun ha-ha."

The old man responds with: That's amazing; you know what street it is on by a chance? Because there aren't too many 100-acre parcels for sale up that way recently.

Jack responds to the Old Man saying: Yeah! It is on Saddlebrook Street, that's the name of the street.

The Old man has not even been looking at Jack during this conversation, but he has been drinking his coffee while reading the newspaper, but once Jack said Saddlebrook Street. You can see from the side of his face that the old man goes wide eyed and slowly turns his head toward Jack.

The Old Man says: Are you sure you bought the 100-acre parcel that is for sale on Saddlebrook Street there? Have you walked the property? And where do you think?? you are going to build your cabin?

Jack responds with: You know of the place?

The Old man responds: Yes, I do.

Jack says: no, I haven't walked the property.

Jack is thinking that it is only land so who cares, drop some logs, mill it up make a small log cabin sit by the fire and enjoy the views, sit on social media, and talk to his friends all day when it is finally done!

The Old Man just smiles and says: well, thank God I won't be around for this one, however kid. I am going to send someone to check up on you there in a few weeks. I wish you the best of luck.

Jack is left in suspense and suspicion. Jack is very curious what is all going on here and what the Old Man meant by the words he just said.

Is this still real life? Jack is enjoying the day finishing his coffee.

Jack says to the Old Man: nice to meet you and hope we see each other again one day.

The old man responds with: I hope so too kid, be safe up there.

Jack gets in the Boxster, turns the key and the engine starts right away with a nice vroom sound, He can feel the mid based engine 6" inches behind him while he's in the leather bucket racing seat the vehicle comes with stock. The vibrations from the foreign machine revs differently than any other normal everyday car, it basically massages your back as you drive.

Slowly and in style, Jack drives out of the gas station, looking at the Old Man he just met in the mirror as he watches him drive away. As Jack drives off in the Porsche Boxster, the old man calls his daughter who he hasn't talk to in a year and a half and on the first ring the daughter answers the phone.

The daughter says: Dad are you okay? Is everything okay? I haven't heard from you.

The Old man responds: Darling, I am okay, it has just been hard since your mother has passed away… But I don't want to talk about that at this time, but I need you to do me a favor. Not for me, for Sophia it's what she would have wanted.

The Daughter responds: What is it dad? Just let me know and please let me know where you are, the family misses you.

The Old Man responds: Trust me, I'm going to be coming around very soon. But I just met a man he is going North to Saddlebrook. He is roughly the same age as you and is driving a black Porsche Boxster, slick gel hair, city slicker look.

The Daughter responds: Why he is going to Saddlebrook? No one goes to Saddlebrook anymore, it has been closed well since Mom had to start Chemo for her cancer. And even after that it was bought by a trust company that just holds land and they promised you they wouldn't build anything on it.

The Old man responds: Listen to me, this man from New York City must have just purchased the property from the trust, because they most likely just wanted to get rid of it and he wants to log it and build a cabin on the top, what Sophia and I built with our own two hands, Isabella can you help.

The daughter of the Old Man is named Isabella.

The old man says to Isabella: Can you try to steer this young man in the right direction for this property as your mom would see fit.

Isabella responds to her father: What does that mean?

The Old man says: I'm sorry dear, it hurts me too much to think about your mother when she is no longer here with me. Still to this day when something reminds me of her, I'll cry. I trust your judgement dear, and I love you with all my heart.

. . .

Jack is driving now at cruising speed to Saddlebrook Street and an hour passes quickly and Jack pulls into the driveway and notices it's an old ungraded gravel road where the Porsche is near close to bottoming out and it is too risky. This vehicle is not good for the conditions of this driveway. It drives in not even 100 feet into the start of the driveway, and you can hear the little 3" minus rocks of the driveway scrapping the under carriage of the Porsche brush guard and heat shield. As the parts are very expensive on these foreign cars, the car will have to be parked and the property will have to be walked by foot.

Jack is eager, young, agile, it is a new adventure. He is in the adrenaline rush of driving the Porsche and jacked up jittery on all the coffee. Ready for a hike and ready to go. Equipped with a backpack with some water and gas station snacks in it, he gets out of the Porsche and makes his way to the front of the car. He opens the front hood which reveals the front trunk of the Boxster and takes out a few more supplies to add to his backpack.

Jack starts to walk up the driveway noticing it is a steep elevated pathway that he is going to embark on. Right now, fitness is key, Jack has his Apple watch on to track his heart rate for this exercise and the number of footsteps that he is going to be taking. He starts to walk up the driveway, it is very overgrown and looks like it hasn't been used in decades if it has ever been used at all. As he walks up the driveway, it seems that the end of the driveway is nowhere in sight. He proceeds to walk up the hill, timing how long this walk takes. As he walks into the land more, it looks like someone has been here in the past as this driveway has been cut in at approximately 15' wide by some sort of heavy machinery perhaps an excavator or a bulldozer and there are signs of chipping on rocks with manmade machinery. Jack notices that the rocks that are cut aren't cut by normal water deterioration over time. Normal water from runoff through a mountainside on a rock surface will create very smooth long cuts. The cuts in the rock Jack sees are jagged and precision cut. Jack is curious to see how many feet in he has already walked on the property. He looks at his Apple Watch and sees he has gone 1,200 feet in the driveway. He notices what looks to be two football field size areas and each of them are filled with sand on each side of the driveway. Literally the whole side of the hill side is just cut out must have been a 20-acre parcel right here just filled with sand.

Jack is thinking to himself, what the heck is this going on, there's one football field size on the left side and one football size field on the right side of the road driveway, path thing whatever this is. He's walking in and around these football fields areas. Along these areas, Jack notices that bordering these sand football field sized areas are entire tree log lumber laid down which was placed to hold in the sand.

Jack is thinking to himself, what in the heck is this, what can we use this part for? a septic field?

Jack thinks wow I really don't need a 20-acre septic field for my small cabin, anyways it is interesting lets circle back on this at a later time. Jack is experiencing this property for the first time, he marks his territory by peeing in this giant sand box that he bought, Jack thinks to himself, this is my mountain I bought this! I'm a dog, an outdoor dog, I pee where I want, no more city for me! Wow freedom!

In total now, Jack knows he is 1,200 feet into the property that he has walked, and he is still climbing up to the next level of the property. He is starting to notice odd things around the surroundings like initials in trees with hearts around them. This is just all foreign news that he was not expecting about this property. Jack is feeling out of his element, its trees towering over him, not city trees either, we are talking 4' diameter 100' tall. Trees that have never been touched before; this property has never been logged before in some parts. This property is like a nature preserve, with nature still in its wild pristine form.

As Jack has walked deep into this property, now he has a feeling that he is no longer alone. The feeling of being in the city is like you are trying to escape from being around all the people there. Every different person has a different opinion, feelings and then there are pressures from everyone around you. Now that Jack is in the country his entire mindset has changed in a very short amount of time. Instead of how he was thinking of when he was in the city and wanted to get away from everyone, now Jack is wondering if he will get attacked by an animal. Who would he call to come save him? Jack feels and knows that he is outnumbered by all the wildlife animals on this property. Jack has realized now that he has made a huge change in lifestyle. Who he is as a person has changed almost immediately.

At his old location of New York City, it was about saying hi to the right people as he goes down to the elevator. Making sure to go through parking security smiling so they know he is a resident there. In the city, those little things are how you survive. Now, in the country, out here is a different type of survival. In this surrounding, Jack is immersed and his issues that he was facing is no longer a worry for him. His primal instincts as a man have opened. He is connected right now to where he is at. He is grounded and this is a very profound feeling. Sitting there looking at these carvings of initials in the trees, he examines them closely to see what they mean. Maybe this property was owned by a couple? Maybe all their friends came to carve the initials too?

Jack continues his walk up the property, he looks down at his Apple Watch. The footsteps say that now he has walked roughly 2,500 feet into the driveway. It hasn't been all straight up; the driveway has curved once. The general direction is up to the top of the hill. As Jack is walking up the driveway, he notices that it opens again, it looks like another flat graded 20 acres that is done, this part isn't sand its gravel, Jack is surprised how nice of condition it is still in. It looks to be ¾" gravel very flat with old cut up log's kind of like the sand field but cut in sections of 8'. It looks to be laid out very similar to a huge parking lot at like a Walmart or something. On the side of the parking lot there are some old bleachers and although they are not still usable, you could see if they were still usable. It is a clear view of the sand fields down below. What were these sand fields used for and why on Earth does it have enough parking up here on this level for what seems to be able to hold 150 vehicles. This is just so perplexing, Jack thought he was buying 100 acres of untouched land to log, mine out and build a small cabin. It looks like half of this property has already been mined and cleared. Jack has been walking the property for quite some time now and hasn't really gotten far into it, for 2 hours and only 2,500 feet in. He is thinking and learning along the way. Jack is trying to develop a plan of attack for this property. After seeing the current state of the property, he is not sure if he wants to even proceed. Jack is also questioning if he is even on the right parcel that he purchased. Jack checks his phone to make a phone call to his realtor but decides not to make the phone call. Jack decides to try to walk as much as he can and afterward will dwell on the logistics for this project and how to move forward. He proceeds to walk up to the top of the driveway; it is set all the way back on the property where it is all graded out flowing overgrown grass like a massive pasture with a structure on the site at the end of the driveway. Jack walks closer to the structure and notices that there is already a cabin on the site at the back.

Jack starts to think that someone is playing a prank on him. He is not sure how to feel about this whole situation, but the rustic vibe is exactly what he was going for. This is one heck of an experience and as he reaches the front porch of the cabin, he sees that it is all handmade, hand milled wood from the site and there are still some nice pieces. Jack sees that this property needs work. He walks up to the cabin and notices that his feet are about to fall through the porch, the front doorknob rusted to the point of not functioning, all the windows need to be replaced. The entire cabin needs full rehab. Jack turns around from the front door toward the porch and sees the view from the front porch. Where this cabin was built, it must be one of the highest elevation points in the town as Jack can see for miles. The weirdest thing is from the front porch of the cabin, Jack can see all the different levels of the driveway, but when Jack was walking up the property he couldn't see the cabin. Jack is perplexed about why you can't see the cabin from the bottom of the driveway as you're walking up, but when you are at the top of the property, at the cabin you can see the bottom of the driveway. It is an anomaly.

Jacks plan of attack for his first day being on his new property was to count the diameter and height of workable trees on the property. He was going to write a list of what will be usable on site for board length cuts between hard and soft woods. Softs for the fast work, structural and hard woods for the counters and finish pieces. Jack was crossing his fingers for an abundance of hemlock wood for easy workability and stability now. Hemlock has a very short drying period. But after the walk, he just went on, it changed his entire plan. It seems the land has been worked and logged already. However, this may be in his favor. Jack is a businessman; he knows the consequences of buying things sight unseen. The realtor has helped him buy over 8 properties now and this will be interesting to see what is going on. The realtor most likely acted in his best interest. Jack thinks to himself that he has seen a good amount for the day and calls it quits for the day! He is contemplating going back to the city for a few weeks to figure out what to do with the property. Jack thinks to call a logging company and order some already milled lumber and to bulldoze the old house to start a new construction home from scratch. Maybe the old foundation could still hold strong, Jack will see if it'll support the metal tracks as its bulldozed by the heavy piece of iron.

As Jack enjoys the nice peaceful walk down to the bottom of the driveway, Jack starts eating his gas station snacks out of his backpack. Jack, still being new to the mountain lifestyle, he throws his half-eaten egg muffin sandwich that he didn't finish eating on the side of his driveway. He proceeds to walk back down the hill at an even 120 BPM heart rate as his Apple Watch dings that he is at cardio heart rate pace for him. He is now back down to the Porsche Boxster where you can see the main road. There is an elderly couple that are about the same age as the Old Man that Jack met at the gas station. The elderly couple weren't really walking by Jack's driveway entrance, they were standing holding hands. The husband is holding his wife close with her head close to his chest and Jack notices that she is crying while she is looking Jack in the eye as he is about to get into his car. The woman didn't have a cry of anger, or sadness, more of a cry of nostalgia and reminiscence. Jack doesn't say anything. He gets in the car minding his own business. There are not many people in this area, so Jack needs everyone to be on his side around his new property in case something happens such as getting hurt. The closest police department and paramedics are over a half an hour driveway away from Saddlebrook Street. The look in the faces from the couple Jack just saw is very mysterious to Jack. He is focusing on trying to pinpoint the feeling that he felt and what this couple was thinking about when he saw them standing outside his driveway. As Jack is driving away, he keeps an eye on the rear-view mirror at the couple. Jack thinks maybe they are neighbors and are curious to what is going on? As Jack drives away he sees on the side of the road about a block, maybe two blocks away a parked vehicle with no one inside and no driveways nearby. It's a Chevy Tahoe, a nice-looking luxury vehicle. It looks to be around the year 2011 for it age. Jack thinks to himself that the Chevy Tahoe would probably be able to get up the driveway that his Porsche can't. Jack figures this Chevy Tahoe is from the couple he saw outside of his driveway. Jack goes about his day and starts to plan what he is going to do for the night. Jack was contemplating going back to New York City to his condo but decided to stay in town by his property. He types in on his phone to search for local hotels nearby. Jack picks a mid-range priced hotel to stay at and starts driving toward the hotel. Jack pulls into the hotel checks in and it's around 4pm currently. Jack knows he will have to eat at around 6pm. He asks the counter staff member at the hotel what there is to do around this area on the weekend. Front desk staff member suggests while looking him up and down. She says for you, your age… go get a hat, some jeans and some sort of boots on, take those dress shoes off and go to The Ranch. It's a local bar and it has country line dancing; it'll be a good time. The front desk staff member also throws in that it is the only place nearby anyways. Jack goes up to his hotel room to take a quick power nap before going out for an hour or two.

…

While Jack is checking into his hotel room for the night, taking a nap before he goes to the local country bar. Isabella the daughter of the Old Man is trying to figure out how to make her father proud. She takes out her cell phone to make some phone calls. She calls any contacts of her mother or father that she can find. Isabella got a hold of a couple and each of them all greeted her with HEY Isabella! Long time no see, how's your father? It is a hard question for Isabella to answer as she tries to dodge the question every time.

Isabella says do you know anything about this new guy who bought Saddlebrook? One of the people who she called responds with: No, no, no someone bought that place after?... Well, you know. It's closed. Did someone pay the asking price for what that land was listed for sale?

Isabella put the feelers out to about 10 contacts and left each person she got in contact saying: please if you hear of anything give me a call back. This is urgent, my dad called me.

Each of them basically responded the same way. Whoa, what? Your dad. called you? Where is he? What is he doing now? I haven't seen or heard from him since Sophia's… passing…

Isabella said: look I can't talk about this, but if you hear anything please let me know. My dad asked me for my help on this.

Isabella was a little sad that she couldn't find anything out, she thought to herself, work is going well, and I can do most of it remotely anyways. She has enough savings that if she were to get fired for telling her boss that she is going to start working remotely, it wouldn't put herself in a bad financial position if she did lose her current job. It is around 4pm and Isabella thinks to herself okay we're going south to Saratoga Spring area. As she packs a suitcase, she thinks about what she should wear, how will she meet this new Saddlebrook guy. She is all packed up and ready to go. She grabs a coffee to go, puts it in her cup holder of her nice Honda CRV and starts to head south on the highway from her apartment in Lake George area! She brings with her what she needs, puts it all in the trunk in the back of her Honda CRV and off to Saratoga Springs she goes. Isabella books a hotel near the Saddlebrook property because her plan is to stay in town to go by the Old Saddlebrook property every day until she sees the new owner there. As Isabella drives South on the highway, she receives a call from a phone number that looks familiar, probably one of the people she just called. Isabella answers the phone and the woman on the other end of the phone call says: Isabella, guess what.

Isabella responds with: What.?

The woman on the phone says: Isabella you'll never get this – my friend Judy called me after I got off the phone with you and told me something. Judy said that she thought she saw your dad at the old Saddle Brook property. Judy wasn't sure but it looked just like a car that your dad would have been driving in the past so Judy and her husband were standing nearby seeing if anyone would come to the vehicle because they didn't even know if they would recognize seeing your dad anymore because it has been so long. As they were waiting, a young man came to the vehicle and Judy couldn't help but cry when she saw him because he reminded her of your father! He looked exactly like what your father looked like perhaps 30 years ago!

Isabella responds to the woman: Do you have Judy's phone number????

The woman responds with: No, no, no I don't think I should give that out. Judy's husband had to finish telling me the story because she was crying while trying to tell her what she saw there, there are just so many emotions tied to that property for our generation since Sophia has passed, it just hurts us to even think about it. So many good times, so many good times came out of that place. But here's something for you Isabella, Judy says this guy is in a Black Porsche Boxster.

Isabella says: Well, that's not going to help he's probably already back in the city now.

The woman responds to Isabella: Well, it'll be the only Black Porsche Boxster that is covered in dirt in the back from driving it offroad today.

Isabella gets a hotel for the night near Saratoga Springs, she made sure to pack her boots, her cowgirl outfit, her hat, and she knows a few steps to a few line dances at The Ranch. She takes a nap and after about a couple hours, she heads down to the local popular bar called The Ranch. (The same bar that the front desk staff member told Jack about) She drives down to The Ranch in her CRV, as she pulls into the parking lot, even with all the cars packed there, she notices the Black Porsche Boxster with mud all along the rear fender.

Isabella starts getting a little nervous. She checks the mirror making sure no one sees her looking at herself. Isabella makes sure that her make up is looking great and her hair is how she wants it to look. The Ranch (The country bar) doesn't look too busy, so she sits at a table and waits for the hostess and orders a side salad trying to figure out what the gentleman she heard about on the phone looks like. All that Isabella knows is what he drives and that he probably looks like a city boy. She knows that there is mud on the Black Porsche Boxster, so there might be mud on the man's shoes/boots as well. She assumes that he is not from around the area so he probably doesn't have too many friends that will be coming up to him to say hello.

Isabella looks towards the bar, and she sees a man at the bar watching the motocross race of Eli Tomac out in first place and he is pretty into the race. Isabella notices that he is alone and there is mud on his shoes, the coat that he is wearing, a nice brand-new jacket. This might be the man. She thinks of a way to get closer to him. Isabella tries to calm her nerves, thinking to herself this is just a guy, guys always hit on her all the time. She should treat this guy the same as any other guy and not to come on too straight forward.

As Isabella is walking toward the bar where Jack is to meet him for the first time, Eli Tomac is in the lead but the second place behind him cuts him off in a turn and Eli Tomac goes down hard getting launched off his dirt bike in a corner. Eli Tomac on the television gets back up and Jack says: thank God go Tomac he's okay! Then after saying that, Jack goes back to eating his buffalo chicken wings, he ordered from the bar. Isabella picked up that Jack must like dirt bikes. She leans into the bartender who immediately notices this beautiful woman and basically stops who he was serving. The bartender says: hello miss would you like anything? Isabella, (having to give the perfect first impression to Jack) says to the bartender: Yes, please can I get an Expresso Martini. Jack notices her and thinks that was an interesting drink of choice. She must be wanting to stay up all night tonight or had a rough day today. He circles back to the television to watch the dirt bikes.
Isabella says to Jack: What's on TV?
Jack responds to Isabella: Dirt bike racing, this is called Supercross.
Isabella responds to Jack: Do you race?

Jack responds: Oh yeah, I race (with a smile on his face)

Isabella is curious about this dirt bike racing Jack does and she thinks to herself that this is the first man she has met who races dirt bikes.

Isabella says to herself that she has to stay focused, she has to control this conversation, short and sweet, everlasting, leave impression, then leave after getting his phone number. Once she gets his phone number, her plan is to call him in a few days.

Isabella comes up with this: Well anyways! You seem very interesting, what's your name!

Jack responds with: Thanks! My name is Jack, what's your name?

Isabella responds by saying: My name is Isabella.

After she said that, Jack almost spit up the drink he was drinking.

Isabella says: What? What's wrong?

Jack responds with: (Laughing) Nothing, nothing at all, I just try to stay away from any girls with the name of Isabella.

(Jack hears the country music coming on in the other room) then says: it was nice meeting you! (As he starts walking away)

Jack waves goodbye to Isabella and veers his attention toward the line dancing, curious to how this dancing goes, and it looks fun! It looks like a great workout. Isabella watches as Jack's attention is not on her and he basically walked the other way. He wasn't rude to Isabella, but she thought that the entire conversation would go in a completely different direction than it did. Not sure what to think, she asks the bartender and waitress who served her just to make sure she is paid in full and she pays what's left of the tab then goes out to her car to call it a night. She decides to go back to her hotel room and think about what happened between her and Jack's interaction at the bar. For some reason, she can't help but shed a tear down the side of her cheek. Not having control over the situation has brought a moment of sadness over her, not about Jack, but more about missing her mother and the Saddlebrook property where people loved to spend time at.

. . .

Back to The Ranch at the dance floor, everyone on the line dancing dance floor took a liking to Jack and the next thing he knows is they are doing the dances extra slow for him for the first night to get him involved to come around more. Jack is thinking wow just wow, he has never been accepted in anything as cool as this! And Wow! What a great work out, he's drenched in sweat. Does a few more dances, a couple hours pass, and it is already time for Jack to go back to the hotel to go to sleep for the night. As he leaves, he grabs his jacket and heads out to his car to drive back to his hotel for the night. As he is pulling in to where his hotel is, he parks the Porsche in an open parking spot. As he is pulling in, Isabella was looking outside the window of her hotel and sees Jack's Porsche pull up and park right next to her CRV. It is assuring to her for some reason knowing that life has kind of brought them back together, it is interesting how they are both at the same hotel at the same time. Isabella also knows that it is one of the only hotels of a few that are around in the area. Isabella watches behind the curtain to not be seen checking on him. Jack came back to the hotel at a reasonable hour, not drunk or even tipsy, but he looked happy. There is a pep to his step and he's showing off a few of his new line dancing moves as he walks toward the lobby entrance. This put a good feeling in the air for Isabella.

. . .

The next day, Isabella woke up to the sunrise in the morning, quite early, and looked outside to see what the day looked like and noticed Jack's Porsche was already gone for the day. Isabella thinks to herself, wow he woke up early today. She wonders what he is up to so early. She just met him last night, and let's be honest it was a forced meet, she literally actively pursued him to talk to him. So, she thinks I can't just show up to Saddlebrook because that would be way too much of a coincidence especially because they are staying at the same hotel now too. But maybe Isabella stays another night and Jack is staying another night at the hotel? Isabella figures to wait another day and see if he comes back to the hotel. She could run into him in the lobby as he gets back to see if he says hi to her again.

. . .

Jack heads over to Tractor Supply – Lawn & garden, animal feed / country store and buys some work boots that would be easy to hike in. He invests in buying a jacket as it is cold in the mornings and in the evenings when working outside. After picking up some new wilderness equipment, Jack heads up to Saddlebrook to see what to do today. He drives in and remembers that the Porsche doesn't make it to the sand field, he says well maybe that's one thing we can do today. Jack parks the Porsche where he parked the first time he came, and he hiked up the hill to where the sand fields are. Standing in one spot he looks over the sand fields and takes a drawing out of his pocket.

The night before at The Ranch, before Isabella got to the bar, Jack was hand drawing a little dirt bike track he wants to attempt to build where the sand is, he used the race he was watching on the TV at the bar as an outline to make the track like. The drawing was already folded up and put in his pocket before Isabella got to the bar that night when they first met.

As Jack stands there looking over this awesome soon-to-be place, he is ready. This will be exciting, he wants a jump between the field on the left and the field on the right, what separates the two fields is the driveway in the middle. Jack wants a dirt bike jump to jump right over the driveway on his dirt bike.

Jack figures that when friends come over to hang out, Jack can jump over their cars as they pull into the driveway on his dirt bike. This is what we will do today, Jack thinks. A bulldozer will be perfect for the job. Jack already perk-tested the material from when he peed the last time in the sand fields, so he already knows that this sand will be perfect to rip up and down on his dirt bike. As Jack is walking back down to the designated Porsche Boxster parking area (The farthest he can drive up the driveway in it before it bottoms out hitting rocks), Jack calls the rental company he has used in the past called Sunbelt out of Connecticut to ask how much a rental would be for a small to mid-sized bulldozer. Jack and the Sunbelt Rental company agreed on a price, and they scheduled the delivery of the bulldozer to be delivered. After the phone call, Jack went back into town to the nearest Chevy dealership to see if any car dealers would be interested in trading in his Porsche for a truck. The Porsche of Jack's is awesome, its fast, sporty, fun, but right now it isn't practical, it was hard enough to fit the three or four things Jack bought at Tractor Supply this morning into the tiny trunk of the sport car.

Jack is hoping today that one of the Chevy truck dealerships will do a straight trade for the Porsche Boxster for a decent pickup truck which he could use around his new property.

Jack arrives at the first chevy dealership, a salesman looks at Jack's Boxster and says to him: Honestly, we wouldn't even make an offer on the vehicle. We have no expertise in foreign sports cars and have no interest in reselling them unfortunately. However, you could try going north to Lake George to the Chevy dealership up there. They might be able to help you a little more. Jack says thank you and uses his phone to verify they would be interested in the car he has before making the drive there. Jack calls the phone number off Google that he finds for the location and a salesman answers the phone. The Salesman for the Chevy dealership there says: What kind of Boxster? Is it the S or the regular version? What liter engine?

Jack gives the salesman the information and the salesman says: Yeah, we would be interested, we know a few customers who like those cars, and we would be able to trade it/ buy it / within reason.

Jack drives up to the dealership in Lake George and the salesman shows a few of the trucks that would be in the similar price range for an even trade. The salesman says: We wouldn't be able to do the top of the line lifted, tricked out truck for a trade but any of the other trucks on the lot would do, whatever you want works for us. The salesman also says: You don't want the lifted anyway, those trucks come back every 10,000 miles with shot ball joints and suspension issues. There not good work trucks. The lifts throw off the tow capacity on them too too.

Jack says in response to the salesman: What about that black one back there?

The Salesman says: That truck is a gas job, don't you want a diesel truck? They are worth more when you go to resell it and diesel engines have much more power.

Jack says: Nope, I don't need diesel, gas is fine and can get gas from any gas station, so I like that, but tell me about that black truck I like.

Salesman says: Sure! Yeah, that black truck is a work truck edition, it is a basic truck, no navigation, no sunroof, a regular radio, 4x4 and it does have power windows!

Jack responds with: I'll take it, a nice brand-new simple truck. I like it. Less things to break down!

Salesman says: Alright, ill draw up the bill of sale agreement and have you on your way.

About an hour later, Jack was waving goodbye and heading back toward the Saddlebrook property of his. Once Jack arrived, the truck went up and down the driveway completely fine, not even having to turn the switch on to activate the four-wheel drive 4x4. Driving up the driveway passing the sand fields just picturing the dirt bike jumping over the truck, Jack makes it all the way to the top of the cabin and sets in for the night at the top of the property. He goes through the cabin and finds some old blankets, supplies, essentials to get through the night to sleep there. At night on Jack's property, it is starting to get cold outside, so Jack looks around inside the cabin to see if there is any firewood to put in the fireplace. This fixer upper of a house was in such poor condition when Jack bought it that the electric power utility company disconnected the power to the house until it is safe to put back onto the grid. As of now there is no electricity, lights, heating or running water until the electricity is back and connected.

Jack doesn't see any firewood laying around the house from the past, but he goes out to the pickup truck to drive it around the property looking for any small twigs, logs, anything that will work as firewood for the night. He is successful in the collection of wood debris from around the property, Jack goes back into the cabin to start up the fireplace to keep the cabin warm for the night as he sleeps.

. . .

Jack had a successful day today. He had a nice trip to the local tractor supply store. He figured out some of his plans for the property. He traded the Porsche for a nice reliable and useful pick-up truck then he made a fire to conclude the day. As soon as he started the fire, he was sound to sleep for the night. On the other hand, Isabella from the previous night hadn't seen Jack since the rendezvous at the country bar where she very shortly got to speak with Jack. She knows that she is staying at the same hotel as him, but she hasn't seen him come back to the hotel since he was gone early in the morning. She thought that perhaps around 4-5pm, Jack would drive into the hotel parking lot in his nice Porsche and hear the high rev of its engine as it pulls into the parking spot by where he parked the day before.

However, as the night got later and later, the sun started to go down and it was getting late. It was a work night and Isabella usually likes to go to bed around 10pm during the week. The time passes fast and before you know it, it was already 10pm. Isabella is a little concerned but figured maybe Jack went out again for the night to a local bar or an event. She also thought that if he was working at Saddlebrook, you would think that he would come home to at least shower before going out right?

Isabella falls asleep with a curious mind but tries not to think about Jack too much as they both don't know each other very well. Isabella also has pressure by her dad, how he wants her involved on the Saddlebrook property. Isabella falls asleep and as the sun rises, she walks over to the window, moves the curtain to the right veering out into the parking lot noticing that there is a fog out and no sign of Jack and/or his black Porsche Boxster in the parking lot. With this, Isabella turns on her laptop and checks for any emails to see what her to do list is for her workday today. She goes through everything and in about 30 minutes she is caught back up to speed on her work from when she signed off yesterday at the end of the day. Finishing up, she goes through her head to see if there is anything left missing. Closes her laptop, and goes to her iPhone email, swipe it down making sure she has coverage, and it updates the new emails. Check is done, iPhone Is working well currently to go mobile for the day and take this to the road. Isabella goes to the lobby of the hotel and grabs a quick bite to eat for breakfast and a coffee. Isabella gets into her Honda CRV and makes her way towards the Saddlebrook property to see if perhaps Jack's Porsche is there, probably at the entrance because it can't even go on the driveway to the top of the hill where the house is. Isabella slowly passes down the street of Jack's property trying not to be noticed or seen but still doesn't see Jack's Porsche in the driveway. Isabella was not too sure what to think or how to react but after finishing her drive she was on the loop back to the hotel. Isabella figures that she will go back to the hotel room on the laptop and check in with her co-workers for the day to see how things are going. As Isabella gets back to the hotel, the daily ins and outs of work go as normal. Isabella has the tv on in the background and is sitting on a chair where she can see out the hotel window in case anyone pulls into the parking lot. In the back of her head, she thinks her hair looks nice, make up looks good, was dressed up but not too much to raise suspicion that she is trying too hard to impress Jack.

Isabella keeps going over in her head what to do when Jack pulls into the parking lot. Her daydream is that she'll casually walk down to the lobby to get into the CRV and happen to run into him on the way to her car where she will say hi to him quick. Hoping, he remembers her from The Ranch Country bar the other night. But the moment never comes, it doesn't come today for Isabella, it doesn't come the next day or the next day. Each day Isabella has been waiting for an opportunity to run into Jack, however it is not working. Three days later, Isabella maintains the same schedule, wakes up, food, coffee, emails, texts, gets up to date and takes a drive to Saddlebrook but nothing has changed. Except for on the third day, Isabella receives a phone call from Judy.

Judy says: Hello, my friend talked to you before and she said you would most likely be happy to hear from me if I did call. She gave me your phone number and I wanted to call you to introduce myself, my name is Judy, I was a friend of your mother's Sophia!

Isabella responds: Thank you so much! Yeah, thank you, I did meet the fellow you told your friend about to tell me, the young gentleman in the Black Porsche.

Isabella says to Judy: I met him once a few days ago but I haven't seen him once since then.

Judy responds: Yeah, I have been checking on the property just walking by or driving by as well and I haven't seen any signs of him being around until today. A big bulldozer got dropped off by sunbelt rentals, I'm not sure what his plans are with that big machine, but I sure hope he isn't going to demolish that house up on the top of the property.

Judy says to Isabella: Could you please go by and see what is going on and report back to us please?

Isabella responds: Sure, what do you think I should say to him?

Judy says: You could ask him if he is a contractor and would like to get paid to do some work around my property with his bulldozer? I don't really have a need for any bulldozing around My husband and I's property, but it's a good excuse to go and talk to him! Then it looks like you don't know it's his property too, your friend just is interested in his machine to take out some stumps!

Isabella responds: Yeah, that works!

In the back of Isabella's head, she's wondering if her story is going to add up or if there are any loose ends to make sure it is crystal clear. But this is important and there isn't much time to think things through, so Isabella walks down to the hotel's lobby to go outside to start up the CRV and heads over to Jack's Saddlebrook property. Once she gets there, she notices there is a bulldozer in the driveway, it is a large machine. Going up the driveway is no problem for Isabella's Honda CRV. It has an automatic AWD mechanism that triggers all four tires to spin into four-wheel drive if the car loses traction. It is an impressive feature that is very innovative by

Honda for an affordable price! Isabella is driving up the driveway in her car and as she approaches the middle of the driveway, she sees a black bear on the side of the driveway picking through a leftover McDonald's burger. Isabella can only see the wrapper of the burger and it says McDonald's on it. Isabella says to herself: You can't be throwing trash outside like that in this area, it'll attract the black bears and racoons. She makes it to the cabin at the top of driveway and there is a black Chevy Silverado pickup truck in the driveway. Isabella walks around the house to see if anyone is outside and there is no one to be seen walking around the property. Isabella figures she should try knocking on the front door, as Isabella walks up the front porch stairs, it is very noticeable the condition of the floorboards as they are moving, tweaking, bending and almost screeching as she steps on them. As she reaches out her hand to knock on the door, before she can knock, she hears a voice coming from inside the house saying: Hello! Is someone there? Hello is someone there? Isabella paused for a moment trying to decipher the tone in the man's voice. This doesn't sound like laid back Jack that she is used to. Isabella thinks to herself: Who is that? She responds to the voice with: what are you doing in there?

Not sure what to encounter now, she clearly doesn't think it's Jack with the tone in his voice, it's not his car, has someone broken into his house? It can't be that maybe there is a contractor working at Jack's house. The man inside the house says back to Isabella: Please help, I've been stuck here I can't move. The door is locked, you'll have to break the window.

Isabella goes into survival mode and grabs a rock nearby and throws it through the window, it didn't take much to blast through the glass window. She breaks the glass and reaches her hand in to unlock the dead bolt lock on the door and sees that it is Jack there stuck. A beam in the house must have fallen on him and has been pressed against his chest and the floor for quite a while now. Isabella is not sure what to do next as the beam looks heavy like you need a crane to lift it. Isabella is standing over Jack in awe not saying a word. Jack says to Isabella: The key to my truck is on the nightstand right there can you go to the truck and behind the passenger seat will be the tire repair kit please get it.

Isabella goes to the truck and grabs the repair kit and hands it to Jack. Isabella stands there looking for answers about what to do next. Jack opens the repair kit and there is a little truck jack with a ratchet that moves the jack up to extend. It is used to lift Jack's truck if he ever gets a flat tire on the road. This 3.5-ton jack should be enough to lift this beam, Jack puts the jack next to his waist and starts positioning it the best he can in the current position his body is stuck in. You can tell that Jack has been going over this for quite some time as he has been stuck under this beam for God knows how long. As Jack has put the jack into position, he asks Isabella to finish turning the jack ratchet clockwise a few more rotations as it'll take some force now. It slightly lifts the beam a few inches off the ground, and it allows Jack enough room to get out of the tight position that he was pinned on the floor.

As Jack is freed, he rolls over a few feet over to his back, looks up towards the ceiling as if he has been saved and his life has flashed before his eyes. Isabella is still not sure how long

Jack had been stuck under this beam for and it is not time to try to start a conversation with Jack at this moment. Jack is speechless, still laying on his back with a clear mind, for a while Jack honestly was unsure if he was going to make it past this point in his life. Stuck under a fallen beam in his own house with a dead phone in his pocket.

How life can change so quickly, he looks over and thinks to himself: who is this woman? If she hadn't come to this house at this instance, I perhaps would not have lived. This fallen beam could have been the death of me.

Jack turns his head from looking upward to the ceiling toward Isabella and says to Isabella:

Jack: Thank you

Isabella says to Jack: It was just a coincidence, I'm glad I came when I did.

Jack (coughing into his elbow from developing a cold from the overnight weather with no heat in the house): No, really, I don't care what brought you here or why, but I'm glad to have you been here to save me, no one has really saved me before.

Isabella: the bulldozer outside.

Jack: what?

Isabella: I'm interested in the bulldozer, can me and Judy use it when you're done?

Jack is thinking what is going on? A girl has come to ask about the bulldozer who just saved his life. This is funny, okay sure, this is interesting. Jack is questioning everything that is going on now.

Jack: What do you want to do with the machine?

Isabella: Judy wants me to push stumps.

Jack: Yeah, we should be able to work something out

Isabella: What are you using the bulldozer for? Are you bulldozing this house?

Jack rolls over onto his side with a heavy cough that doesn't stop for two, three, then four coughs. Jack gathers himself and rolls back over to where he was.

Jack: Jumps

Isabella: Jumps? What do you mean jumps?

Jack: I want to make jumps. Two of them for now.

Isabella: And what is a jump?

Jack reluctant to explain what a "jump" is, she wouldn't get it. But she did save his life, so he owes her for that.

Jack: I'm trying to do a big jump on a dirt bike.

Isabella had a little smile on her face and wasn't expecting this childish answer. But she is relieved, number one she is making her father happy she is on the property looking after it. Two she now knows that the house won't be getting demolished today and three is happy to see Jack again.

Isabella: sounds like a plan.

Jack rolls over to his stomach and pushes off the ground with his hands in a push up position to get his feet underneath him to get back on his feet to stand. Once standing, Jack proceeds to walk back to his truck and Isabella is still in the chair just watching Jack in awe as she sees Jack get up very weak and make his way to his truck like he has stuff he's got to get done still. Isabella waits a minute as she knows it might take some time for Jack to make it to his truck. She stands up and walks to the front where Jack parked his car and walks up the truck's driver side window where Jack takes a hair brush out of the center console of the truck and starts brushing his hair in the mirror.

Jack says to Isabella: what day is it today? I look like crap.

Isabella: Its Thursday

Jack: wow that's not good.

Isabella: do you need anything?

Jack (drinking what's left of a water bottle that was in his cupholder in his truck): probably. As he throws the truck in reverse and turns his head over his shoulder to back up the vehicle.

Isabella says: Where are you going?

Jack completely forgets that Isabella was standing right there as he is disoriented and out of it. And says to himself: dang don't want to be rude to this lady. Jack slows the truck to a stop and switches back into drive and pulls up next to Isabella.

Jack: sorry still little out of it, Isabella from The Ranch, right? You were at the Ranch the other day.

Isabella: yeah, your right

Jack: And you want to borrow the bulldozer?

Isabella: yes please

Jack (chuckling and laughing) thinks to himself that this is a very different type of woman then the last Isabella he was in a relationship with.

Jack (laughing a little while responding): Yes, you can borrow the bulldozer.

Isabella: well, where are you going? Can I have your phone number?

Jack: Tuesday 6pm, not this Tuesday but next Tuesday

Isabella: what do you mean?

Jack: Go to The Ranch not this Tuesday but next Tuesday at 6pm, bring your dancing boots and ask if your friend Judy wants to come too

Long pause looks as if Isabella is not sure if Jack is playing a prank on Isabella and is just messing with her.

Jack: I would go this Tuesday, but not going to be nowhere near able to, I got rest up a bit. I have no idea what is going on with work as I have been out of any contact for days now. I'll be rested up for next Tuesday though. You should come by if you want to borrow the bulldozer!

Isabella: Okay I'm going to ask Judy if she wants to come, but please be there because Judy is on the older side compared to you and I, she doesn't go out much most likely so this could be a big deal for her if I can get her to get out of the house.

Jack: Noted – I'll be there.
Jack: Thanks for saving me.

. . .

Jack makes his way to the hotel room that he has been paying for since he was stuck under a beam in his cabin. He goes to the hotel room to shower, eat, shave, and hydrate drinking water. He is still very weak but after about an hour and a half of touching up on his hygiene, Jack is back in his truck heading south to the city to check on his company. He feels as if contacting his employees would not mean anything and he must show his face to get his respect back.

Jack headed to the hotel immediately following his interaction with Isabella. When Jack left the cabin, Isabella called Judy asking if she could come over to talk to Isabella (Isabella is also knowing that she must kill some time before going back to the hotel to not run into Jack again). Once Isabella gets to Judy's house, the two turn into little gossiping teenagers, Judy leads Isabella into a room where her husband can't hear them talk and Judy and Isabella talk about every detail of the interaction.

Isabella: and there was a large beam that fell from ceiling!

Judy: and he was alive?

Isabella: Yes!!!! He didn't even seem phased.

Judy: And how was the house?

Isabella: the house was close to how I remembered it.

Isabella: and I used the jack from his truck to lift the beam and jack got right up.

Isabella: get this!

Isabella: he just gets up and walks to his truck after being stuck against the floor for days

Judy: (Doesn't get a chance to say anything)

Isabella: he didn't even say goodbye he just got in his truck and started backing up

Isabella: Oh, Oh Oh! Get this.

Judy listening intensely:

Isabella: he invited you and I out.

Judy: really? Why? When?

Isabella: I told him that you and I want to use his bulldozer that he had in the driveway.

Judy: me and you want to operate a bulldozer??

Isabella: Yes, that's what you said.

Judy: hire him to use it!

Isabella: it's easy!

Judy: when did you use one?

Isabella: nope haven't done that one.

Judy: (laughing)

Isabella: So, he wants to meet with us soon.

Judy: Okay

Judy: he is a nice guy?

Isabella: I really haven't talked to him much. But anytime he opens his mouth it's funny whatever he says.

Judy: okay well is it tonight?

Isabella: Oh no, it'll be on Tuesday. Not this coming Tuesday but next Tuesday. 6pm at The Ranch, it's not too far away.

Judy: Ok, yeah, I'll go.

Isabella: We're doing a line dancing lesson there, bring your boots, if you'd like we can practice before together, I know a few of the dances, I could teach you!

Now the next meeting between the two is almost a week and a half away. Isabella is unsure where Jack will be, so she doesn't want to return to the hotel in case she runs into Jack again, one time accidentally bumping into each other is a cute coincidence, when it is happening two, three times then it can become a tad bit odd. To play it safe, decides to stay at her place in Lake George and visit

Judy to do some practicing for the lesson coming up at The Ranch with Jack.

Isabella calls the hotel and asks them if they can clean out her room either mailing her belongings to her or holding them until she's back in town. Expecting to pay a massive cleaning fee, the hotel was very nice and said if you reserve your room for when you are coming back, we can hold these items for you no problem, no extra fee and sorry for your sudden change of plans, hope everything is okay. Isabella makes it back to Lake George with a feeling of success and excited over the next couple of days to follow until she gets to see Jack again.

Jack on the other hand, Jack heads to his business in New York City, he goes into the office of his business, and no one is there. The trash trucks are out on the road working doing what they are supposed to be doing. He finds a chair and starts logging into the manager's account on the computer to review the accounts. Almost as soon as he sits in the chair, Jack falls asleep, a few hours pass at the end of the day and the staff walk in. The manager nudges the boss (Jack) on the shoulder and says: You good jack? You look like crap.

Jack wakes up and looks at the guys in front of them and holds out his fist. Saying: pound it, gives the guys each a pound it and says: it nice to see you guys. The guys smile and sit down just to hang out for a little bit, Jack listens as the guys tell their shop drama, their baby mama drama, and the waste company events that happened.

Foreman manager says to Jack: I have been trying to reach you, we got a few things to go over, hope you're not mad I had to make some executive decisions, I waited as long as I could, but wasn't sure if I was being tested or what was going on.

Jack says: yeah, that makes sense, I was busy, was tough getting to my phone, sorry about that. So how did you guys make out?

Foreman responds: Well National Waste again, had 4 dumpsters go missing, we are thinking that they have been taking them from us. We didn't want to call the cops because that was not the right way to handle it.

Jack sat there listening and still a little out of it.

Foreman continues talking: So, we did what we would think to do.

Jack getting some humor out of this, kind of excited to hear what they did I mean 4 dumpsters if they are 40-yard dumpsters (the largest dumpsters they rent) with the price of steel right now that's roughly $10,000 a dumpster times 4 equals to about $40,000 worth of inventory that has gone missing.

Jack knows that these dumpsters turn up usually, but inventory is low, so it is good to get the dumpsters back. Anyways... The Foreman continues talking.

Foreman: I sent a guy to their yard over there in Greenwich

Foreman: The driver pulls up to the yard and you can see our 4 dumpsters clear as day with our company lettering right on them from the main road

Foreman: The driver calls me asking me what I want to do with this, I tell the driver to drive in as the gate was open and grab the first dumpster and to start doing trips back to the shop. It would be a full day's work for this one driver.

Foreman: Anyways, he goes to back in to hook the truck onto the dumpster to bring the first stolen dumpster back to the shop and guess what

Foreman: Guess what happens

Foreman: As my driver who I said to go into the gate goes to back up and hook the dumpster up to the truck to bring it back, those guys I'll tell you what! Those guys you want know what they do? They close the gate locking one of our trucks in their yard!

Foreman: Over the loudspeaker of the gate, they say please exit the vehicle or the police will be called as this is a no trespassing zone, please read the sign. Please exit through the walkway. Thank you.

Foreman: I had to call an uber drive to get the driver to make it home, because now they locked one of our trucks in their yard too!

Foreman: One of our trucks and four containers is at National Waste's yard! Man, if I had an ounce of what I was when I was 19 years old again bam bam right left hook that sucker. No doubt about it, no doubts abouts it!

Foreman: How mad are you at this? I just didn't know what to do without you here on this one boss.

Jack: That's a funny one. He was probably mad; I haven't talked to him in a couple days. I'll see if I can help you guys out get that truck back for you guys.

Jack: How have you guys been getting by without that truck? Happen to get that back up truck we were working on back on the road?

Foreman: Yeah, yes sir, that was my first instinct to get that going. So, we installed two new rear tires, brake pads all around, oil change, air filter, rear brake light bulb, thermostat and then got it aligned. We haven't passed it through annual inspection yet, but it's on the road. (Foreman yells to the other room to another staff member) Hey bud come in here.

The driver staff member walks into the room where the Foreman and Jack are talking.

Driver: yes sir

Foreman: That truck you were in today, what do you think of it, we got to pass it through inspection in next couple of days

Driver: seemed good

Foreman: (Looking toward Jack now) We are hoping to set up the annual inspection early next week for that truck, we just waiting on that DOT kit, flares, extinguishes to come from an internet order we placed.

Jack: Do you guys need anything around here for the next day or two? I'm going to stay around town for the next couple of days, trying to help be productive get little back into it.

Foreman: yeah, we could use your help boss, just keep your phone on you.

Jack: thanks, appreciate you guys

Jack clocks out from the office and shop last as he is the last one there for the day. Jack takes his truck back to his apartment that he still rents not too far from the shop where his work is. On the way back to the apartment, he texts his buddy saying:

Jack: Your crazy

National Waste buddy: Lol, so that's what it takes to get you to text me back.

Jack: been away from my phone buddy

Waste buddy: When are you coming to get your truck?

Jack: Soon

Incoming picture message from Jack's waste buddy

Jack: opens message

It's a picture of a key with looks like grass, field, and horses in the background.

Jack responds saying: looks nice there.

Waste buddy: that's the key to the gate your truck is locked behind, come, and get it.

Jack thinks that he is a little too tired to play these types of games.

Incoming picture message

Jack: Opens message

It's a picture of a plane ticket from New York City JFK Airport to Ocala International Airport

Waste buddy: Come down and visit me! You haven't seen my farm down here, it'll be fun! Only a few days

Jack: I'm in, I must be back within a week I believe, I have an important meeting I must go to.

As Jack starts making his way to sunny Florida, he goes to pack his luggage for the time away.

Isabella, the lady who saved Jack at Saddlebrook the other day, is back up at Lake George working hard at her current job and cruising through the week getting her deadlines done.

Jack boards the plane to Ocala International Airport and lands with his National waste buddy at the gate ready to pick him up when he lands. As Jack gets in the truck, Jack goes do you have the key or what?
Waste guy: whoa slow down, it's at the farm don't worry there. By the way you look like absolute crap, are you okay?
Jack: yeah, I'm fine thanks for asking
Kind of a silent type of ride, can feel in the air that Jack is kind of forced on this trip and not in the mood to be playing these types of games. As the two got to the driveway entrance after the quick 20-minute drive from the airport, Waste guy presses the remote on his sun visor button and it opens the gate to go down the long driveway with fencing along both sides, the entrance to the driveway has pillars on each side decorated with horse carvings on the top with their family name plated on a plaque. They pull in and slow down the driveway, not to kick up too much dust along the driveway or scare any of the horses. Pulling in there are the stables on the right side with a few equestrians looking over at the truck to see who is arriving and they look the other way to try not to catch the

attention of the owner of the property. Waste guy comes to a slow halt, moving the truck into a parking spot, putting it into park, checking his phone quickly then getting out of the vehicle to Jack's side of the truck to signal it is okay for him to come out of the truck and follow him towards the barn.
Jack follows waste guy toward the barn and waste guy goes, there's a lock box up here for this property, come on jack, walk a little faster, waste guy opens up the lock box, takes out the key that unlocks the gate for Jack to get his garbage truck and four dumpsters from behind the gate.
Waste guy says: here's the key.
Jack takes the key and sighs of relief. He is glad that there's no more games being played here.
Waste guy: sorry for messing with you.
Jack: no big deal
Waste guy: Do you think you're going to stick around here for a couple days, or do you have to go back right away? I do appreciate you coming down here, I heard that you bought yourself a horse property, I didn't know you were into horses.

Jack: What do you mean? What did you hear about buying a horse property? I mean my ex-Isabella was into horses, but I never thought too much about it.

Waste guy: You bought Saddlebrook I heard in upstate NY, that used to be the place to be in the equestrian world.

Jack: Yeah, that would make sense, seems people think very highly of that property in the area

Waste guy: it hasn't been popular in a while; I think one or two generations ago was when it was popular. I heard it was sold and wasn't supposed to be built on or something.

Jack: yeah, I wasn't really expecting that when I got there, but whatever

Waste guy: what you are doing with the property?

Jack: I mean after last week after being there, I'm not sure if I'll be doing anything up there to it. I might just sell it.

Waste guy: anyways, you want to go to the springs down here that the locals go too? Nice little place we like to go relax. I was thinking head out around 10am tomorrow morning?

Jack: yeah, that sounds good, you have a car or truck or something I can use in the morning

to take into town to run a few errands before
leaving at 10am?

Waste guy: yeah, the code to the lockbox for
the staff is 2020 and there's a Ford key to the
work truck we use around here. Just try fill it
back up with fuel when done, the truck is
around the back of the barn and oh yeah.

Waste guy: Follow me I'll show you where
you can stay, we have some living quarters
that are empty for farm staff right now or I
have an extra room in the main house.
Whichever one you prefer.

Jack: The living quarters is good, I'll stay there,
I appreciate it

Waste guy unlocks the door for the living
quarters where Jack will be staying and goes
up the stairs to second floor above the barn
and says: the Wi-Fi password is 2020horses.

Jack: thanks, I'm going to fall asleep, I'll be
back here in the morning tomorrow by 10am,
going to go grab a coffee and do a few errands.

Waste guy: you got it bud. Sleep well my
friend.

Jack sits down in the chair and figures out
how to turn the AC on, the weather in
Northern Florida this time of year is perfect.
Jack pulls his phone out and notices how

spotty the coverage is in this area for whatever reason, so he opens and puts the password in to get the Wi-Fi connection on his iPhone. He goes through his emails, there are only a few emails for bills he must pay, and he pays them quickly. Jack then checks his social media accounts and then goes through text messages. He sees that his Ex Isabella from North Salem, NY has been messaging (Don't get it confused, this is the Isabella from North Salem not the one from Lake George who Jack recently met at the bar) …

Jack notices some text messages that he didn't get the notifications from, he forgot that he silenced/ muted the text messages from her. So, he opens the texts from his ex-girlfriend from North Salem and there are 23 text messages. Jack thinks oh wow, she's mad, she is going to absolutely freak out.

Jack is alone, still a little worn down and clearly not thinking straight. He thinks he can't text back all these messages there are too many. Jack sits there and thinks of the solution and his solution is to call her.

Jack hits the call button on his cell phone to call the Ex-girlfriend Isabella:

Isabella: Hey Jack

Jack thinking to himself, this is an odd tone in her voice, not sure what this means:

Jack: Hey sorry I just checked my phone, works been busy

Isabella: no no no its okay I'm glad you're answering I was getting worried.

Jack thinks to himself, something is fishy, she has never been nice to Jack or even showed one care in her heart for him.

Jack: So, what's new? How is the new boyfriend?

Isabella: It was nothing, we went on a few dates and every time I thought of you. I really regret how I left things with you and hope you find a spot in your heart to forgive me.

Jack: yeah, it's no big deal things happen

Isabella: What are you doing tonight? Would you want to come to the barn again to see me?

Jack: I wish I haven't really been with anyone in a while, now that I think about it, I think you are still the last girl I've been with, I've just been, I don't even know what I've been up too.

Jack pauses for a little and he gets a little distracted, remembers that the ex-girlfriend does have a nice and amazing body and all his rational thoughts go out the window.

Jack: yeah, I'm in to come see you, oh snap…
Isabella: what?
Jack: I'm in Florida, I completely forgot
Isabella: are you okay?
Jack: no no not really, but yeah, I'm down here right now
Isabella: where in Florida?
Jack: Ocala

Isabella knows Ocala. Every equestrian in the world knows Ocala. The horse capital of the United States in the wintertime is Ocala. Ocala is miles and miles of horse pasture; over the years the real estate has just skyrocketed there especially after the Covid-19 Pandemic. Seems like people are flocking to Florida to move there. Isabella's mind starts to spin, who is this man? He's in Ocala? This is different. Curiosity flows through her.

Isabella: are you staying with another woman?
Jack: I don't think he is a woman, but if he is he would be the biggest and tallest women I've ever seen (Jack is laughing when he is saying this)
Jack: My friend flew me down here, so I'm visiting

Isabella: Can you or he fly me down there too?
I love Ocala, I've competed there before too, I
can show you the spots.
Jack: I can ask, I don't think I'm staying long,
I'm going to do some errands in the morning
then probably head home after
paddleboarding
Isabella: At the springs?
Jack: yeah, were going to the springs, you been
there? Are there alligators there you think?
Isabella: just don't fall in and you'll be fine.
Yes, all the guys used to take me there in my
hay day when I was in the area competing,
that's where we would hang out.
Jack starts to think of the timeline from when
Isabella and he were dating as to when she was
competing down in Ocala.
Isabella: so, you're coming back tomorrow
night you think?
Jack: I'm not too sure, you want to call me
tomorrow night and see what I'm up to?
Maybe I'll leave tomorrow or maybe after a
few days I'm not too sure yet.
The next day Jack wakes up early and has a
quick breakfast out of the food in the pantry
in the living quarters, a bowl of oatmeal and a
glass of water. He then heads outside, the sun

is just coming up and he is trying to be quiet to not wake anyone. Once Jack swung the door open, it made only a slight creaking noise and immediately footsteps came running to the living quarters door. There are two sheep farm dogs running to Jack. One with a frisbee in its mouth wide awake and ready, wanting to play fetch. Jack is in his running gear wearing Asics shoes, shorts, and a t shirt. He grabs the frisbee that one of the energetic farm dogs brings him and throws it in the air. As the dog runs the other way, Jack slowly starts his jog before the dog's return. You can tell the dogs have their morning zoomies and want to run around. Jack goes for a nice jog, a 10-minute slow jog and 5-minute faster pace to train the heart rate for an intense work out. He keeps doing that for a 30–40-minute run and ends the run back at the farm. As Jack gets back to the horse farm, he is greeted at the property boundary line by the two farm dogs, one with the frisbee in its mouth and one that likes to follow the other dog around. When he gets back to the farm, Jack grabs the work truck to head into town. When he gets into town he goes to the post office to overnight the key that unlocks the gate to where his truck is locked behind to his foreman back at work to make sure he was given the right key. After mailing the key, he heads back, when he gets back to the property, he opens the door to the apartment to walk upstairs, takes a shower and drinks water to stay hydrated. The time is nearing 9am so he combs his hair, changes his clothes, and goes outside again at 9:30am to go see what the waste guy is up too.

Jack is feeling nice after the workout runners high from the exercise he just did. He makes his way over to the main house with his dog friends and their frisbee following behind him. Jack knocks on the door and the waste guy yells "Jack come on in buddy the door is unlocked." Jack enters the nicely furnished house and

Waste guy says: here's some food if you want any before going out, how was your run?

Jack: nice, I like the weather here, you were awake at that time?

Waste guy: were in the waste industry, you know how it is once you're in it, you're in it, that sleep schedule doesn't change, I was reading the newspaper when you were going

out, that's a good thing you do, I'm not motivated enough to go on runs like that.
Jack: thanks, I appreciate it, is there anything new in today's paper?
Waste guy: not much in the paper down here, but did you know Bill Malone? He was in the New York times magazine this morning.
Jack: sounds familiar
Waste guy: he died last weekend; they found his body over a bridge in New Hampshire with a "suicide note" on the driver's seat in his Porsche.
Waste guy: there is no way he committed suicide. There is no way he would do that. You think our industry is crazy, you should hear about the industry he was in. He was going head-to-head with that private equity hedge fund backed competitor United Site Services.
Jack: Are you talking about William Malone? The guy who also had the first natural gas station open to the public east of the Mississippi in Bridgeport, Connecticut? The guy who had a fleet of trash trucks that ran on natural gas? He also had his own powerplant that can convert biodegradable waste to natural gas? The owner of A Royal Rush the

largest privately owned portable toilet company in the United States?

Waste guy: yeah, that is Bill Malone

Waste guy: well, he died over the weekend, and I guarantee you there won't even be an investigation.

Jack: He was in our industry too, he had a trash company too, I agree that doesn't sound right

Waste guy: all those customers of his are going to go right to United Site Services, sad, real sad, he was one of us basically in the waste industry.

Waste guy: So, keep your ears open if you hear anything regarding what happened to him, it's the least we can do to pay our respects.

Jack and Waste guy finish up their chit chat and make their way down to the springs to have a good exercise on the paddleboards throughout the water ways.

Afterward paddleboarding at the springs near Ocala, Jack and the waste guy make it back to their living quarters and they both sit down with their laptops doing their work while watching tv and hanging out.

. . .

Back in the Northeast, Isabella from Lake George is spending time with Judy having some laughs and learning one of the easier line dances together called Ready for it. Hop forward, three hip swings, hop back, three hip swings, two touches one two three sailor, other side one two three then sailor. Slight ¼ turn counterclockwise and cross overs. Pretty easy and they have a good time, having laughs and their confidence builds in the dance which is a good thing as they look like they know what they're doing!

Isabella shows Judy the new makeup and lip gloss line for a famous music artist that is coming out soon. That's what Isabella does for work, she works for a company that helps bring products to market and she is more on the marketing side of things. Isabella helps bring the customers to new products, sometimes for celebrities, sometimes for large companies or corporations. Isabella is good at developing certain niches and sales channels.

It is quite interesting, some of the famous artist's songs went viral on TikTok as when someone translated one or two of her songs into Spanish, it developed a want or a need for makeup in that region. This famous artist has been a client for the firm that Isabella works for, for merchandise and products. So, while managing her brand, they picked up an influx of a new following and followers on this music artist's Instagram from a lot of Spanish speaking fans! This was interesting and that is something the company is gearing some of the new product toward!

Judy: Soooo! Tell me

Isabella (Lake George Isabella): tell you what Judy?!

Judy: What is she like? (Referring to Isabella's famous music client)

Isabella: Oh, she is a true class act.

Isabella: Just the way she talks, acts, and flows is incredible. She sang for us the other day just acoustic with guitar and something about the conviction behind her voice. You can feel every word through your soul.

Isabella: she's a great woman, really keeps to herself, hardworking and is respected.

Judy: incredible, I've heard her music, and it is good.

Judy: Have you thought about Jack at all? How much do you think the bulldozer is going to cost for us? Did you talk to him more, what is he doing with Saddlebrook you think?

Isabella: (smiling) yeah, I've thought about him, I still don't know much about him, I don't even know if he is single either. But he is handsome I would give him that. I'm excited for Tuesday.

Isabella: no idea what the cost for bulldozer is, not sure what he's thinking either. I'm very anxious.

Judy: do you think he'll let me paint the fences there? I want to change the color to a dark green. My husband and I have already bought the paint (chuckling laughing).

Isabella: I mean his attitude from what I have gathered is I don't think he cares at all and will most likely be okay with it.

We are going to do a quick summary and fast forward the clock to Tuesday. At the Ranch Line Dancing lessons night, Judy, Isabella from Lake George, and Jack are meeting. The subjects to be discussed at the meeting are the bulldozer borrowing, Saddlebrook and finding out who Jack is dating.

Before we can fast forward to Tuesday let's bring it up to speed with everything.

Isabella from Lake George focuses on her work. Jack's ex Isabella from North Salem is keeping herself occupied by focusing on chasing another man to date. The Waste guy he's down in Ocala all winter, his company NATIONAL WASTE is massive with more than enough infrastructure to manage itself. Jack takes a plane flight home back to New York City after spending a few days in Ocala and resumes his work.

The only thing that has changed in Jack's schedule is that he has been in conversation with his ex from North Salem almost daily on the phone around 7pm each night. It is none of our business what they are talking about currently. However, let's note it for the record they are "talking".

Tuesday comes around and the meeting is on! Isabella Lake George, Judy Saddlebrook fan and Jack the Saddlebrook owner finally get to meet! Jack pulls up to The Ranch in his truck and walks into the bar to watch the people there playing pool.

When he gets there, he looks, but it doesn't look like Isabella or Judy are there yet. After a few minutes, he sees them come in seeming to be in a good mood and dressed nicely for the occasion. As Judy and Isabella walk into the establishment, the front door attendant asks them for their ID. Judy has hers; Isabella hasn't been able to locate her ID or wallet for the past couple of days. Isabella says to the front doorman, I can't seem to find my ID this past week, is it still okay for me to do the line dancing lessons tonight? I won't be at the bar just pointing to the dance floor, will be over there. The front door attendant gestures for them to walk on by and it is not a problem. As they are walking past the entry way, Jack makes eye contact with them, checking to make sure they are the right people he is meeting there tonight, and it is. They look back at him and change the direction they're walking now towards Jack. They're walking toward him; Jack stands up and starts walking toward them to greet them.

Jack: Hey, how are you guys?

Girls: Good, thanks for inviting us!

Jack: The lessons don't start for a bit; do you guys want to sit over there across the room at the tables? It looks like those are the people for the lessons, they sit over there at the tables. They walk on over across the dance floor and sit down as the instructor of the dance lessons for the night says: Hey, guys come sit over by us!

Jack thinks to himself awesome, a nice group setting, he doesn't have to be hounded by these two beautiful ladies about the Saddlebrook property. Jack is here to have a good time, get some good exercise doing the line dancing and figured it would be a good idea to invite these ladies to keep him company here tonight. They also do seem to be looking out for Jack's interests.

The dance instructor passes out a piece of paper to the lesson goers and says: If you could go over the steps, this is the first dance we will be going over. Just a quick 1-hour lesson after the lesson the dance floor opens for line dancing to the public for the night.

The first song in the lesson they are going to learn is called Shivers and a little under 10 people in the group line up to learn the dance. The instructor leads in the front and goes very slow as the people in the lesson follow her footsteps. It is a great atmosphere, low key only about 10 people and the skill level between everyone is very diverse. Some people here have never danced before, and it is their first time. On the opposite side of the spectrum, there is one person in the lesson who travels the country line dancing as a career. They do the lesson to stay fresh on their skills.

As the hour lesson passes, the group has a great time and worked up a sweat being active. As the lesson ends, the group goes back to where they were seated previously and sits down to have a quick bottle of water. The group that was doing the lesson pretty much splits apart for the night, as some of their friends come to The Ranch to hang out and get food, others go home for the night. Judy, Isabella, and Jack move to a table by themselves. And Jack asks the waitress who comes to serve them.

Jack: Could we get some water? thank you (The waitress at The Ranch goes to get water for the table)

Jack: How did you guys like the lesson? Both of you were incredible at dancing I must say.

Isabella: thanks! We were practicing the dances and it paid off! It made the lesson nice and easy. Judy you were incredible too!!

Judy: So, Jack!! I don't see a wedding ring on your finger.

Jack: Ha-ha (Jack laughs) very observant

Isabella: are you going to still let us borrow the bulldozer? Well, when your done with it of course.

Judy: Whispers to Isabella – ask him about the paint, don't forget the paint.

Jack: yeah, you girls are welcome to us the bulldozer. Where's it going too?

Isabella and Judy not thinking the whole using the bulldozer thing through and Isabella looks at Judy.

Isabella: it's going to Judy's house.

Jack: Does Judy's house have an address? The metal tracks on it can't go down the road, the town usually will call if we leave the track marks on the road.

Isabella hands her notepad from her purse to Judy to hint to Judy to write down her address for Jack.

Jack: do you guys want to provide a contact phone number for the delivery driver to call when he's on the way?

Isabella writes down her phone number on the notepad next to Judy's address to where the bulldozer is going.

Isabella: Do you know how much the payment is going to be to use it?

Jack: I rented it for one month but I'm not using it anymore, I'll call Sunbelt in the morning, that's the place that it was rented from. I would want you guys to pay the delivery to get it there, they come with a tractor trailer low boy bed that they'll have to move it with. If you would like, I could have them call you and if you like the price just give them your card information over the phone to pay for the move.
Jack: I rented it for 30 days, so at the end of thirty days it'll be getting picked up if that makes sense
Isabella: Yeah, it shouldn't take too long.
Judy: So, Jack! What are your plans for the property?
Jack: I don't have any plans for it
Judy: Why not? You're not going to open it again?
Jack (sipping on his water, watching the dances going on): Don't think so, haven't really thought of it much.
Judy: Well, what was the plan with the bulldozer?
Jack: Oh yeah! I was going to make a big dirt bike jump over the driveway.

Judy and Isabella kind of look at each other and didn't know what to respond.

Isabella: so, no more dirt bike jump?

Jack: nope no more dirt bike jump

Isabella: have you been staying up there at the house?

Jack (still veering over watching the dances): nope been down hanging out in the city lately. Last time I was there is when you saved me. You been up there lately?

Isabella: haven't been there since I saved you.

Isabella: I didn't know I was allowed there.

Judy: when you're not there Jack, would it be okay if I checked in on the place occasionally?

Isabella: when are you going there again? Do you know?

Jack: Don't really have any intentions going back to that place

Jack: Yeah, Judy you can go there, just be careful, maybe don't go alone?

Judy: yeah! Isabella, or my husband, I'll bring someone with either way!

Jack: you guys have any questions? I had a good time, but I think I'm going to be getting out of here, I'm going back into the city for the night I'm thinking. Got hour or two drive ahead of me dependent on the traffic.

Jack: oh yeah, keep your phone on you guys, I'll have the rental company call you tomorrow about the bulldozer getting moved.
Isabella: yeah, sure not a problem.
Jack stands up looking toward the exit way and turns around back toward the table where he was sitting.
Jack: Hey, I had a really nice time here tonight, thanks for coming out. You both look great tonight too.
As Jack walks out before he makes it to the door to exit the building, he turns with a smile to Isabella, gives a slight head nod goodbye with a hand wave of a goodbye.
Heading out of the building, Jack opens the door to his truck, sits down and starts driving back South to the city. As he is driving South, Jack looks back in the rear-view mirror with a smile, almost laughing thinking of that interaction he just had with two ladies. Jack thinks to himself, now that is a different breed of woman up there compared to the city. Talking about using a bulldozer and wanting to paint stuff. Too funny, Jack is a little concerned for their safety using a bulldozer without any training, but it will be interesting to see how their project ends up.

As he is driving, its nighttime and the lights are bright in the oncoming traffic. He tries to get more focused for a safe drive home and remembers it is about time where he normally talks to his ex-girlfriend around this time. He opens his phone with his left hand and goes through the call log, to hit the name on it for his Ex Isabella so the phone starts calling.

Jack: Hey! How are you!

Isabella (Ex): hey what's going on, you sound like you're in a good mood? What have you been up too? I hear you're not home are you driving?

Jack's mood kind of shifts where he's feeling that he is dragged down and almost gets defensive to these questions for some reason.

Isabella: Hello, are you there?

Jack: yeah, what's up?

Isabella: are you going to answer my questions?

Jack: oh yeah, I'm driving back to the city right now.

Isabella: where were you?

Jack: Kind of near you actually: near Saratoga Springs, I had a meeting there

Isabella: you should have let me know; I would have asked you to stop by to see me.

Jack: Yeah, you could have come to the meeting it would have been fun!

Jack: We went line dancing tonight!

Isabella: I never knew that you line dance.

Jack (laughing while saying this): It's funny, I've been sending my meetings to my line dancing lessons. It is working quite well actually; I think it's awesome. Great work out too!

Isabella: who was your meeting with?

Jack: We're working on a little project up there, and two of the locals were asking to use my equipment for Judy and her husband's property.

Isabella: Is this up near your new Saddlebrook property?

Jack: Yes! Exactly

Isabella: Yeah, I figured. Everyone in the equestrian industry has been talking about that place.

Jack: that would make sense. Seems people get excited about that property. It is interesting.

Isabella: So, what are you doing with the property? Are you building a new house on it? I heard the old house there is atrocious.

Jack: No plans, Hun, I got to get off the phone, I'm just getting a headache now, not sure why, might be the bright headlights this time of night. But yeah, what are you up to next week? Do you want to meet in person to talk?

Isabella: Yeah, can you come by the barn like old times? Regular time any day of the week!

Jack: I would, but I don't think that is a good idea at this time. I don't want to give anyone the wrong impression that we are dating. You told me you have been seeing someone in our time apart. I think for us to try to get back together to work it out, perhaps we go on a date somewhere to talk more about it?

Isabella: what were you thinking?

Jack: Ice skating? There is a rink by your barn your usually at. Brewster ice rink I believe it is.

Jack: Thursday night? I can let you know day before what time open skate is, but I believe it starts 5-7pm

Isabella: I haven't ice skated in a while.

Jack: Get practicing! I haven't either, we can just sit, eat a hot dog or something at the rink if we don't have to ice skate too.

Jack & North Salem's Isabella date is planned for Thursday 5-7pm: Ice skating at Brewster Ice Arena Brewster, New York

Soon enough Thursday rolls by and Isabella, the ex or soon to be girlfriend again of Jack's goes to where she is living after a day at the barn being with her horse and freshens up in the mirror. Jack was at work in the city most of the day and he clocked out early, freshens up in the mirror in his apartment in New York City then he starts to head up to Brewster Ice Arena to meet his Ex-Girlfriend Isabella.

When he arrives at the ice-skating rink, he goes inside, pays for the rental of skates and the time to skate, he arrives pretty early perhaps 4:30pm before the open skate starts. He hangs out in the lobby with the staff then he makes his way over to the rink where the Zamboni is driving around, icing the rink, and giving it a great finished coating that'll be smooth to skate on.

After a few minutes watching the Zamboni, Jack gets a text from his Ex Isabella

Isabella (ex) – text message: I'm here where are you?

Jack doesn't text very much, so he decides to call her as it is easier.

Jack calls Isabella: Hey I'm inside by the lobby.

Ex: Can you come outside to walk me in?

Jack: Ok be right there

Jack walks outside and tells the staff at the front desk that he'll be right back, he must go grab someone who just got here. Jack walks up to the side of Isabella's vehicle and waits to see what mood she is in tonight:

Jack: Hey! Are you ready? Its skating timeeeee

Isabella: Yes gosh, this isn't exactly what I consider "a date"

Jack thinks to himself, oh jeeze well this is going to be a fun date (sarcasm)

As they walk in, the mood between the couple gets worse and worse, where it starts to feel bad. Walking in, Isabella asks where her skates are, and Jack explains there over there by the rink and that he had already paid for them to get in. With entitlement in Isabella's voice:

Isabella says: I hope you got me a good pair. Jack doesn't say anything because he is just counting down the clock until this date is over, but he is thinking why does she need a good pair of ice skates? I mean all that is going on here is beginner ice skating, no one here between Jack & Isabella are pros, so not sure if it really matters. However, Jack is smart, he doesn't say anything, keeping his mouth shut.

The two tie up their skates, as open skate is about to happen, the Zamboni is all done, and the staff has opened the door to signal that its open to the public for the next hour or two.

Looks like a laid-back night here, small perhaps 15 people are ready to give skating a shot. Like line dancing, not too many people, and with a wide range of skills amongst them. A few elderly individuals out skating, Jack and Isabella, some other people who are decent.

There is a figure skater that is out in the middle of the rink doing her elegant twirls and a few young hockey skaters coming out to zip around warming up before their practice. Isabella and Jack take the next few minutes ice skating at a slow speed and as the time goes by, they pick up on their skills and get a lot better. After about an hour in the open skate, they notice a lot more of the younger hockey player skaters coming out on the rink. The young hockey players start getting competitive racing each other and around this time Jack and Isabella decide it's time to exit the rink. The two did share a good moment. Isabella had a moment where she was happy, proud that she could still ice skate and she was smiling. It was a good moment for the time being that was shared.

As the younger hockey players were coming out to the rink, the hockey parents started coming to fill the bleachers. It looked like the next reservation for the hockey rink was reserved for a local youth hockey team for their practice for the night. Isabella and Jack were sitting in the stands as the parents started coming in and these kids had some skills for their age that's for sure! It looks like it will be interesting to watch the practice and Jack & Isabella decide to stick around for little bit to watch.

Jack gets up and asks Isabella if she would like anything from the concession stands and she says yeah hot chocolate or coffee is good.

After a few minutes, Jack comes back with hot chocolate and hands it to her, still standing as Isabella is sitting, Jack says did I miss anything? Anything exciting happen?

Isabella responds: Georgina is here, Georgina, her son must play on this hockey team.

Jack responds: Oh! (Isabella has talked about Georgina before, Georgina is Isabella's main competition in the equestrian series Isabella competes in)

As the kids line up for warmups, every 30 seconds or so, Isabella is looking towards Georgina sitting all by herself, just there for the next hour or two to watch her son who was at practice.

Jack gets a bad feeling; Isabella isn't usually a friendly competitor when it comes to her competitions. Knowing that Georgina has beaten her every single show, this could get out of hand here. Trying to deflect and end the night on a good note, Jack tries to distract, change the subject, anything. But this is going downhill.

The practice changes from warmups to a scrimmage next. Where offense is going over plays, as one of the plays calls for a pass from across the front of the goal and the other player grabs the puck as a little fake out to throw the goalie off, the other play accepts the pass and shoots the puck to the back of the net. The players are going over this play and as the pass goes across the line of the goal to the accepting player, one of the defensive players sees the play happening and hard hits the receiving player to the ground. The parents watching you can hear," ooooooooooouch and ooooooooooh". Then a frantic woman in the bleaches is yelling "HAHA, I hope you broke your back just like your mother did in 2002."

The coach goes over to the kids skating backwards while eying the frantic woman who said that disgusting comment. Jack is looking for who said that comment and it's Isabella – the woman he came to the ice-skating rink with. As the coach is skating backwards, he says in a slow calm voice to ease the atmosphere in the rink "and that kids are why you always keep your head on a swivel. Always must be on the lookout. "

As the moment has passed, you can feel a shift and Isabella is getting looked at by the other players' parents in the bleachers. One of the other mothers walks over to sit by Georgina and puts her arm around her. Isabella is now in the wrong place and her actions were clearly uncalled for.

Jack says to Isabella: I'm not sure what or why you just said that.

Isabella: His mom Georgina is an utter cheater.

Jack: At horses? This is hockey here.

Jack: you just said you hope the kid broke his back, that's really messed up

Isabella: that's what she deserves.
Jack: look, that's a weird thing no matter what the circumstance for what you just said, I think you should say you're sorry
Isabella: There is no way that will happen, unless they take all her gold medals away from every time she has cheated, all the judges are in her back pocket.
Jack: It's not only this right now, but I don't think this is a good idea
Isabella: what do you mean this?
Jack: You are not the one for me, I am sorry. Isabella living in the ego doesn't feel what is going on and quickly leaves, heading back to her car to leave the ice rink.
Jack sticks around the hockey rink until the practice is over, sipping on his hot chocolate and the other parents come by after a while to make small talk with Jack. After a little bit, Jack tries to slip in the conversation an apology for the crazy lady he was on a date with. Jack laughing a little he says yeah, I don't think it will work out between me and her on that one. The other parents chuckle and Georgina doesn't say anything but shoots Jack a glance saying thanks for sticking up for her.

After practice, the kids come back to their parents and Georgina's kid walks by Jack. Jack puts his hand out for a fist bump and says good job kid. Jack goes to use the restroom before the drive back into the city and as he is walking out the exit of the ice-skating rink, he sees Georgina there and Georgina says to Jack:

Georgina: Was that Isabella who was saying that?

Jack: Yeah, it was

Georgina: I know about her.

Georgina: Nice choice buying Saddlebrook by the way.

Jack: Thanks, funny how people know about that

Georgina (Looking up towards the sky): Sophia would be happy right now about it.

Jack: Who's Sophia?

Georgina: When I was a little girl, she was the one who taught me how to ride a horse.

Georgina: It was at Saddlebrook.

Jack: Very cool, I didn't know anything about that, it was nice talking to you, I have to head out, couple hour drive until I get back, try to keep it on four legs!

. . .

It has been quite some time now since Jack has seen Isabella, who is friends with Judy up at Saddlebrook. Jack has forgotten about her a little and about their meeting at the country bar The Ranch. The whole Ocala trip has taken Jack by surprise, he forgot about his Saddlebrook property altogether. A few months have already gone by, and Jack finds himself with a week off work around the holidays. The guys at the garbage company Jack owns are off work for the week between Christmas and New Year's so Jack was going to take a vacation. Jack's friend the Waste guy was still down in Florida, so perhaps Jack goes there to visit? But Jack is trying to think, and he remembers, then says to himself, let's go North and check to see how the Saddlebrook property up there is doing.

He packs his belongings, not sure where he is going to stay when he gets there. It could be the hotel he was at last time or he might stay in the cabin like he did before when the beam fell from the ceiling and Isabella (Not Jack's Ex, the Isabella from Lake George) came to rescue him.

As Jack drives North, his life in NYC is forgotten about and he starts to remember the tad bits of the interactions he had with people up at The Ranch. Jack starts laughing and smiling, thinking about the ladies using the bulldozer. I wonder how that one made out. Smiling, thinking about how that probably went, wondering if they got anything done! Jack pulls into the driveway of Saddlebrook, and the entrance is decorated with some Christmas decorations and the property looks like it is somewhat maintained. As going up to the cabin, he notices the fencing has been painted white as well, Jack thinks wow that looks much better, very neat, wonders if anyone is around. As he gets to the top of the property, he sees no vehicles on the property and goes up to the cabin, the cabin looks untouched, no maintenance done, fallen beam still in the same spot from before when Jack was pinned under it.

Thinking about it now, Jack hadn't been up to this cabin in months now, ever since while he was sleeping, and a beam fell on him. He was pinned underneath the beam for what must have been 4 days. Someone came knocking on the door and Jack yelled: help me. Isabella from Lake George came into the cabin and helped him get the car Jack to lift the beam from off him.

What else has happened, up in this neck of the woods Jack is thinking to himself, we went line dancing with Judy and Isabella, oh yeah, they rented the Bulldozer! Anyways… Trying to stay occupied and to find something to do while at this cabin.

Jack looks around for a project to do to be productive. As he is walking up on the porch to the entrance, he sees the floorboards are a little moldy, old, cracking and as walking on them. He can feel them flexing, the noise is a faint creek which throughout time if left unattended will deteriorate fast too. Makes a short list on his notepad, front porch floorboards. Looks at porch front and it would look good to be painted white, he adds white paint on the list as well. It'll match the fencing. Looking through the living room, its dusty, get a broom, some rags and water or chemical, looking where the beam fell from the ceiling, trying to see what else it could need to make sure it is safe to be inside this cabin structure. Adding to his list: hammer, 6" spikes, 2" nails, 3" nails, more floorboards for inside the cabin.

Jack takes his truck into town to the nearest Home Depot to gather a good number of supplies for the projects he wants to do. After he gets out of Home Depot and loads the truck, all the seats are full of shopping bags, materials, tools, the bed of the truck is full. Jack even got a couple bags of mortar to fix the fireplace bricks in the back and a couple loose stones in the walkway coming up to the house front porch. He purchased a little more at Home Depot than he anticipated, the truck was feeling the load too, the back end was sagging a low. The suspension on the rear of the truck compressed down due to carrying a good size load! Still within the legal limit of the vehicle's capabilities and Jack makes it safely back to the cabin.

The dust was too much on the floor and around the walls, he takes the broom and starts sweeping almost every spot, the floor, the walls, the furniture, opens the front door and sweeps all the dust outside. Jack's thinking that he wishes that he got a vacuum at Home Depot too, but then he starts wiping down everything to bring out the character in the cabin. When the dust is cleaned out up and wiped, it starts making the wood pieces to the cabin shine. Jack brings out the hammer and starts looking for weak spots in the structure to investigate what needs to be supported better, checking for any shifts in the foundation throughout the life since it was built, the cabin seems pretty level still. Jack doesn't seem to find any major shifts in foundation from freeze and refreezes. A lot can happen, and it can happen quick to deteriorate a cabin fast! It was a long day, Jack drove up from NYC, went to cabin, went to Home Depot, worked at the cabin for a good majority of the day. Stopped tidying up, made a quick fire in the fireplace before it got too dark and cold. Jack is more prepared this time! He brought a battery powered system to power a lamp, his laptop and charge his phone. After a short while, the fire is lite, the cabin is nice and cozy, Jack falls asleep. Before you know it, Jack has been staying up at the cabin for almost a full week, he has been waking up early going into the town nearby for coffee and working out at the gym, then going back to work on the cabin for the rest of the day. It is very nice and very peaceful there, so far, no visitors have yet to come and say hi.

Each night before falling asleep, when the sun goes down, the coyotes howl out to communicate their location to each other. The coyotes seem to figure out where each other is and find each other during the nighttime. Each night it seems like a different type of howl, their moods seem to have been changing each night as they come out too. One time, it seemed like their communication was a short greeting and that there hadn't been any news in the wildlife arena for the area. On the other hand, another time it seemed to sound like they were celebrating that one of them got a good kill. Each night the communication in the woods listening to the coyote's howl's, their life seems to be very active, and they are not always nice to one another. It seemed as if one was getting bullied or punished by another coyote, just hearing from the howls, and screeching from being in pain. Perhaps one coyote went in for a kill and was not successful so that coyote was told by the leaders that it needs to shape up and get in better shape if wanting to survive out in the wild.

This seems to be a part of Jack's normal schedule, where he would like to get home before dusk because that is when nature comes out. It isn't a good idea to run into an animal in the dark, not that the animals are too dangerous that Jack couldn't handle one of them but running into wildlife by accident in the dark may startle them. Sometimes in life, it's about keeping the peace to not start any fights.

As a few days of Jack's cabin refurbishing have gone by, checking the calendar, it is New Year's Eve Day, meaning at midnight it'll be the new year. Jack goes to The Ranch to celebrate with the locals to watch the ball drop on the television screen and celebrate with a cold refreshing drink. After midnight happens, he drives back to the cabin and falls asleep quickly as his days have been filled with lots of hard work from tender love and care to the cabin.

Jack falls asleep basically the second he gets into the cabin, starts up a fire to heat the place up and lays down. He's sound to sleep, the sun starts coming up quickly and around 9am, he hears a car pull into the driveway and looks outside, it's Isabella and Judy coming to the cabin. Jack sees who it is and goes to put on some decent clothes. While he is changing clothes there is a knock on the front door, he finishes buttoning his shirt and puts on a jacket, because it is cold outside. He opens the door; Isabella is standing there with a broom in her hand and Judy is there for moral support for Isabella.

Jack says: come in, please its cold out there!

Isabella: (Kind of just in awe) wow you did some work in here that's for sure.

Isabella and Judy both are walking in while they are having this conversation. Their eyes light up as they touch the wall with their hands as they walk around the living room as if seeing this place in this condition for the first time in a while. Thoughts from the past must fill Isabella's mind as she breaks out in tears.

Jack: What's wrong? What happened?

Isabella: (wiping tears from her eyes), I just can't believe it, it looks so nice here, I just wasn't expecting all of this.

Isabella: It looks beautiful.

Isabella laughs and sets down her broom: I don't think I'm going to need this broom today. Our plan today was to sweep it out, but it looks like you were way ahead of us, and you polished and cleaned up everything.

Isabella: How did you move the beam?

Jack (Laughing while he says this): I made a pulley system and lifted it back into place where it was drilled back in

Jack: but I wouldn't stand directly under it still, not sure how well my work is yet (laughing again)

Jack: I'm so glad that you guys came, I was thinking about you guys and was hoping to run into you guys again!

Isabella: You mind if Judy and I stay around for a little while? I'm sure we can find something to work on around here.

Jack: Yeah, sure do you need me here or you think it is okay if I run into town? Was thinking about going to the gym for a quick work out.

Judy: Yeah! Go for it! We'll be here if we leave by time, you get back, we will make sure to lock it up!

Jack looking over towards Isabella.

Jack: I had a good time last time when You, Judy and I went to The Ranch before. I would be okay with going again if you guys are up for it?

Isabella and Judy look at each other smiling.

Isabella responds with: Yeah, I think we would be okay with that, what do you think Judy? When are you wanting too?

Judy: Yeah, sounds fun, I'll bring my husband!

Jack: Hmm, what day is it today? Hmm, it's Friday I believe (looking around trying to find a calendar, he has no idea what day it even is). If today is Friday, would you guys want to do tomorrow night? I would say tonight but I must freshen up on my dance moves.

Isabella: You've been dancing still?

Jack: I have been watching this line dancing instruction lesson on YouTube to stay in shape! So, I was going to freshen up on my skills before tomorrow night!

Pause . . .

Jack: Have you guys been dancing at all?

Judy looks at Isabella and you can tell on their faces that they haven't been dancing recently.

Isabella: Oh yeah! Definitely!

Judy: Have a good time at the gym! We'll be here!

Once Jack pulled out of the driveway in his truck on his way into town to get some breakfast before working out at the gym, Judy and Isabella started to look to see what else the cabin house needs. Isabella goes upstairs into a room and sees there is a still a desk in the corner. Nothing else, the room is quite bare. She opens the closet door and sees some old picture frames. By the time Isabella is picking up the old picture frames, Judy walks into the room and sees the pictures. Judy recognizes the picture, it's a picture of Sophia (Judy's old friend/Isabella's mom) teaching Isabella how to ride a horse. This picture brought so many memories to each of them, it was tough to hold back tears, a mixture of tears of sadness and happiness because of the reminiscence of those times.

Judy: I'm sure Jack would be okay with you keeping those pictures, Isabella.

Isabella: I'm not sure if I have already told Jack or if he knows that this was my parents' house that they built.

Isabella: I don't know how to have that conversation with him.

Isabella: I have my iPhone; do you want to practice dancing for tomorrow night before Jack comes back?

Judy: (laughing) yeah that is probably a good idea if he has been practicing!

Isabella: If Jack asks, we'll say we found all these old picture frames in a closet here and we are wondering if we can hang them up in the barn here, so visitors know the history of this property!

Judy: There isn't a barn here I thought?

Isabella: (A very mischievous smile) There isn't a barn here… Yet!

Judy and Isabella practiced their line dancing for tomorrow night's outing with Saddlebrook Owner Jack. They practiced the four most popular dances that everyone likes to do! It seems like the DJ at these country bars where they do line dancing, they'll do a popular song then play an older song. I feel as if the DJ does this so that the dancers don't get too worn out. Changes up the songs so that the dancers don't know all the songs of the night! As Judy and Isabella are upstairs rehearsing for tomorrow night, they are keeping a look out at the driveway from the upstairs window. Once they see Jack pull back into the driveway from working out, they finish up their dance practice and start walking downstairs.

As the front door opens,

Jack says: Find any fun projects you guys were looking for? Hopefully it wasn't as tough as the bulldozer project! That one sounded rough.

Isabella: (A little out of breath from dancing) Yeah, we started working on a room upstairs! We found some nice picture frames of the property from the past and we were hoping to hang them around this property.
Isabella: But wait! You can't completely say no, we still haven't even figured out where to hang them up, they're just so awesome and it'll really bring out the history here! and…
Jack smiles and tries to gesture that it's not a big deal at all.
Jack: Sounds cool!
Judy: You don't care if we hang them up or where we hang them up?
Jack: Yeah, I trust you girls! You have better eyesight for those type of things than I do!
Jack: To be honest (looking at Isabella), I am pretty much trained to sleep anywhere, I don't really see materialistic things anymore, all I see is like a car can drive from point a to point b, a house I view as a shelter. Real weird perspective I have right now, all that really matters to me is how I feel in every moment and who I am with if that makes sense.
Judy: That is neat Jack, most people don't learn that until they are much older in their life.

Jack: Are you wanting to start working on the picture frames right now?
Judy and Isabella: No, no, no, soon though! Any plans today that you have?
Jack: Not really, lay down take a nap, get ready to see you guys tomorrow at The Ranch
Jack: Isabella guess what.
Isabella: (almost rolling her eyes) what Jack.
Jack: the power company crews are putting back on the electric power to this place they said, so if I get stuck somewhere like I don't know under a beam, now my phone will at least be charged! (Jack is referring to the time Isabella saved Jack from when he was stuck underneath a beam and his phone was dead)
Isabella: You're funny!
Isabella and Judy proceed to leave saying their goodbyes and that they're excited for tomorrow night. Judy talks to Isabella saying that Jack must like this place if he's putting the power back on! That's a good sign.

. . .

The next day they all meet up at The Ranch and it doesn't look too packed at all for a Saturday night, nice low-key vibe going on at the country bar now. Jack is dressed up in his western cowboy boots, jeans, and a black western hat. Isabella and Judy have their make up on! A little bit of blush, eye shadow and eyelash darkening. Both are wearing cowgirl boots, jeans, and a nice country shirt.

They meet at a table away from the DJ's speaker so that it is a little quieter than it was the previous time that they met. Isabella and Jack kind of hold their eyes a little bit longer than usual then the last couple interactions between the two. Judy picks up on this as well. Not sure what this means, Jack asks if they are ready to dance because they all know this song and they all go out on the dance floor to have a good time. After the song ends, they make it back to the table where they were sitting at.

. . .

Jack is purposely making this meeting with them awkward on purpose, like he is teasing them or something.

Jack says to Isabella:

Jack: Isabella I would like to talk to you about something

Isabella just looks at him and doesn't say anything, but you can see it in her eyes that she is wondering what the heck is this kid about to say!

Jack: is it okay if I put my dirt bike jump in at the property? I can't stop thinking about it, ughhhh.

Isabella lets out a sigh of relief and her shoulders drop down to a more relaxed position.

Jack throws in before she can respond about the dirt bike jump question:

Jack: How did I forget! How did the bulldozer project go? I am so fascinated by it, so proud of you girls for being able to use it all by yourself!

Isabella starts coughing, she accidentally drinks the water that was in the cup down the wrong tube of her throat and is coughing, looking at Judy.

Judy: Easy! Real quick!

Isabella is done coughing now from the water from the unexpected question.

Isabella: Yeah! We pushed over trees, stumps, graded the whole back yard! It was awesome only took us two days.

Jack is sitting there just laughing to himself, it got to a point where he was trying to stop himself from laughing so hard and then a small tear crying rolled down his face from him laughing so hard.

Jack: that's a good one
Judy and Isabella: what's so funny?
Jack: Nothing, nothing, I'm not sure why I am laughing, I just think it is so cool that you two were able to operate the machine all by yourself!
Jack: Did you happen to take any pictures! We can frame them and add some of the frames onto the walls where you guys are going to hang the other ones!
Jack: Isabella, I have been meaning to ask you something as well.
Isabella looks up at Jack, his laughing has stopped now, and he looks like in a more serious mood with a slight smile.
Jack: I don't really know much about you, but my drive up when I came up here, I was reminded of you, and I couldn't help but smile. I want to say that I would like to get to know you more, because you seem to always be here for me and are looking out for me. I hope you may feel the same about me a little bit at least. I just really enjoy your presence and hope you will allow me to start seeing you a little more if that makes sense.
Isabella smiles back at Jack.

Jack says to Isabella: I came up with a good pick-up line as well. (Jack holds out his hand next to Isabella's hand) I see you also don't have a wedding ring on your finger.
Jack then holds Isabella's hand for a second and gives her a wink.
Jack: Yup that's all the pickup line was! I even went to the grocery store to get hand lotion so my hands wouldn't be all chalky dry when I held your hand right there! Can we talk after dancing, and you take some time to think about it? I really don't want to put you on the spot or in an awkward position too.
Isabella: It was a decent one, don't worry.
They walk back to the dance floor to do more dancing, and Isabella & Jack occasionally exchange glances at one another.
After a few hours on the dance floor, the night is coming to an end. On the way out of The Ranch, Jack pulls Isabella aside and hands her a letter. Jack says to Isabella.
Jack: You know the bulldozer story?
Isabella: Yeah
Jack: I can feel what you are always thinking before you say it. For some reason, I have a weird connection to you. Like I can feel what

you're thinking when I look into your eye if that makes sense.

Isabella: What does this have to do with the Bulldozer?

Jack: You and Judy did not use the Bulldozer.

Isabella: (She starts to get defensive) yes, we did!

Jack: It's not only my intuition that is telling me what really happened, but I also know things.

(Judy is behind Isabella in the background overhearing this conversation with the expression on her face that is reassuring Jack what he is saying is the truth that they did not use the Bulldozer.)

Jack: Us equipment guys can tell if their equipment was used.

Isabella: Oh yeah is that right Mr. equipment man?

Jack: Yes, did you open the letter I gave you yet? That is for a refund for the delivery charge, Sunbelt rentals where I rented the Bulldozer from felt bad that we rented the bulldozer for a month and didn't put any hours on it, so they called me to mail me a refund for the delivery to Judy's residence to be nice.

Jack moves in and leans into Isabella's ear and says: I'm not mad.
Jack leans back away from Isabella's ear and she notices that he is crying.
Isabella: what's wrong? I'm sorry it was the only way we could think of introducing yourself to us, we didn't think you would let us use it all on our own.
Jack (wipes away the tears from his face and starts laughing while saying this): I know what you girls were doing and I thought it was one of the cutest things. But the white lie brought up a past thought in my head from previous years and it just really hurts me when I am being lied too.
Isabella: I understand, do you still think you want to see me again?
Jack: I haven't met someone in a long time that intrigues me and what excites you as a human being I find very interesting. So...
Yes, Isabella
Isabella: (No words are needed here, as Isabella lifts her hand up and holds his arm for a second holding eye contact)
Jack: Goodbye Judy, thanks for coming out!
Bye Isabella

The ladies: Jack! Where are you going? When will we see you next?

Jack: Thanks for the work you've put in up there too! I painted the porch the same color as you girls painted that fencing not sure if you noticed that!

Isabella: Jack! When will we see you?

Jack walks away from them to his truck and as he smiles, he turns around while still walking over his shoulder he says to them: We have a big Spring ahead of us. I'm hoping to see both of you a lot this coming Spring!

Jack: I'll contact you if I need help with the plans for the property!

Isabella runs towards Jack and says: Jack how are you going to contact me? You don't even have my phone number!

Jack: That is true! Well life seems to be bringing us together on its own!

Isabella: well, take this Mr. Universe! (Isabella hands a note to Jack), take this, it's my phone number. You can call me!

Jack: Thank you Isabella.

Isabella reaches in for a hug and kisses Jack on the cheek. After Isabella leans back out, Jack reaches in and kisses her on the lips with his right hand on her waist and his left hand holding her right hand.

Isabella: can't wait to see you again.

Jack nods to Isabella, as he gets in his truck, Judy says goodbye to Jack and Jack gives Judy a nod goodbye.

Jack: See you soon Isabella!

. . .

As the next month went by, Jack had thought about Isabella and Isabella had thought about Jack. Jack doesn't hesitate to call Isabella or play games, but he still hasn't contacted her. Not sure why no contact has been made by Jack to Isabella as Isabella is very successful. Jack could be losing his chance if she forgets about him. On the other hand, Jack perhaps could still be getting over his Ex-girlfriend Isabella who he did date for about 5 years. Either way, if jack is interested in Isabella, it would be a good idea to say something!

. . .

Around February time, a week before Valentine's Day Jack calls Isabella. Calling the phone number that she had given him the last time they saw each other.

Jack: Isabella

Isabella: Yes

Jack: How are you?

Isabella: I'm good.

Jack: I have been thinking about you

Isabella: Yeah? What about me?

Jack: I have been wondering what your plans are for the barn.

Isabella: What barn?

Jack: The barn at Saddlebrook.

Isabella: How did you know I was going to build a barn at Saddlebrook?

Jack: Remember when I said I can sense what you are thinking about, I can feel that's what you want to do.

Isabella: Ok, so yes. Yes, I am building a barn there.

There is a little bit of a pause there as Jack is hesitating the next words, he is about to say, as it could be life changing.

Jack: I am hoping you can come up with some plans for a barn for the property. After the middle of March and the last frost, I have been thinking of sending my saw mill up to the property to cut lumber to build with.

Jack: I am not sure how you feel about me or if you feel the same way I feel when I am around you, but I am being drawn to you. My question that I am calling about if you could be around the property with me this coming spring? It seems like it has already been your home and you've saved my life once there already.

Jack: I am not sure if I am trying to ask you to live with me there or how I am wording it. But you can live in the house with me, or I can rent an RV outside on the property that I can live in, or I'll live in town at the hotel. But what I am getting at is, I'd like to have you around as much as possible. The plans that I have for that property, I don't think I can do it alone.

Jack: You don't have to answer all of that right now, can take some time to think about it. I have been thinking of how to communicate this to you and wasn't exactly sure how to go about it if that makes sense.

Jack laughing: yeah, that probably came off little more serious than I meant it to be.

. . .

Isabella: Okay, so the plan is to use a sawmill, build a barn and you're asking me to live at Saddlebrook?

Isabella: Am I the one doing all the work?

Jack: I like to do most of the work, it's good to have someone there in case I get hurt again. I figured Judy would come by to keep you company too, she likes seeing you.

Jack: I know you're not usually in the area, but I remember you saying you've been working remotely most of the time?

Jack: It was just a real rough idea I had (Jack looking down, maybe his idea is a little crazy)

Isabella: I just need electricity to do my work to be honest, you said the electric company is coming to connect it?

Jack (responding with enthusiasm after Isabella seems to be open to this idea): Yeah! I could drive up and check, I paid the bill for them to connect in, the electrician who put a new box on the house, oh I could call him he would know that answer. But yeah, it should be all done by Mid-March for sure.

Isabella: There is a bedroom upstairs that me and Judy started cleaning, do you think that I could stay in that bedroom?

Jack: Yeah, that's fine! I was thinking of having a little work out area in the basement, I'll make myself a bedroom for myself down there too, so then we'll be spaced apart at opposite sides of the house!

Isabella: So, you are thinking March 15th?

Jack: Yeah March 15th! I can let you know when it gets closer if the date changes but yeah, I think that should work great.

Isabella: Can I invite Judy to help with the barn?

Jack: Of course

After getting off the phone with Isabella, Jack has a smile on his face and a wave of calmness falls over him, for some reason he feels as if he is living in a dream.

Jack is reminiscing in his head about the past couple of years and how his life has changed completely. 10 years ago, he was starting his business in the back of a pickup truck working for neighbors who needed help throwing out old furniture. Now ten years later, he has a few great employees still doing trash for work, but in much bigger trucks and for larger customers. He has two best friends or close acquaintances you could say across the country. He lives in NYC, a new business partner Isabella and his waste friend in Ocala, Florida. Waste guy he may or not be a friend, he is a little crazy but entertaining for sure! Jack knows the clock is ticking! Mid-March is only one month away and it's time to close the projects he's working on to make way to spend time developing the Saddlebrook property with Isabella. Now Jack is going to be spending more time up North working with Isabella on the land.

Wonder how Waste Guy down in Florida is doing! Maybe he has some ideas for Saddlebrook.

Jack makes a phone call to Waste Guy:

Jack: Hey Amigo!

Waste guy: Hi Jack

Jack: You, okay? You don't sound very happy.

Waste guy: everything alright no need worry, what do I owe the pleasure?

Jack: You still want me to come down and visit? Remember you were saying I can come down anytime I want to say hello.

Waste guy: of course, amigo, when do you want too?

Jack: sometime next week? I'll book the plane ticket and let you know a couple of days ahead of time. I can stay at a hotel too, no need to barge in on you guys.

Waste guy: We should have some open living quarters come, come. I'm excited.

Jack: Awesome! Will let you know couple days ahead of time to give you a heads-up notice.

. . .

Jack lands at Ocala International Airport and Waste guy is there to pick him up to take back to the property.

Upon arrival, Jack gets in Waste Guy's car. The two-exchange small talk and here is something that was said.

Waste guy: I didn't want to tell you over the phone, but the mood will be a little different around the farm.

Waste guy: I am not sure if you know this but accidents in the equestrian industry can happen at any moment.

Waste guy: We had a death at the farm last week and it is very sad. It was a long time basically family member here, he has been at this farm working and living even before I bought it. It is just sad, he managed a lot of responsibility here, ran most of the lesson programs. It will not be the same here for a long time without him.

Jack: I'm sorry to hear that, what happened exactly? (If you can talk about it)

Waste guy: Hold on a second

As they pull into the property, the gate has security in front of it and the Waste guy gives the main gate guy a head nod giving the security guard a thank you for the work done. As they approach the barn, they drive towards the main house as one of the barns looks like a crime scene taped off with caution crime scene tape from the police department.

They park in front of the main house and Waste guy waves to Jack to follow him towards the golf cart that's on site.

Waste guy: Get in, let's go for a drive.

The two drive the golf cart on the carting road between the double fences of the property around the border. As they are near the back of the property where the horses tend to go to get away from the owners.

Waste guy: You see Jack everything we do here is not normal. This life isn't normal, you see this isn't just a business to me, this is my life, and this is the lifestyle I choose. We have taken on a lot of different horses here, all sorts of different kinds. Some come from boarders who rent a stall, some are left by boarders who

abandoned the property, some of these horses
I brought here are fresh from the mountains
rescued from the wild who have never seen a
human in their entire life. Some horses come
here because they got hurt and our staff is the
only one in this area who can rehabilitate it.
We get all sorts of different kinds, most of our
clients are eventers / jumpers here probably
80%, but I love a great project. Give me the
worst horse that's wild and we can turn it into
something, which is a skill not a lot can do or
want to do.

Waste guy: But the worst horses we get
through these doors are an OTTB. Off-Track
Thoroughbred, the new owners will scoop
them up right off the racetrack when they
have a bad race, or they get hurt and their
owners don't want them because they're mad.
They'll sometimes sell the horse right there at
the racetrack.

Waste guy: The reason why I am saying this is
the new owner will buy that horse, the OTTB
right then and there, then bring it here with a
blank check wanting us to train that horse.

. . .

Waste guy (Looking around while he is saying this): This is the most dangerous horse here when we first get it.

Waste guy: Granted this is the first death regarding an OTTB. But when we get it, the horse takes some time to come down and it acts like a crack addict, a druggy where you can't rationalize any behavior or predict the next thing it will do. The horse is just straight wired, primal instincts, could be from all the adrenaline from the races, the crowd cheering and being in that environment. Not sure I just overhear the trainers here talking about it, only the old timers experienced guys will try to untrain and train straight off the racetrack.

The customers pay for it too.

Jack: Was it an OTTB that caused the accident (Looking over towards the barn that is taped off with crime scene tape)

Waste guy: Between me and you, I shouldn't be saying a thing because the investigation isn't over yet. I can only tell you what I heard, being the owner of a horse stable this size comes with liability and the less I know is better sometimes, (looking down) unfortunately. From my point of view, I was inside talking to the team at work up in the

Northeast, seeing how their day to day was going. I saw people crying and an ambulance came in. Then the fire truck came, then the police came and then a private looking Tahoe blacked out truck came, which I would think would be the crime scene investigator.
Waste: My manager walked in here with his head down and looked me in the eye and I could just feel it that whatever he was about to say would be bad.
The manager said: Boss, you give me permission to give a statement about what happened.
Waste man: Yeah, turn your iPhone voice record on while you make the statement so we can add the exact transcript to our file. Has any staff made a statement yet?
Manager: No one has talked to anyone
Waste man: Call all staff to the meeting room and close it in until all officials leave the property. Go pull the camera footage and watch it before making a statement. Before you give your statement, dot your I's, and cross your t's on that one.
Waste man: Talk to all staff in the meeting room and have everyone agree on your statement. (Looking at manager with a

serious expression) Everyone here must agree on your statement. If there is a discrepancy you need to figure it out before this statement is released.

Waste man: This could shut us down. Take this seriously. You know what happened. I know what happened. We need to be clear to the officials as to what happened. Review the footage and I do not want to hear about it. I already know what happened as I can feel it and have overheard rumors already. Luckily, all the rumors seem to be adding up.

Waste guy: After you release your statement to the police, go upload it to transcribe it to a word document and send over the original statement recording sound recording and the transcribed word document to the companies email so I can put it in our system as our insurance company lawyers would appreciate a thorough paper trail on this. Plus correlate your statement with the video footage if the cameras were able to see the angle of what happened. I want the video footage to be put on an usb flash drive and erased from the system. The police will have to get the original footage through our lawyers should they request it.

Jack overhears this conversation as it is happening right in front of them. Waste guy looks over at Jack to see what his reaction is as Jack was not anticipating entering this circle of trust in this room with Waste man's staff.

Waste guy: Keep me in the loop.

Waste guy: Go drink some water and calm down, take a deep breathe, accidents happen, and this was an accident, you are doing well manager. Report back to me tomorrow on this.

As the manager leaves the room to go gather staff and do as the owner requested, Waste man takes a deep breath and sits down.

Waste guy says to Jack: You want to know what happened on this one.

Waste guy: I overheard in the tack room as I walked by, so you ready for it? Can you handle this?

Jack: I don't need to know

Waste guy (starts getting agitated with Jack and changes his demeanor): You listen right here; I know what you're doing up at Saddlebrook. I know. You want to get in the game, you need to learn what can happen. It's not just about oh you're going to open and let anyone with a horse come to your property.

What if. Let's say you're doing lessons, right? Lessons for kids? One of your staff starts doing lessons there and she or he puts a kid on the wrong horse and it's not the guy who died here this week, it's a kid that one of YOU put on a horse. Imagine calling the parents and telling them there isn't a need to pick up your kid from lessons because they are DEAD. Imagine making that phone call Jack.

Waste guy: You need to think about every situation that can happen before it can happen, you need to learn each horse, there like humans with personalities, it takes time to develop an eye. You as an owner don't need to learn that. All your responsibility is, is to make sure the water system doesn't freeze in the wintertime, and you order enough hay for the herd. Jack, what you need to look for is someone or a few who has an eye for horses, you'll feel their competence with them and that's how you'll know you're ready. Once you find that person, you need to listen to them. They will manage your investment.

Waste guy: I shouldn't even be in this business; I should have listened to my insurance agency and closed out this business. But we do this Jack, it is what we do.

Waste guy: This horse that killed him.
Waste guy: fresh off the trailer, it was an easy ride getting the horse in, its trained for trailering, walked perfectly fine going into its stall.
Waste guy: first day not an issue, normal horse
Waste guy: then after the second day when the horse was coming down, it started acting differently and kept cutting itself on the side of the stall.
Waste guy: what it sounds like, is he was putting a new bandage on the horse's side and the horse slammed him against the side of the stall over and over, when he fell, the horse trampled him crushing his skull with all its weight.
Waste guy: That is what I heard. After the report, it'll be documented what truly happened and whatever the report says is what will be recorded for the stable's files.
Waste guy: It is sad, sad. It was a risk we took and this time we did not win. Nothing we can do about it now, except get smarter about it and try not to let that happen again.
Jack: What do you do with the horse that killed him?

Waste guy: Every situation is different. After the report is posted, I am going to call the police department who were on the scene to see what their recommendation is for that horse. If they don't have instructions, then I am going to call the family of who the horse killed. In their country, they most likely have a way to deal with that. They might keep it for training to ride, or they could sell it for meat which is very common in other countries. I am not sure, but that horse is not welcome on my property, and the horse will not stay here, if it was my decision, we would put that horse down. We can't have that lingering pain that horse caused around here.

Waste guy: most of these trainers on this property don't work for me, they usually run their own business and it can be very lucrative for them at times. Every deal is different, but sometimes they take in their own horses or buy one from me then they train it and resell it, show it. You name it, you got to be creative to make money in this business. It's sad, he was good at what he did.

. . .

Waste guy: Well, that's some of the negative in owning a horse ranch for you Jack. It can also be rewarding as you'll see glimpses of happiness in everyone around you here, which is a priceless thing to create.

With the events that occurred here recently, Jack stayed around the property for a couple more days which ended up being a week. One other conversation is still lingering in Jack's mind. Waste guy what he does for fun in the waste business he does, is he buys small businesses, it is a great way to take up market share and is common in the waste industry. The Waste guy presented Jack with wanting to purchase Jack's company.

The waste guy gave Jack a check while he was staying at the Ocala property. The check was written out to Jack's business's name and the memo was purchase of business thank you.

The check was written out for $1 million dollars which is a discounted price for what Jack's business is worth, it should be selling for 3 times annual profit which would be higher, however Jack would be getting a three-year salary and benefits to help as a manager to make sure customers transition smoothly to the new owner.

As Jack is flying home from Ocala International Airport and into John F Kenney airport, he keeps thinking of what even a million dollars will do for Jack. Now a days you can barely build, buy, or make any money with only a million dollars. So, throughout the course of the flight, his attention keeps being brought to his front jean pocket where the check is in.

Jack is trying to picture his life without his New York City trash company that he owns, which is what really has made him stay in that area. The one thing that Jack knows that is on his mind, is that he is excited to see Isabella again and thinks that his future is with her.

The connections, the bond, the trust, the feelings, yeah, he has just met her, but the communication he is feeling between Isabella and himself he has never felt that with anyone else. The time away from her seems to go by very slowly and the time with her seems to flow so perfectly. It is just such a noticeable positive effect just being around her that the feeling of being with her again is longing and getting stronger as the time goes on.

Jack knows that he has about three weeks until Mid-March comes around and until he starts his new project up at Saddlebrook.

Jack is strongly considering depositing the check from Waste Guy for $1 million dollars to sell him the waste company that Jack started years ago. Jack knows that with a million dollars, he can make a 10% return annually minimally in the real estate business buying a property or two and renting it out long term. Jack goes through his personal expenses to see how much he needs in his monthly income. 10% a year on one million is $100,000 a year profit, which is a little over $8,000 a month net income in Jack's pocket if he goes that route. That is a steady $8,000 a month for the rest of Jack's life with this money. Jack calculates his expenses and all he has is food, phone and fuel bill which living a comfortable low-key life at maximum is $2,000 a month in expenses. Jack's truck is paid off and his Saddlebrook property is paid off. Jack does own his apartment in NYC which will most likely fetch him another $600,000 when he sells it as that is paid off as well.

Jack's plan of attack moves forward. Cash the check for the sale of the trash company. Collect the 10% profit on rental income with a rental or two near the Saddlebrook property in towards town, perhaps leave one as an Air BNB on a lake so Jack and Isabella (IF the relationship pans out! It is still very early on) can vacation there when the Air BNB is not being rented out. Sell the NYC apartment to pocket $600,000 in Jack's pocket to start either another side business on the side, invest and grow Saddlebrook property or to leave in savings in case of an emergency. Jack sitting there in his apartment in NYC after his Ocala vacation, leaves the check on the coffee table in his living room. He knows this is a big decision and he will leave the check there for the next couple of days. Every time he walks by the coffee table, sits down to watch tv, gets up to leave the house, he veers over at the check on the coffee table intimidated by it, because that check represents a major life change for Jack. This decision will decide the rest of Jack's life right then and now.

A few days have gone by with thought and meditation on the decision. Jack drives to the bank to deposit the check knowing the next few months will be an identity change for Jack which he will be going through. Just when your life changes so much, it is a lot of movement to get used to.

After leaving the bank, Jack looks in the rear-view mirror at the bank in the background wondering to himself if he made the right decision. As Jack looks away from the bank towards the future, he never looks back. That life is behind him, and it is time to move forward in life.

This is the turning point for Jack. He's all in. The next morning, at 8am. Jack receives a phone call from an Enfield, Connecticut phone number. It is the main manager of NATIONAL Waste.

Manager: Jack

Jack: Hello, Good Morning

Manager: Thank you for making the right decision, I am the decision maker here at NATIONAL Waste.

Jack: (Not sure how to respond)

Manager: For the next three years, if I have a question, it will be emailed to you. You must respond to the email within 24 hours. If you do not respond to my email if we need anything, your salary will be cut. You will no longer receive your 3-year salary as an add on during the transition period from this buy out.

Manager: Can you do that?

Jack: Yeah, shouldn't be a problem

Jack: How often do you think you will email me you think?

Manager: If everything goes smoothly, we won't email you once.

Manager: I am hoping to never speak to you again. Save this phone number, if there is a mess up in payroll give me a call, we have your routing and account number from the check you deposited yesterday, keep that account open as that is where your direct deposit will go on a weekly basis for the next three years.

Jack: Ok yeah that works, I appreciate it

Manager: Good work in this company Jack, you left it in good hands. Good luck up there.

The phone hangs up and Jack thinks to himself wow totally forgot about that salary coming from that buy out deal that was made, add that into the budgeting equation and Jack has peace of mind that he made the right decision. The one thing that Jack did not want was to be in the struggle again where it was tough at first as a new business owner.

This is a great cash flow, savings, no debt situation Jack is entering and no matter how it pans out, the great thing is that he knows that his bills will be paid off no matter what, which is a great feeling as an adult.

. . .

One of the weirdest feelings for Jack is that he no longer goes down to the shop where the waste business of his was, so he has been trying to change his schedule to figure out what to fill his time with. Jack texted and called the guys at his work to let them know what was going on and they were happy for him. Jack says to them to stay in touch and helpfully they will work together again down the road as life is always changing who knows! Jack is trying to think what his priorities are now. And the only team he must make sure is doing well right now is Isabella and Judy up at Saddlebrook!

Jack calls Isabella:

Isabella answers the phone.

Jack: Hey

Isabella: Hey, how are you!

Jack: Good just wanted to touch base it has been a while since we talked last. I've been working on putting together a plan for the building at Saddlebrook and wanted to see how you feel about everything that is going on at your end?

Isabella: Yeah, I was hoping to be there around Mid-March and I have a lot of nice-looking barn building ideas for the property. I wasn't too sure what you were thinking so I was going to save all the ideas on my laptop and show you, see what you thought of it too?

Jack: Oh, that's awesome, yeah, we have a good supply of lumber for the new build, if we can find the labor to mill it. For the roof, I was thinking metal roof, looking for a rustic type of look and as the business grows, we can always cash flow to improve the work that we did if that makes sense.

Isabella: Do you think we could start small with just one stall and see how that goes? If it goes well, we can set up the farm to be expandable, so if we get a boarder or a horse to train, then if it works out and another customer wants to bring their horse, we can expand the barn as the customer base grows? That way we don't have 50 stalls sitting there empty if the demand isn't there.

Jack: Yeah, I am going with the flow these days, I think that is a good idea. I will start putting out feelers up there to get a staff member to work full time milling and building there. I think having manpower to help around the place will be a good start. I talked to a tree company owner that I have met before, and he offered to bring us the hard wood mill able log lengths at a discounted price if we let them dump wood chips down in the back where our manure pile is.

Isabella: That could work if we can mix the two, it helps the compost break down and help keep the smell down as well.

Jack: With the millable wood, the staff can focus on milling it up into workable pieces for the barn, siding, structural, then we can stack, cure, dry put away for whenever it is needed. If there is any leftover we can keep for spares, build more with it, or even sell the wood down the road too.

Isabella (smiling while talking on the phone with Jack envisioning the hand-crafted wood, rustic nice barn that will come out of the mill): I think that is a great idea, the price of lumber these days seems to have skyrocketed and it isn't even real lumber. I think having our own mill at the farm will be incredible and something that will add a lot of value to the property.

Jack: Awesome! I wasn't sure what you were thinking, and we still don't have to mill it all ourselves if we don't want to. That was just an idea if you want to take some time to think about it as well, we still have some time before we must decide on any of this!
Isabella: No, no, no, I think that's a great idea. I 100% approve, my dad has experience with that as well! I could ask him too for advice.
Jack: Awesome

. . .

The time is Mid-March the 14th and Jack starts making his way up to Saddlebrook, he has hired a realtor to sell his property in New York City the apartment, which will almost sell immediately within 2 days guaranteed as the housing inventory has been low. Jack says goodbye to the apartment and starts making his way up North. He is really excited about the new property, new beginnings, new relationships, and most of all a new family. Upon arrival up at Saddlebrook, Isabella was also coming up a day early or perhaps she had already been in town and already started working at Saddlebrook. Jack was pleasantly surprised to see her there and with a smile

Jack greeted Isabella with a smile and a nod saying Hello Isabella.

Isabella says to Jack: Nice to see you around here, Jack.

Jack to Isabella: Good to be around.

As the two are both moving into the residence house at the top of the property at Saddlebrook, it will be a transition to get used to. Both Isabella and Jack have moved a couple hours away to a new location, new surroundings, and a new environment out in the country away from any neighbors. Just the two of them alone on a very large piece of land.

Jack offered to help Isabella with her belongings moving them in, and Isabella offered to also help Jack with moving his belongings in. This step may have been a little too fast, however running this property is not a one-person task. As it will take a small team to grow this property and the only place to live on site is in the main house.

The day to day is taking time to get used to as Isabella and Jack have just moved in together, you don't think about this until you make the move. Yeah, going on dates to get to know someone is good! But do you really get to know them when you're dating, seeing each other for 2 hours twice a week? The true colors of who someone is are usually like what they are like all the time. How do they react in certain situations? What time do they wake up in the morning, fall asleep, what kind of food do they like? Do they like to have music playing throughout the day?

Altogether the move in together up at Saddlebrook has gone quite smoothly as they are both professionals. Isabella is on her laptop either in her bedroom or in the living room where she can glance out the window to the large field outside enjoying the view. Isabella does not say much to Jack as she is minding her own business. Jack does not say much to Isabella either as they don't want to offend one another as they are living together in close quarters in the middle of nowhere. They are each taking it slow as both do not know how long they will be living together for.

As Isabella still has her main job which she is now doing remotely and is currently keeping her occupied. Jack is now basically somewhat retired, has not received an email from the company who bought his waste company and each day when Jack wakes up, he tries to figure out what to do next to be productive. Lately, Jack has been on his laptop looking at barn and farm property ideas for Saddlebrook and then walking or driving around the property to see how they would turn out after it is built.

Jack has no idea what he wants for the property ideas as they all look so nice. Jack is waiting for an opportunity to discuss it with Isabella but doesn't want to overstep by getting too much in her way throughout her day. Jack waits for good timing for when the opportunity for the conversation is right.

It was around dinnertime and Jack walked upstairs to Isabella's bedroom and when he knocked on the door it opened slightly as the door was cracked and the knocking opened the door. As the door opened, Jack looked away, as he didn't want to come off as strange peering into Isabella's bedroom unannounced.

As Jack knocks, he says to Isabella: Just wanted to see if you wanted any takeout from the Chinese place in town?

Isabella: Yes, sure, I like take out.

Jack: what do you usually get?

Isabella: General Tso's chicken, rice and an egg roll would be good.
Jack: You got it, be back in about an hour I would guess.
Isabella: Be safe.

. . .

About an hour later, Jack gets back from the Chinese restaurant with the takeout for them to eat for dinner. When Jack gets back, he notices that the house is cleaned up, the lights are dimmed a little bit and there is a candle lit on the kitchen table. When Jack gets to the kitchen, Isabella is standing there with her hair up, jeans on, her indoor slippers and a nice long-sleeved shirt on.
Jack says: This food smells good, you look very nice tonight too.
Isabella: yeah, I love Chinese food! How was your day today?
Jack: It was good! Thank you, how was your day?
Isabella: It was good, I had about an hour worth of work to do today where I signed in online to a video conference and then I was on Pinterest for the rest of the day until I talked to you about Chinese food!
Jack: Anything good on Pinterest today?

Isabella: Oh! There are these impressive designs for the house, the barn and yeah! I saw lots of cool things that would be so cute.

Jack: Feel free to show me anytime too! Would love to see what they look like, sounds interesting.

Isabella: So! Anyways. What do you do again for work? What was your day like?

Jack: Yeah, that's a good question! I sold the company I had for 10 years and now I just like to try to stay busy during the day if that makes sense. Today, I was looking at barn and property building plans and then walked around to try to picture what it would look like in real life after it is built.

Isabella: Oh, that's awesome! Very neat you don't have to work too! That's a major accomplishment selling your business as well.

Isabella: I have been looking at building ideas as well, did you find any that you like? There are so many different styles to choose from.

Jack: No unfortunately, I was hoping you would help me decide, I can't decide either.

Isabella: What kind of parameters or things are you looking for?

Jack: Well, I know I want to grow our staff here, or allow more people to live on the property, because it would be nice to have more people or family around to come visit. So, the only thing that I was looking into was like adding little apartments or living quarters for friends, family, visitors… What are your ideas?

Isabella: My idea was to build a stall for a horse and then maybe we could attach an apartment beside it or above it on the second floor?

Jack: Yeah, that's a good idea!

Isabella: What are you up to tomorrow?

Jack: Open schedule, what about you?

Isabella: Online mentor to a new hire for an hour 8am-9am, would you want to show me what you are thinking of plans that you like for property? I would love to see them.

Jack: Yup that would be great!

Jack and Isabella finished their conversation and meal at the dinner table with the candle lit in the background, afterward they worked together to do the dishes and tidy up a little bit around the house. Both look forward to the day together tomorrow and wish each other a good night as they both go back to their own bedrooms to settle in for the night.

The next day rolls around, Jack was up this morning when the sun came up and went for a quick 30-minute run, then took a quick shower when he got back home. Looking through his wardrobe, Jack paid more attention as to what to wear today, because today for Jack seemed like a big day. It was one of the first times he and Isabella were going to spend time together.

Around 8:45am, Jack went to the kitchen to go to the fridge to get a quick breakfast. As Jack is walking to the fridge, Isabella is sitting at the kitchen counter with her laptop and as Jack walks by she looks at Jack with a smile. Isabella still has 15 minutes left of her meeting on her laptop on a zoom call, her camera and microphone are muted as it isn't her time to speak, she has her headphones in. So, she's at work, but has enough freedom to eye Jack while he is walking through the kitchen to the fridge. She sees Jack pour a glass of orange juice, get a banana out of the fridge, and go to the pantry for a granola bar. Jack takes a drink of the orange juice glass and is looking back at Isabella wondering what she is thinking about.

Isabella: be done with this work in about 10 minutes by the way.

Jack: Want a glass of orange juice?

Isabella nods yes with a smile

Jack pours the glass of orange juice and then slides it across the counter to Isabella.

After Isabella's morning session is done, she closes the laptop and goes, "Work complete."

Isabella: Jack!

Jack: Yes

Jack: Isabella

Isabella: Whatcha want to do?

Jack: Horse Farm Stuff

Isabella: Sounds good!

Jack: be right back, I'm going to grab my laptop

Jack goes downstairs to grab his laptop and comes back; he walks over to the couch in the tv room and waves for Isabella to come over to the tv room.

Jack opens the screen on the laptop, and it had his notepad notes up and he is about to exit out of it.

Isabella: Whoa! What is that??

Isabella: No don't exit that I want to see it.

The picture on the screen of the laptop is a handwritten drawing Jack made of a dirt bike jump that goes over the barn and in the picture, there is a dirt bike rider launching off a jump clearing well over the barn and in the air the rider has one foot off the dirt bike showing off!

Isabella: Is that you in the picture?

Jack: (Smiling and laughing) yeah maybe one day!

Isabella: The barn in the picture looks cool too, we should do that!

Jack (smiling): cool that was easy, works for me!

Isabella: So, no more jump over the driveway, now it is over the barn?

Jack: (Laughing) I haven't ridden in a while, so let me get back in the saddle first.

Isabella: I understand that I haven't ridden a horse in years. I don't think I've been on a horse since my mother died.

Isabella: It might be time for me to get back in the saddle too! And this is the perfect place for it.

Jack: I'm sorry to hear about your mother as well. I'm here if you ever want to talk about it, just want to let you know that.

Jack: Do you want to take a walk with me? I am curious to get your input on where to put the first barn here.

As they are walking outside, Jack is talking while walking with his head turned behind him towards Isabella as they are walking so, she can hear him.

Jack says: The thing to think about is the distance of the barn from the house, because as it is starting out it'll mainly be you or me checking on the barn for feed checks. Also, we might not want the horses to get close to the house, because it might be smelly!

As they walk out, Isabella catches up to Jack to where her shoulder is rubbing against his while they are walking, and Isabella turns toward Jack looking up at him with a smile as she lets him lead as they walk toward where Jack is thinking of placing the first barn on the property.

Jack reaches the spot where he is thinking and turns to Isabella and says: I think this would be a good spot.

Isabella: which direction do you think the barn should face?

Jack points with both of his arms and says: in this general direction, what do you think?

Isabella: I think it should go like this… hold on!

Isabella runs to the tree line and grabs a stick. She then walks over back by Jack and says: let me draw what I'm thinking.

After walking the outskirts of the potential new barn location dragging the stick on the ground, Isabella looks up at Jack from about 20 feet away, holding the stick still in her left hand.

Isabella: So, what do you think? That's the outline for the new barn.

Jack shakes his head up and down saying: Yeah, that works.

Isabella: Does that leave enough room for a dirt bike jump to go over the barn? (Teasing Jack)

Jack: Oh, don't worry, we'll get it figured out!

Jack picturing where he will put the dirt bike jump when he's ready to build it.

Jack: (Laughing) You know I haven't ridden a dirt bike in years, right?

Isabella: What kind of dirt bike did you ride?

Jack: Yamaha!

Isabella: Are you thinking about getting the same one again?

Jack: (With a sly smile on his face) Yeah, I am thinking about it

Jack: What kind of horse did you ride?

Isabella: I'm not sure what kind she had, I used to ride my mother's horse. Nothing competitive, we would just go trail riding with her, and her friends a couple times a week.

Jack: Do you miss it?

Isabella: Yeah, we had a lot of friends.

Jack: Do you think you'd want too again?

Isabella: (looking down at the ground) yeah. Yeah. I think so, it would be nice to do it again.

Jack sensing sadness in her tone: how is Judy doing, have you talked to her?

Isabella: No, I haven't, would it be okay if I invited her to come say hi and look at the place?

Jack: Yeah of course, it's basically your place here too, it's your home too, I wouldn't be here without you

Isabella smiles

A couple of days later, a Saturday morning, Judy drove up to the farm to say hi to Isabella.

Judy: Hi, how are you! You look fabulous!

Isabella: thanks Judy! It feels like I haven't seen you in forever! Come, come take a look!

Isabella: Do you want to come inside to see what the house is like now?

Judy follows Isabella inside, Isabella shows Judy how the house has come alive as it is now being used and each day Jack and Isabella are making the house a little bit better and better, just by using it and being there.

Judy is looking around and follows Isabella into her bedroom where Isabella shows Judy the old pictures that she has hung up on the walls.

Judy walks over to the wall and takes time looking at each photo that is hung up as she gets a glimpse of all the memories that her and Isabella's mom had in the past.

Judy says to Isabella: I think your mom would be proud of you! You made something nice of this property, it's neat seeing the progress that is being made.

Isabella: Do you miss mom?

Judy: I do, it hasn't been the same without her.

Isabella: What do you think of me getting back into riding horse again?

Judy looking into Isabella's eyes: Are you sure? Once you're in it, you're in it.

Isabella: it's been a while, but I think I am ready to get back on the saddle again.

Judy: What horse are you going to ride? Any ideas?

Isabella: I was hoping you would have an answer.

Judy: I can find a horse; I would be open to trying out riding again too. What do you think of doing a 50 / 50 lease. I could pay half of the board, feed and help with stall checks. That way it would be half the responsibility of each of us.

Isabella: What if one of us doesn't like riding anymore after we try it out again?

Judy: Laughing, do you think you would not like riding again?

Isabella: Not a chance, it's awesome.

Judy: I'll find us a horse.

Isabella: Any ideas?

Judy: (Laughing) Something laid back and trustworthy, so if we end up not riding then we can at least do lessons with the horse!

Isabella: Smart! That's a good idea! Who would teach the lesson? (Looking at Judy)

Judy: Don't look at me! How about you!

Isabella: I'm not much of an instructor, I barely know anything about horses myself.

Judy: Oh, stick to beginner lessons, teach kids how to brush the horse, feed it, and then have them sit on it. That right there is enough to do lessons with them for an entire year. By the time, they're ready to move on to more advanced stuff just stay ahead of them! Learn what you need to teach them before they must learn it!

Isabella: I could do that it wo…

Isabella pauses what she is talking about as Jack is walking up to them,

Jack: Hey ladies, what are you talking about! Anything good

Isabella looks over toward Judy to hint to Judy to answer the question.

Judy: Not much just girl stuff! Don't worry, all is okay!

Judy: Isabella tells me that you're thinking of putting a barn right here?

Jack: Yeah! What did you think of the plans?

Judy: I think it's a good idea, there should be a horse moving in here real soon!

Jack looks over at Isabella saying: Oh yeah?

Isabella nods and looks at Judy.

Isabella: Yeah

Jack: You going to ride the horse? (Asking Isabella)

Isabella: Yeah, I'll take a shot at it.

Judy: (Laughing) I might try too.

Jack: Let me know ahead of time so I don't startle you guys while you're riding with my dirt bike!

Isabella: Oh yeah? You bought the Yamaha Dirt Bike?

Jack: (Getting a little nervous thinking about the answer and stuttering slightly) well. Well. Not yet. But it's in the works. It's in the works you'll see!

Judy and Isabella are giggling, and Jack starts backing away from their girl time to go about his "chores" he must do. Which will probably be working on researching what type of dirt bike to get!

It is interesting how woman can be great motivators to men!

Judy says to Isabella, it is just them two alone now: Jack is funny, I like him.

Judy: I don't see any of his belongings in your bedroom, are you two sleeping in separate rooms?

Isabella looks at Judy, not sure if she should answer or not.

Judy: He's a good-looking man, it's about the time for him to settle down.

Judy: He has a lot of options right now; what I am trying to say is not to let the opportunity pass.

Isabella: I do like him.

Judy: Tell him!

Isabella: It's different now since we live together, I don't know how to hint that I like him while we live together, I just don't want it to be awkward between us.

Judy: Do what I do to my husband when I want his attention!

Isabella: What is that?

Judy: Where does Jack usually sleep?

Isabella: In the basement

Judy: hmmmm (thinking to herself) Do you know where the fuse panel is?

Isabella: nope, I do not know where the fuse panel is. (Laughing)

Judy: Okay! Do you have a space heater?

Isabella: Yup, love the thing, it's amazing.

Judy: Okay! So, this is what you do, before bedtime before Jack falls asleep so not too late, take a shower, then when you get out of the shower wrap yourself in a towel, turn on the space heater and start blow drying your hair at the same time and it'll blow the fuse.

Judy: When the lights go out, run down to the fuse panel and Jack will be there.

Isabella (Laughing): I just stand there with my towel on?

Judy: Yup!

I'll try that one out tonight! Hopefully that gets him interested!

Judy: Looking forward to hearing the story!

. . .

As Judy and Isabella are out in the grass fields, Jack's in the basement, he joins a dirt bike forum on the computer of locals in the area. Jack posts in the forum: What type of dirt bike should I get? Not sure what I like to ride, but I want to do a big jump.

Jack gets an overwhelming response from tens / almost fifty people commenting and messaging him on what he should do. Jack is thinking wow impressive new friends! With a lot of great advice from these online strangers, he is confident with what he wants to buy now! As Jack finishes up his laptop research, he goes to the kitchen for some dinner and as soon as he finished eating dinner, he is tired, he starts getting ready for bed. He gets into what he usually wears to bed at night and starts to read a book before settling down to fall asleep. As he is reading his book, he has a fan in the corner of the room and a lamp by the side of the bed to supply light so he can see the words on the pages of the book he is reading.

While Jack is reading the fan goes out and stops working, following that, the light turns off at about the same time. Jack puts his legs to the side of the bed to put them on the ground and he feels around the basement in the dark to find the staircase to go upstairs.

Jack forgot that his phone has a flashlight feature. He figures that he can feel around the house to get to the breaker box to check the fuse panel. As Jack makes his way to the fuse panel, he sees a light that is shining at him as he walks to the fuse panel. Jack didn't know that the fuse panel had this lighting feature. As Jack gets closer to the fuse panel, the floor that he is walking on feels damp or wet for some reason. When it is already too late and he is moving too fast, Jack slides, loses his balance and slides into what feels like another person by the fuse panel. As he slides into the other person, they both fall and Jack at once realizes that it is most likely Isabella, as it smells like her shampoo or conditioner that she uses. Jack is in what he wears when he falls asleep which is his briefs and Isabella is in her towel that she was wearing when she gets out of the shower. Jack sliding down on his back and Isabella fell on top of him, their faces are very close to one another, and Isabella says to Jack:

Isabella: (In a whispering noise) I was blow drying my hair when I got out of the shower.

Jack: That would explain why you're a little wet

Isabella: Oh my gosh, I'm so sorry. (Isabella on top of him, in only a towel)

Jack: I'm not complaining about this position at all!

Jack: I'm surprised you knew where the fuse box is. That is real smart of you to think to check this.

Jack: You smell good right now too.

Jack moves Isabella's hair to the other side of her face to be out of their way as they talk. Isabella moves one of her hands onto Jack's hand and puts her fingers between his fingers and moves her face close to his neck so that Jack can feel her breathing on his neck lightly.

Isabella: Do you know which fuse it is? I couldn't figure it out.

Jack: Yeah, your flashlight would help, that is nifty you thought of that too. I should have used my phone as a flashlight.

Isabella moves in towards Jack's face where her lips are almost touching his lips, as she gets close to kissing him. He can feel her nose touching his, Isabella then stands to her feet and in a now professional manner says.

Isabella to Jack: Friday

Jack stands to his feet abruptly still in the dark, using Isabella's flashlight moving it toward the fuse box responding.

Jack: Friday? (Thinking to himself) What about Friday?

Isabella: I had a good time seeing you today and it brought up a lot of good feelings. I want to see you on Friday. Like outside of the house!

Isabella: A Date. Would you want to go on a date?

Jack finds the right fuse in the fuse box, turns the correct fuse to the off position and moving it towards the on position. The lights come back on, as the lights are on now and Jack can see, he turns to Isabella.

Jack: What do you have in mind? I think I could arrange to make time.

Isabella: Can I pick?

Jack: Sure

Isabella: I'll see how our work goes this week and I'll let you know the day before what to wear!

Isabella: Just remember, Friday 4pm we'll be leaving to go out!

Jack: What do you mean about our work this week? (With a puzzled look)

Isabella: Judy and I bought a horse, and we need a place to put it, so we must ramp up our building, ASAP!

Jack: (Knowing about Judy and Isabella's prior little "white lies" – Remember? They "Used" the Bulldozer to grade out all their pastures, pull stumps, and put in an incredible new lawn? Well remember that the bulldozer logged 0 hours!) (Jack thinking to himself, sounds fishy! But let's go along with this one, see how this plays out) You and Judy bought a horse?

Isabella: Yes!

Jack: Oh okay! What kind of horse did you two get?

Isabella: (stuttering and taking longer than usual to answer a common question)

Jack: Remember when I told you that I can feel what you're thinking, and it is usually right.

Isabella: Yeah!

Jack: You remember when you and Judy did work with the bulldozer at her house (laughing)

Isabella's eyes light up and she stares with an open expression.

Jack: You sure you guys already bought a horse? I mean, I just know you haven't seen her in a while and seems like moved a little fast!

Isabella: Okay, Okay. You're right! We are going to buy a horse! We decided today, but we can't buy it until the barn is done, or at least one stall, or anything, just must fix a couple fences posts so there's not an opening! We can find a shelter for it for bad weather too if the barn isn't done yet!

Jack rolling his eyes and laughing a little

Isabella: Please, please, please can we build the barn a little bit more, I want to help too!

Jack: Yeah, that sounds like a good plan, I had a lot of the wood already milled up down by the end of the driveway where you turn off

into where the mill is. I can ask the guys
working down there to help us out too.

. . .

As the months went by, the property where
Jack and Isabella lived continued to grow. It
grew from Isabella and Judy's one horse and
one stall too two stalls and another stall and
another stall. As fast as the next year went by,
Isabella was able to quit her job and make
enough money working the property that the
two worked very hard creating. The
Saddlebrook property made headlines in the
local newspaper, the energy in the air, the
horses and the shows the riders from the
property went too performed well.
Jack and Isabella no longer sleep in different
rooms on opposite sides of the house as they
sleep together now in the same bed. In one of
the barns that was built, it already has two
apartment style living quarters for visitors or
boarders. As the property is full and there is
no available stall to board any more horses,
the demand for people wanting to board their
horses there skyrocketed where there is a
waiting list with deposits not only to move in,
but to build their customer's own stalls. As
the property has grown and grown, Jack and

Isabella's relationship has remained very stable, for a little over a year now, each of them has become more stable and their day to day lives have been filled with love and enjoyment. The mutual respect between the two has been unheard of in both of their lives and they both have never found anyone who was able to relate to one another this much, understand and be able to get along with. As the good times have gone by in this period they have lived together, whenever you are on a peak of the mountain, the other side is always going down. Life sometimes comes in a wave, when it is up, it is up and when it is down it is down.

As success in the property has grown fast, the amount of work and effort put into keeping and evolving the business of Saddlebrook has brought new deadlines, wants, and needs of their staff & customers, goals/desires, new requirements, and standards. When Judy and Isabella first got their horse to Saddlebrook, it was a fun, laid back atmosphere with a great bonding experience. Jack was able to ride his dirt bike after they were done riding to show off on the little jumps he would make.

It is just interesting how fast life changes and how what is going on around us changes.

Now it seems Judy and Isabella are out competed by the boarders and everyone who moved into the property, it became a liability for Jack to ride his dirt bike around the property because it was hard to know who was riding a horse and who wasn't. It wasn't worth risking spooking a horse with the loud motorcycle engine causing a rider to get thrown off. Jack was leaving the property to ride his dirt bike elsewhere; Judy & Isabella were riding their horse in private when no one was around, which was very rare.

It is not a bad thing! As the business has grown at Saddlebrook so have its needs!

Isabella and Jack tended to the business's needs and have continued to throw wood on the fire to ignite the growth of it, it has been prosperous, profitable, successful. The riders at Saddlebrook are gearing up for a winter show series at WEC the World Equestrian Center in Ocala, Florida. The children, young adults and even parents have all pitched in roles to make it all happen. Isabella is going to take the trip with the young adults to Ocala for the wintertime and Jack is staying at

Saddlebrook in Saratoga Springs area for the wintertime.

With so much going on at the Saddlebrook property, Isabella and Jack's communications have been very minimal, to the point of only talking a couple times a day and every time they are talking, it isn't about learning more about each other. It is talking about what the property needs, what customers owe money for rent/ lessons/ hay/ feed etc. When the two are at home alone, one of them is usually catching up on the laptop for invoices, paying bills and other than that just simply too tired and wanting to rest watching tv or sleeping when they're home. Their weekends are filled with great amazing times, but it isn't in depth personal time, it's going to horse shows with hundreds of people around them with their horse showing team Saddlebrook, cheering on each rider. Making sure everyone is ready and has what they need to compete for the day.

When they are not at a horse show for the weekend, they go to events with the families in the industry, fancy dinners. It isn't a bad thing! It just isn't the same as it was when it was just Isabella and Jack alone in an old house that they were just starting to fix up,

Isabella popping the fuse and running into Jack by the fuse box. The times of them spending quality time together seems to not have happened for a while.

. . .

As Fall time nears, the trucks and trailers show up to Saddlebrook to load up the horses. As soon as the dually pickup trucks pulling in with the horse hauling trailers with living quarters arrive, the horses that are going to compete at WEC (World Equestrian Center) this series were loaded. They are headed down to Florida for the Fall, Winter and potentially the Spring if the Saddlebrook Team does well. Jack and Isabella didn't seem to think about it, or at the time it didn't seem like a big deal, neither one of them noticed. But when Isabella left in one of the trucks with the Saddlebrook Equestrian Team, Jack, nor Isabella, neither of them remembered to say goodbye to each other. Jack was on site talking to the newly appointed manager of the property, Isabella was helping loading hay in the changing areas on the trailers. As the tasks for the trip seemed overwhelming, it was prioritized over Isabella and Jack saying goodbye to one another.

As the days went on, the communications between the two of them seemed to be even shorter and less meaningful when they were living together seeing each other for 30 minutes a day at most. Jack was still up at Saddlebrook property making sure everything was getting done, checking with the customers to see what their reviews are on the current barn condition with new temporary management. Jack was curious how Isabella was doing, but every time he would try to call it seemed to be a bad time. Whether Isabella was at a show, the background was too loud to hear her or there wasn't cell coverage where she was at. The main communication between Jack and Isabella were a few text messages throughout the day and a snapchat occasionally, showing each other a picture of what their day is like going that day.
Jack's view for where he is in his life right now isn't where he would like it to be. The woman he has grown to know and love, he no longer sees her or even communicates with her. Sitting at home at the top of Saddlebrook, Jack stares at the wedding ring in the brand-new box in front of him that he got Isabella for when a good opportunity came to ask her

to marry him. At this point, Jack feels as if he doesn't even have a relationship with her anymore and they have become so distant, he doesn't even know who she is anymore. Thinking about it more, Jack doesn't even know where Isabella and the equestrian team are staying while they are in Ocala, Florida competing this winter.

Tonight… Jack sits alone in the cabin unsure about his life. Unsure about his future. Unsure about what is next and sitting here in stillness questioning how he has gotten to this point. It has put him in a hard place. It feels as if a month has already passed since the trucks pulled out of the property to head South and Jack has been left behind.

. . .

Let's move our attention over to the Saddlebrook Equestrian Team in Florida. As Isabella has gone with a few of the parents and trainers with the team. As they arrive, they take the horses to a boarding facility about ten minutes from WEC (World Equestrian Center) and it is working out! Their living situation is scattered throughout Ocala. They rented a total of 2 apartments and 2 houses with everyone pitching together as a group, they were able to get discounted prices. They wanted enough bedrooms for their families and significant others to be able to stay as well when there were shows and they were visiting. Some of the team members picked up part-time jobs at WEC to help at the new bookstore that was opening where they needed more staff. Most of the other moms were either stay at homes wives or worked remote jobs on their computers when they weren't at the barn training. Some of the riders at Saddlebrook who are competing in the winter series are making decent money with sponsorships. As their Instagram and TikTok accounts have taken on thousands of followers for the show jumping videos they have created! The new relationships and tight quarters of the first winter series trip of the Saddlebrook team is starting to get acquainted and used to the living arrangements in good ole Ocala Florida! Isabella and her now close friend have found out not to be at the South end Walmart past 7pm as there can be crazy Walmart shoppers there! Their usual spots they are figuring everything out and what food they like to eat there. Where they fit in the most, the outdoorsy best place to ride their horses when not competing, the local events, farmers markets, the local laws… There is a lot to it when moving across the country! Much Logistics! It is understandable that communication between Jack and Isabella has slowed a little as she is going through a major move, and it isn't just her. Isabella oversees all the riders who came with Saddlebrook to Ocala, Florida to compete.

The first month in Ocala has passed and the Saddlebrook team is nearing the middle of the second month since they moved south for the winter season. As there has been some drama in the close quarters, the team that originally came from Jack's Saddlebrook Farm seems to have lost a few riders, not due to injury but because they got better offers and deals from local barns in the area. A few barns offered the riders free living quarters, a salary for riding for them and full horse boarding with supplements. Any rider would take that offer! It is sad that Saddlebrook lost a few of their team members because they moved onto a bigger and successful team. However, when Saddlebrook goes home come late spring or summer time, it will help build the brand of Jack's barn up there. It means that the barn is doing something right and their training is top notch. The equestrian competition in the Northeast is easy, with low to little competition. However, in Ocala it is the complete opposite. At WEC (World Equestrian Center), it is the best of the best in the world. People come from all over to throw down their skills and take it to the next level, it is very amazing the facility that has been built there. If Saddlebrook team riding members can compete at the World Equestrian Center, it shows that Saddlebrook is one of the top training facilities in the country in the equestrian industry.

Isabella has been helping with the team and the eventing. She doesn't compete, in the equine realm she likes to joy ride for fun when she has a chance.

. . .

Back up at Saddlebrook Jack's Farm, Jack has been working out 2 hours a day, weightlifting, core balancing, cardio and doing laps on his dirt bike around the property. He is training three days a week, eating healthy and focusing on technique to get better. Jack has a lot of spare time on his hands and is trying to learn how to get faster at dirt biking. He joined the local dirt bike club that meets near his town called CATRA which is a Northeast United States Woods riding hare scramble club. It is noted in the NETRA dirt bike race series that CATRA is one of the most technical, hardest, steepest elevation out of all the Netra races. ANY rider that can train with CATRA goes through the ranks fast and gets better quick. Jack has been training with the best in the meantime while Isabella is away with the Saddlebrook team.

The great thing about the two sports of dirt biking and horse riding is there isn't an age. There are riders who are 7 years old and there are riders that are 65 years old. It is such an odd concept, where your age doesn't determine how good you are, it's about how much you can let go of what is around you and focus in the moment on what you are doing. One mistake, not thinking about what you are doing can lead to a disaster. If you lose traction or if you are off balance and you can be thrown off possibly to get injured. During the day, right before noon. Jack was at the house. The manager of the property comes running up to the house crying, screaming, JACK, JACK help. Jack throws his shoes on and runs out of the house, as the manager turns waving to Jack to follow him, Jack gets to the barn and one of the kids who was riding the horse, she was holding her arm. Crying. The arm was limp and not moving, she was holding her nonresponse arm with her other hand.

Jack to manager: What happened?

Manager: The horse bucked and the next thing she was on the ground

Jack: How did she land?

Manager: She fell backward and put her hand down on the ground to catch her fall.

Jack: alright let me look

Jack goes over to the girl crying and holds her hand. Lifts her arm and says does it hurts when it moves this way.

Youth horse rider: nope

Jack: What about now

Youth horse rider: nope

Jack: So, it just feels limp, like no pain?

Youth horse rider: yes, no pain at all, I just can't move it or feel it (saying while she is crying)

Jack: Okay take a deep breath. In. and out.

Jack: On the count of three, one,

Youth rider: wait wait, what are you doing?

Jack: Were going to pop it back in are you ready? Must go quick, if don't do it soon it won't go back in

Youth Rider: Okay I'm ready.

Jack: Okay deep breathe in and deep breathe out, On the count of three. Oneeeeeee, Two Right when Jack hit two, he swiftly pulled on the hand quick, and it made a small thud popping the shoulder back in place.

Jack: What do you feel?

Youth horse rider starts moving her hand around and slowly moving her arm around normally again: It… It feels better!

Jack: You got lucky. There are mainly two things that happen when you fall that way. Number one you can't move your arm which is dislocated which can be popped right in. The next one would be if fell the same way but couldn't move your arm above your shoulder. If it was that, it means a broken collarbone. With a broken collarbone, you wouldn't be able to ride again for 6 weeks and would be in a sling or must get surgery.

Youth rider: How do you know about doing that?

Jack: (Laughing) Oh, I've broken both of my collarbones before.

Youth rider: No, about popping the shoulder back in place.

Jack: Oh, my little sister fell not too hard at all and the right angle it made her shoulder get dislocated and the doctor taught our family how to pop it back in place right away in case it happened again.

Youth horse rider: Thank you for helping, sorry about your horse.

Jack: What about the horse?

Youth rider: He went running, he hasn't come back.

Jack: Okay it's a horse, we're glad you're safe that's all that matters! Take the rest of the day off from riding though to regroup. Tell your parents what happened and ask them if they think you should see a doctor. We have a doctor that makes house calls, well a sports medicine doctor, they do all the injuries for the athletes at the local college here. Let us know if you want his phone number. I'll be back, I'm going to go help find that horse.

Jack to manager: Hop in (the farm gator utility vehicle)

Jack and the manager drive the gator around the property but can't seem to find the lost horse. It has been over an hour, and they are starting to lose hope with no signs of a trace too where he went. Jack calls Isabella to see if she knows where he might go, maybe it has a favorite hiding spot or a neighborhood friend he likes to go say hi too. Isabella doesn't answer her phone and Jack gets the voicemail recording.

Jack turns to the manager: Have you heard from Isabella at all by chance since she left?

Manager: (shaking her head) nope

Manager: Maybe ask your friend who bought your trash company? (Saying with a hush tone, hinting something)

Jack: Why should I ask him?

Manager: Word at the farm here is that Isabella has been staying at his farm with him. Not sure if that is true or not, but I am about 85% sure. I have heard it from a few reliable sources. I heard that Isabella is living at his property and my friends have seen both (Isabella and Jack's friend who bought his trash company) at the World Equestrian Center events together. Not only together but showing up to the events in the same car together too.

Jack looking at the manager of Saddlebrook
while he presses the call button to his friend in
Ocala who she says Isabella is living with.
Jack places the cell phone on the dash of the
John Deere Gator machine, the machine is
shut off and Jack presses the Speaker button of
the phone. The phone rings. Rings and rings
and then goes to voicemail.
Jack looks over at the manager and gives her
the look that she could be onto something.
Jack: Just because she is living on his property
or seen with him in public doesn't mean that
anything is going on. However, you could be
onto something. I do not believe she left a
single thing of hers here at Saddlebrook and I
haven't spoken to her more than 10 or 20
words since she left here over two months ago
now.
Jack: It doesn't sound good. It doesn't look
good. You are probably right, but she has put
in a lot of hard work on this property with all
of us and let's at least give her the benefit of
the doubt. However, if you get any concrete
evidence about this situation can you bring it
to my attention?

Manager: (Nods in approval of getting the job done seeing what is going on with Isabella in Ocala Florida) What about the horse?

Jack: That's Isabella's horse?

Manager: Yup

Jack (Not in a good mood about what he has just heard, and it is hard not to believe that Isabella is with someone else now, sometimes your gut feeling is always right): Do you know Judy? It is her horse too I believe.

Manager: I believe we have her contact; she knows the hay supplier; I think Judy places the hay orders for us

Manager calls Judy while still in the Gator with Jack trying to find the missing horse: (Judy answers the phone) Hey Judy, it's the manager over at Saddlebrook, we can't get a hold of Isabella and there was an accident on the farm. We couldn't seem to find your horse, it ran off.

Judy: Is everything okay?

Manager: Yeah, we have it under control, but when we were tending to a fallen rider, the horse got loose, and we can't find your horse

Judy: (Is at home, looks outside the window towards the yard) God dang horse, get out of my flowers, I've got him, he's over at my place. If I ride him in, can one of you give me a ride home?

Manager: Sure thing! Glad we found him.

. . .

About a half hour later, Judy comes in riding her horse into Saddlebrook and puts him away in his stall for the night.

Judy to manager: Thank you for calling me, he would have been eating my flowers all night.

Manager: Anytime! Hey! You still want a ride back to your place?

Judy: Yes Please

Manager: Hope on the gator let's go!

Judy sits in the gator, and they start taking it up the road back to Judy's house.

Manager: Sorry we had to call you to find him. We tried calling Isabella and she didn't answer. Have you happened to hear anything from her?

Judy: I have not heard from her. No. But I have heard about her. Have you heard who she is living with down there?

Manager: Yes. However, living on someone's property doesn't mean anything. That is a large property there.

Judy: That is true, but there are still a couple of ladies on our team there that are my age

and they have told me things. You have heard that we lost team members from Saddlebrook?
Manager: Yeah, they got better offers I heard.
Judy: Yeah. Or their parents didn't want their children around Isabella because of setting a bad example for their children.
Manager: When you talk to the friends on our team that are close to you, can you ask for more information. They have phones like cell phones, don't they?
Judy: Yes, we have learned to use phones, we are not that old!!!!, we all have smart phones with cameras.
Manager: Try to get pictures or record a conversation? Or get someone to talk to Isabella about it and hear it straight from her?
Judy: I don't want this information to come from me. I don't want to spy.
Manager: We owe it to the team here, if she is doing what we all think she is doing, it is putting a bad name on our farm, and we can't have that up here. That isn't right. Think about Jack too, he's a good guy. He doesn't care what we do here with the horses, he doesn't deserve to be treated like that and to be cheated on.
Judy: I'll see what we can come up with.

Judy and the manager see Jack coming back from the house to where they are. The manager and Judy stop what they are talking about and turn to Jack to listen to what he is about to say.

Jack: I wanted to let you know that next month in the middle of February, we are going to host a meeting here at Saddlebrook. Just going to summarize the direction of management of this property, a few changes here and what it will be doing moving forward. If you two want to spread the word to friends and family, there's going to be free food, and a local country band playing. It should be a good time! If you want to help plan the venue and details more, then you girls are welcome to as well! We are looking to rent a hall that could be in a VFW building or wedding venue. We want to keep it at a reasonable price and there will be 200 people max at this meeting! Friends, family, suppliers, boarders, trainers, and any stakeholder that may be affected over the change of how the farm here is run.

Over the course of the next month word spread throughout the farm that there is going to be a gathering and event for everyone involved to come to. The staff came together to plan arrangements and Saddlebrook rented a beautiful venue for the event.

. . .

At the start of the venue, Jack gave a toast to summarize everything that was going on to get it out of the way. This event wasn't meant to scare anyone, but more of a time to come together with one another in the winter month of February to touch base.

Jack: (Raising his glass) Thank you for coming to this gathering, it really means something that you are here. (As he is dressed in nice clean jeans and a nice button-down shirt)
Jack: I wanted to gather this meeting today to touch base with everyone who cares about this property of ours. I wanted to thank everyone for their hard work and the time they have put in helping to develop, using, being a customer of Saddlebrook or a supplier, just getting to use the property in general!
Jack: I did not intend to buy the Saddlebrook property for what it is used for today, I am not saying that it is a bad thing for what we use it for now. So much joy and goodness has come out of the property for I would like to say, to

everyone in this room, that property is what brought everyone here together. It also brought Isabella and I together, the woman who I have been with for the last few years now.

Jack: So that brings me to my next point. I figured honesty here is the best policy, sugar coating things and dancing around it is not something we should do in any situation. But before the Saddlebrook team headed south, I had a wedding ring that I bought, I was going to ask Isabella to marry me. I don't want to put a damper on this event, but I felt this is something that should be said.

Jack: I have not heard from Isabella since she left months ago, and I treat everyone here as my family. I find it sad that she left and hasn't talked to anyone here since she left. There have been rumors circulating about who she is living with, and I don't think it matters, all that matters is that she hasn't been in contact with anyone, I could be wrong, perhaps someone here has been in contact with her here? (Jack looking around to see if anyone in the rooms eyes show that they have been in contact with Isabella and most everyone he noticed was looking at the ground agreeing that it is true what Jack is talking about)

Jack: I am not sad, or mad, but just feel very different, having lost a huge part of me now. I have returned the wedding ring to the jewelry store which was very nice of them to allow me to return it. I do not see getting back with Isabella again as I have lost a horrendous amount of trust in her.

Jack: This brings me to my next point. I'm not about drama, gossiping, talking lowly of other people, but I would like to communicate with everyone in this room about what I am going through. (Looking around to meet the eye contact of the Saddlebrook members who came to this meeting) Unfortunately, as you can imagine this property really reminds me of my ex-Isabella and I feel as time goes on, I will learn to detach my feeling of this property being associated with Isabella. At this time though, it is hard for me because Isabella and I helped create this place on our own, before anyone was here it was just her and I. It has been hard for me being alone here all by myself on this property these last few months.

Jack: I am not sure if anyone here noticed, but I have been training hard on my dirt bike in the evenings. Riding with some top riders, training, cardio, and I am very excited that I am going to be able to get the opportunity to travel to compete in a pro race series called the GNCC (Grand National Cross Country) which is aired live online on TV if anyone ever wants to watch! It is a tough series across the country that has 13 races to complete the series. So, I am very excited that I will be able to go compete in this series!

Jack: I am going to be focusing on that coming up, a dream I have had for a while and that may alarm you that I am not going to be around. That is true, I have bought a small house in The Plains, Virginia where I will be staying mostly when competing in the series as it is more centrally located.

Jack: That leaves the last thing I wanted to discuss. The main house where Isabella and I stayed is going to be left empty as I do not feel comfortable living in the same house as everything there brings up old memories. It is not good to leave a home vacant as there meant to be used, the main house will be available for rent and of course if anyone here wants to rent it feel free to let the manager here know. Any of the empty stalls on the farm are going to be rented to a horse trainer or someone who wants to start their own horse boarding business. We are going to try to free up one entire barn to be rented solely to the new leaser, essentially whoever rents or leases the property will be treated as the new owner.

Jack: How will this affect you? We may have to move some horses around to different barns then where they are at now, early this coming week, we will start asking everyone and communicating ideas of what we come up with. We would like to do this deal off the record, no public for rent / lease post, no realtor, I am not in a rush, this property is entirely paid off and we do not need any extra money or are we in a bad financial situation here. I would like this property to be used up to its full potential and everyone can keep their ears open and talk to people they know who may be interested and suitable for this opportunity!

Jack: I didn't mean to scare anyone! This is a good thing for this property to bring it new life and hopefully bring us all closer together as well!

After Jack gave this speech, it helped everyone to be on the same page. The farm felt like a family again and there weren't any unknown changes, before with the main leader Isabella just MIA (Missing in Action). Everyone was left in suspense, no one knew who was really in charge and the farm lacked competence and strong leadership. There is still one unknown as to who will be the new head of the farm! Saddlebrook isn't for sale, but it is open for a long-term lease which is basically the same thing as under different ownership! (To put it into perspective, almost all franchise like in malls, local auto part stores, the businesses usually only lease the property, for Example Subway franchises usually lease their locations where they sell their sandwiches, it is a very common thing!)

A few weeks later, the farm got a call from someone interested in renting the entire farm. Competition, boarding, training, showing, Saddlebrook Team, leadership, competence.

Georgina. She was inquiring about the property as some of their turn outs and runs could use a year off to recuperate the fields and grass, let them grow out a little. Her and her staff have been looking for another location to hold more horses they would like to acquire. Her current farm staff has the infrastructure to easily add and manage another property much smaller than the property they have managed in the past.

Jack talks to the manager about it to see if the staff and members of Saddlebrook would be open to the property being leased by the G. Equestrian Management team.

Jack receives a warm felt and greatly accepted response from the team there, filled with great stories from previous years and generations. It turns out one of Georgina's family members is from Judy's generation and the family member remembers and missed the Saddlebrook Ranch.

Jack asks the manager to have her, and her team set up a meeting to see if it is a good fit to discuss more! Saddlebrook's temporary manager sets up the meeting for later in the week.

. . .

About a week later, two black SUVs pull up the driveway and the driver step out of the SUV that was behind the leading SUV to open the door. Two ladies get out of the SUV to walk toward Jack. The two ladies are Georgina and Isabella. Isabella (Jack's ex from years ago) Remember? The one who despised Georgina, the one who left Jack for another man? Yup! That is her, here with Georgina. This is odd! Let's see how this interaction plays out.

Jack notices that his ex-girlfriend Isabella, who rarely ever left the farm, is here with Georgina. Jack is not too sure what to say. He looks in his Ex-girlfriends Isabella eyes and he sees a major change in her eyes from who she was before years ago.

Jack: Long way from North Salem, Isabella. (Looking at Isabella) Nice to meet you (Looking at Georgina)

Jack: So, what is going on here? Is this just a prank or something?

Isabella: (moves towards Jack, holding onto both of his arms) no, no, no Jack.

Jack doesn't say anything and still a bit confused:

Isabella: I didn't think you would take the meeting with me, but I figured if my friend called that you would be interested and have her meet with you.

Jack: Yeah, true, your probably right (laughing a little)

Isabella: I think it is incredible what you did with the place here and I am sorry for the way that I treated you.

Jack: It's okay, I would have responded to your messages that you sent me, but I was dating someone, so I figured it wasn't a good idea to respond if that makes sense.

Jack: Is your friend or you interested in renting the property?

Isabella: Georgina is all set with her own property she has, I am the one interested in the lease or possibly purchasing the property down the road if you would be open to the idea.

Jack: I really haven't seen this side of you. Ever. And I was with you for a long time. If I may ask, where are you going to be getting the money? I don't think it would be a good idea for you to run the property here if it is someone you just met or your parent's money funding it if that makes sense.

Isabella: I have had my own business for a few years now, boarding, training, lessons, sale horses, competing. Look here are pictures on my phone of where I am renting now, and it is too small! Here is a picture of us and our team last year for Christmas, we had a great Christmas party.

Jack looks through Isabella's pictures on her phone and must step back onto the porch to sit down to look at them all.

Jack: Isabella. This is incredible of you, like when we broke up and stopped seeing each other, you were not like this at all. You didn't have much responsibility at all, you are sure that this is something you're able to handle?

Isabella: Yeah, I think so, I am hoping that we can figure it out, this would be a great thing for my riders and for me.

Jack: I hate to ask this, it isn't about knowing each other personally as well, I would ask anyone who is looking to do this deal. I would recommend your business size to support this property would be around $500,000 a year in annual revenue. To prove that you can do that, I would have to see tax returns... Do you happen to have the last three-year federal returns for the business? And as for equestrian industry competence (Jack looks towards Georgina), If Georgina can vouch for you that your competent to run this business and you know horses that is good enough for me.

Georgina: Am I allowed to visit and help Isabella when I want to?

Jack: (Laughing) Sure.

Isabella walks towards Jack handing him a folder: Here are financial reports, cash flow and current equipment. Last year we hit the half a million a year mark, but the last two years were shy of it as it is a new business if that makes sense.

Jack: Is Georgina signing the lease with you here or just you by yourself you think Isabella?

Jack: (Looking at Georgina) If you're going to sign as well, I must see proof of income other than money from family members such as your father.

Georgina: I think Isabella can manage this all on her own, I wouldn't sign the lease. I do want to come visits my friend here though! But! To respond to that, yes, our family's money comes from our father. However, I do have a business on my own and it does generate money.

Jack: I know I keep up with you girls in the equestrian industry, very impressed with both of you. Just wanted to see how you would react to that. (laughing)

Jack (Looking towards Isabella): I am happy for where you are in life, and I am okay with having a personal relationship with you as well. With this professional part of it, if don't meet income requirement, which your real close just it is a newer business, which has higher risk, but all business is high risk. Anyways. I just want a few months down payment on rent. I was going to say first and last, but I would like first, last and a security deposit. If you're not okay with it, or need to save up money, I can hold the property for you for three months because I think this is a good thing for you Isabella. Also, if you want to go home and think about it, even if you decide that this property isn't for you, it isn't that big of a deal. I am still hoping you want a personal relationship too ha-ha. I am really turned on right now by all of this, and if you would like to know. I guess I have been single for like 4 months now too. (Looking down shaking his head)

Georgina: Oh, we know Jack.

Isabella: Yeah, rumors are rumors. But when we also heard this property is open for a new lease for the entire property (Isabella looking at Georgina when saying this) we knew the rumors were true.

Georgina: Jack, you have been racing we heard?

Isabella: You were just getting into riding dirt bike when I was with you.

Jack: Yeah, I haven't talked about it much here around this property, but yeah, I've been racing (Saying that with a smile on his face). I have met hundreds of people doing the races I do, kind of just like having this property. It has brought many people together here which has been awesome. Yeah, I wanted to talk to you about that next. But yeah, I'm just in the amateur class right now, nowhere close to going pro in the sport like you two are in your sport doing your horse jumps. Now, that takes skill. On the dirt bike, if I want to go faster, I just twist the throttle.

Jack: So yeah, one of the major reasons why the property is open for rent or lease is because yeah Isabella and I are no longer together… I am not sure what she is up to, who she is with, where, and please don't tell me what you know because I don't want to know. I just know that she has not touched base or talked

to anyone from Saddlebrook since she left here months ago, including myself. And I know she has seen my messages, because she left me on read on IMessage text message and on Snapchat! So, it is super official!
Jack: Anyways, I have a race next weekend in Union, South Carolina and it is called GNCC which stands for Grand National Cross Country. It is on TV; streams live on your computer or iPhone too if you girls want to tune in. So anyways, I am going to get away for a little bit, try to forget about some old memories here in this place with the ex-girlfriend. I think I'll be able to get over them, it might just take some time. So, I have another property in The Plains, Virginia which I am going to be staying there for most of the year because it is more centrally located for the series. It is a warmer there in the wintertime. Not as cold as it is here, maybe in the 40s on the real cold days in January. If this deal works out too, I will have some horse stalls available there to rent out if you girls ever want to rent them. I'm going to bring my sawmill down there to keep me occupied when I'm bored, we'll mill up lumber again to build another facility in our free time.

Isabella: What do you want for monthly payment for Saddlebrook?

Jack: Not much. $15,000 a month with the three months down payment to start. $45,000 would be needed when you're ready to sign. The going rate for this property is much higher than that, which I am sure you know. I own this property free and clear, so my expenses are paid. I have some other real estate that pays all my bills right now. Just explaining why, it is so inexpensive rent here.

Isabella: That is very fair.

Jack: I have stipulations though. The first month all the current boarders here will go to current Saddlebrook management just to ensure the transition goes smoothly for the first month. After that the boarders are yours to manage. The next stipulation is that I don't want to be involved in the farm here. I might come around to visit to say hello, but for management and responsibilities, I am not available. When you sign the agreement, every detail of the property is yours to manage, lawn, property maintenance, water, sewage, etc.... You essentially are the owner of the property. That is about it, the manager that has been running it here since Isabella has been away, she knows everything about it here if you have any questions. I am sure she would love to stay employed here if you girls see fit, but it is ultimately your choice and up to you.

Jack: Are you still interested?

Isabella: Yeah, I'm going to do it Jack. Thanks for forgetting about the past.

Jack: (Laughing) I have no idea what is going on right now (looking down Jack cries a little bit, not a cry of sadness but of happiness actually)

Jack: (laughing) haha, I have no idea why I am being emotional, I completely forgot about you, but I have no idea what is going on right now, this is intense.

Jack: I'll sort out these emotions don't worry, I want you in my life, I haven't talked to you in I don't know? What has it been 5 years now?

Isabella: It has been 4 and a half years since I left you.

Jack: You have the $45,000? It's a big amount...

Isabella has a slight smile on her face and turns around and starts walking towards one of the SUVs that her and Georgina came to the property in. She opens the back door and leans in to pull out a briefcase. Walking back to the front porch.

Isabella says to Jack: Do you accept cash? I can write a check if that's better.

Jack: Cash is king

Isabella: Do you mind if we go inside to sit down to count it?

Jack: Like right now? I don't have the lease agreement or anything ready, we never even officially listed the property for rent yet haha.

Jack: What day is it today? Like Tuesday? I'm probably leaving Thursday to head to South Carolina to race. Do you think maybe in the middle of next month we will do the deal? I must get a lawyer to draw up the paperwork and he/she will figure out the legal aspects and what not.

Isabella: Whatever your lawyer comes up with we'll sign. Were in the business. I'm ready tomorrow. I'll get a hotel nearby until Thursday, so I don't move in while you're still here if that's alright.

Jack: (Jack always trusts his gut instinct and his instinct says to do the deal) Ok. Let me get this right, you want to pay me $45,000 now and start here tomorrow?

Isabella: Yeah

Jack: This is business, this puts you in a bad bargaining situation if you don't like the lease then there's basically no going back for you
Isabella: You're a reasonable person.
Jack: Hold on
Jack pulls out his cellphone and says into the phone:
Jack to the Saddlebrook manager over the phone: Hey, how are you, sorry for bugging you, I'm guessing night shift has started for the night and you clocked out for the day? … ok. Um was wondering if there's a way to meet you right now… Okay yeah that's fine, what time do you think your going to get there? … ok … Is it okay if I meet you there? Should only take 15 minutes, I'll be coming with two visitors… Yup… Her and my Ex-girlfriend… No, the ex-girlfriend before her. Yeah
Jack: We are going to go down the street, do you want to leave the cash here or bring it with you?
Jack: If you leave the cash here you are accepting the deal, the manager here that's been running the place since the other Isabella left, she clocked out already for the day, but

we are going to go meet her, because you'll need the run down if your starting tomorrow.

Isabella: Yeah, the money is yours, whose car do you want to take there?

Jack: Doesn't matter to me, if I go with you guys, just make sure to bring me back here haha.

Isabella, Georgina, and Jack start walking toward the SUVs and the three of them get in the SUV in the back and then Jack asks the driver if he knows where the dog park is nearby?

Georgina: Dog park?

Jack: Yeah, her dog goes there twice a week, we can't mess up his social life! Dog's lives matter too!

Isabella starts laughing at that joke, it was a clever one!

Jack: It should only take 15 minutes.

. . .

The drive to the dog park wasn't too long, about fifteen minutes, when they got there.

Jack says to them: Soooo, what should we do in the meantime?

Isabella: What do you mean?

Jack looking at his watch while responding to the question: Well, I didn't think we would get here so soon; they'll be here in probably twenty minutes still.

Jack: What do you girls do this time of year? Don't you usually stay in Wellington or Ocala for the winter circuits down there to compete?

Isabella: Taking this off season to heal our bodies. Georgina's back is acting up a little again and my body is just pretty worn down.

Isabella: So, we're staying up here in the cold this winter close to family, which isn't bad either!

Georgina: What do you even do? Do you work? (Looking toward Jack when she is asking these questions)

Jack: (Laughing) Been working since I was 18, since, I moved out at that time, but I mean I pretty much just make sure things are running smoothly business wise these days. Sometimes, I wont work for an entire month, sometimes I'll work for a week straight in whatever location work brings me too, with minimal hours of sleep if any at all. But, right now if I wasn't here collecting your hard-earned money today, I would be watching dirt bike videos on my phone or computer most likely.

Georgina: For the race next weekend?

Jack: Yeah, it is the Big Buck Union, South Carolina race Grand National Cross-Country GNCC race.

Isabella: Are you ready? What's the race like?

Jack: Oh yeah, I've been training hard, so I'm excited to go throw down to see how I do down there, I have my phone in my pocket if you want me to put the race from last year on

Girls: Yeah sure!

Jack takes his phone out of his pocket and goes into the YouTube app on his phone and puts it on the screen, the three are in the back seat of the SUV Georgina is on the left driver's side, Isabella is in the middle seat and Jack is on the passenger side back seat, the driver is remaining quiet in the driver's seat of the car. Jack turns on the video and places the phone in an upright position on the center console.

Isabella: This isn't on the TV.

Jack: Yeah, we can watch that if you want. But most guys run a Go Pro camera so if you know them, they'll send you their race footage from last year. This is a racer I met in Rhode Island at a race, his name is Kurt Damkoehler. This isn't his favorite type of races he does, but he usually places pretty good in this series too.

Georgina: What kind of racing is this? This isn't the kind of racing everyone does on the TV.

Jack: (Laughing) yeah this isn't the meat grinder, this is woods racing. What you're probably thinking of is supercross, small track lots of jumps in it?

Georgina: Yeah, that's it!

Jack: Yeah, that's a fun one, but I call that the meat grinder. Most athletes in that series are ground up and spit out in 3 years. This series is different, yeah, we break bones, legs, and ribs, but you can see a lot of guys race in these series for 10, 20, 30 years. Longer track, couple jumps but more about dodging through trees at 40 miles per hour.

Isabella: Is Kurt going with you to the Union South Carolina race this weekend?

Jack: No. He's out right now. Broken Femur and shoulder I believe. The doctor said six months before he's back on the bike I believe.

Georgina: Wow that isn't good. What happened?

Jack: Yeah, lot of the riders got pretty banged up in that race. Kurt was racing with GasGas, just an easy type of race. The series he was racing in usually is easy, but I think they added a few more difficult parts to the course and after the race started, the rain started to come down heavy, making it slick. He was out in front in the lead, and I heard he slid out off a rock in 5th gear which is around 50-60 miles per hour, thrown off bike. I wasn't there, I've never raced that series that he was doing.

Jack: Yeah, it's sad it happened, sometimes riders after a hard fall like that won't come back to race. So, I'm going to wait and talk to him next time I see him, see if he's going to come back to racing again. It's ultimately up to him if he thinks it is a good thing for him. I'm not sure who he's going to ride for the next time around though. He was riding GasGas, but even as a professional rider, I remember the bike he was on, he was having starting issues and his team couldn't get the electrical issue sorted out.

Jack: Oh perfect, the manager is here.

Jack rolls down the window to wave over to the manager and her dog to come over to the SUV they are in.

Jack gets out of the SUV and closes the car door behind him.

Jack: (Leans down toward the dog) Hey buddy, how are you!!! (The dog runs up and jumps up on Jack getting his jeans all dirty from the dog paws)

Manager: Get down

Jack: He's okay haha

Manager: how is everything?

Jack: Good, the day today I was not expecting, that's for sure

Manager: Is everything okay? How did the deal go?

Jack: Well Georgina and Isabella are both in the SUV behind me.

Manager: Isabella your ex who just left for your friend in Ocala?

Jack: (Laughing) we don't know for sure that she is with him, but no not her, the ex before her! The one that competed and can also ride horse well.

Manager: Wow, okay. And what do you think of it?

Jack: I asked for 3 months down payment, they got the money. Isabella has changed since I knew her, developed a respected equestrian business it looks like too. I approve, but I wanted your opinion, because you'll be working for them or with them. I'm leaving for a couple months.

Manager: Do you remember what her horse business is called?

Jack tells the manager the business name that was on Isabella's Instagram.

Manager: I'm going to be right back, mind if I take my doggy for a quick walk?

Jack: Yeah, no rush!

The manager walks away from the SUV and whistles to the dog that it is time to run and exercise, do a couple laps around the park. Jack gets back in the SUV and sits down, looking out the window at the manager playing with the dog. Jack sees the manager get on the phone to make a phone call for a few minutes. Jack has a feeling he knows what she is doing, calling her girlfriends to see what kind of thing she finds out about Isabella's current business she has been running.

Isabella and Georgina are asking Jack about what the manager is doing.

Jack: We are interrupting the dogs exercise schedule so just waiting for the dog to simmer down get worn out from all the running

Jack is stalling a little, not trying to let them know that he is doing his due diligence on this deal before the manager meets them.

The manager starts walking towards the SUV and her dog has found a new dog friend that it's playing with

As the manager gets closer, Jack opens the car door, steps out and closes the door behind him.

Jack: How did the dog's exercise go?

Manager: (laughing) oh good, the dog met a friend over there so he's happy now, he'll never want to leave here now.

Jack: What did you find out?

Manager: Yeah, she runs a good business. I called a friend, and she told me to call her friend. So, the other friend I called said it is a good business, lot of young riders look up to her right now for learning to ride which is a great thing. She has sold some sketchy sale horses though. Not sure if she is still training horses for sale, but that could be something to keep an eye on.

Jack: What do you think?

Manager: It's a lot of responsibility, so it's hard to find anyone who wants to tackle the whole property. They clearly have the experience and I guess the money.

Jack: Yeah, if it doesn't work out, we just take back the property? I'll put a 90-day default on the lease that goes back into our ownership and eviction is started.

Manager: Do you want me to talk to them?

Jack: Believe you're going to be showing them the ropes tomorrow. So can meet them in the AM tomorrow or now.

Manager: Just in the AM is good, tell them 6am be there.

Jack: Okay, I'm leaving not tomorrow but the next day, so can you just keep me in the loop these next couple of days on your thoughts about everything that is going on?

Manager: Yeah Jack. Thanks

Jack and the manager part ways for the day. Jack goes back into the SUV and the manager goes back to play with her dog in the dog park.

Jack closes the door behind him as he goes into the SUV.

Isabella: She is not going to talk to us?

Jack: She approves of the deal, so we are good to go. She's not working, so it would be good to give her some free time out of work.

Jack: Oh, she said you clock in tomorrow around 6am. I'm assuming it'll just be you, Isabella?

Isabella: Yeah, Georgina is going back to her own farm.

Jack: Yeah understandable, I'll be around a little tomorrow, but packing and moving things into the basement at the main house at Saddlebrook. I was wondering if it would be okay if I rented the basement from you? I'm not going to be living there, but if I'm in town I was wondering if it would be okay if left it open for me? There's a back entrance on the side door too so you wouldn't have to see me around the house as well.

Isabella: Yeah, sure, it would be nice to see a familiar face around here too, I don't know anyone in this area yet. Don't worry about the rent, you gave me a great price on leasing the facility.

Jack: You don't have to keep the manager around if she gives you a hard time. She is very professional and has always treated me well and managed this place great. However, I am not going to be around, lot of places I'll be at, I won't have cell coverage for most of the day. Do you want another local contact for someone I know? She would love to come around, I haven't seen her car here in a while, she used to be here 2,3, 4 times week grooming and riding her horse a little.

Isabella: Yeah of course!

Jack: (Opens up his phone and shows the contact for Isabella to save in her phone) Yeah, her name is Judy, she's a sweetheart. Judy and her friends from her generation used to all ride here, they met their spouses here, like their whole social group, so it means a good deal to them to be included.

Isabella: Yeah, I'll touch base with her in the morning tomorrow, hopefully she'll come down soon so I can meet her!

Jack: (Smiling) alright, are we ready to take me back to the farm?

Georgina: Yup! Ready!

. . .

6 months have passed.

. . .

Where we left off 6 months ago Jack, Isabella and Georgina were talking, the manager was walking her dog in the dog park. Isabella was excited to start taking over the new property, Jack was excited for starting his dirt bike races.

Life was calm. Life was moving, evolving, new experiences and changed people.

. . .

It is the middle of summer now.

. . .

Jack opens his eyes to the pavement level with his face, bruised legs, hip, shoulder slide down on the pavement high revs fill the air and his dirt bike shooting in the air off to the side. The onlookers at the motel Jack is staying at run to his help, lifting him off the payment to his feet asking if he is okay, the other hit the kill switch on the dirt bike and assess the damage to his bike for him. One of the bystanders yells he rides Yamaha, two stroke, dad get out here! The father runs out to Jack yelling no wonder you fell your running that stank gas. That bike needs race fuel, are you okay?

Jack: (Limping up to rest on the pole, overlooking toward the parking lot where he just fell) thanks guys, I think I would have still been laying there

Crowd: What were you doing?

Jack: Had to show off a little bit unloading the bike

Crowd: you're racing this weekend, aren't you? We saw the gncc sticker.

Jack: When I was unloading the bike to put in the room for the night, so it doesn't get stolen, the guys over there were eying the bike. I figured might as well start it up and show off for a few minutes. I jumped over the curb and cleared the sidewalk, revved high and the bike spun a little sideways. I was wondering why it spun a little easier than usual. When I came back around, I jumped off from the grass using the curb and tried to go up into a wheelie and the bike instead of going up, the rear wheel spun too much turning the bars in making me go into the ground. It wasn't until I was on the ground with the asphalt to my face that I noticed that the parking lot here was just seal coated. Made it slippery.

Crowd: This weekend is snowshoe, have you done it before

Jack: Nope I haven't done this race before

Crowd: Set your gps in your phone ahead of time, going into West Virginia to that mountain, you won't have cell coverage within 2 hours of getting to the race. You will need to keep an eye out as the terrain changes in that area very fast. When you're driving there, the roads from here will take you up and down through the mountains. The terrain, textures, wetness, and soils are all different at different elevations. Did you do your jetting for this race?

Jack: Just the JD Jet kit, its just a carb on here

Crowd: Notice when you're there, a lot of your friends will have issues because of the elevation difference. The Yamaha is just bulletproof. The only thing you must watch out for is to not blow up that engine. The weather isn't looking good for that race this weekend, I wish you the best of luck. Don't go out too hard in that race. The key to a survival race which that race is going to be is just finishing the race. Keep your pace, don't give up, it's a three-hour race and it gets muddy there.

. . .

Lined up at the starting line at the race in Snowshoe, West Virginia for GNCC. This series brings racers from across the country. It's streamed live for friends and family so they can watch from back home, each racer's name is listed off over the loudspeaker which can be heard by the people at the race and from the people who are at home watching online.

Jack's bike is running well, his energy is a little off today at the race, tired from the travels, he took a fall in the parking lot the other night and his support system is a little low now. Jack is riding well, right from the start. He is in a flow and doing well. The course is a rough 12-mile course, and it goes up and down a mountain, its muddy, the competition is tough, the crowd is ecstatic with so much energy in the air. Jack has no idea what place in his class he is in, but he knows if he can just finish the race without the bike blowing up that he will be in a great position. Most athletes who race GNCC can't complete all the races in the season, so to win a top 3 championship position for the end of the year, Jack knows that all he must do is finish every race with a decent position. Ride smooth, ride smart, ride on the edge and at the end of the day, keep going.

Jack is two hours into the three-hour race, feeling of loss in his body starts, sweat almost stops, because he has sweated so much, he can't sweat anymore. He's running an oversized gas tank but that is not enough. He rides into the pits to grab a quick water bottle to drink while his pit crew are filling up his dirt bike with more race fuel to keep going. Jack starts the bike and drops it into 1st revving high on his bike out of the pits, banging it into second and now holding the top of third gear in front of a small spectator jump where the crowd and photographers like to hang out. In the middle of the air, Jack notices if you come up short, you'll go over the handlebars, in the middle of the air Jack realizes he doesn't want to get hurt because he won't be able to make it home to see Isabella. The moment passes, Jack revs high bringing his front tire up to absorb the landing with the rear shock of the bike, feathering the clutch now to see how he should react on the throttle come the landing and its smooth sailing. He lands in a balanced position and can rev high, drop the clutch, and move his momentum forward at a great speed. Jack finishes the race doesn't place top 3 in his class but a respectable 5th place finish which will suffice for the top three championship position he is aiming for this GNCC race season.

After the race, Jack says goodbye to the new friends he met at the race where he parked his race rig set up to move his bike around to the races he does. Jack was planning to make the three-and-a-half-hour drive back to his home in The Plains, Virginia but about an hour into the drive, he starts throwing up from the intense three-hour work out. He pulled the vehicle over and on the side of the road opened the driver's door, vomiting all over the gravel pullover area. This is nothing new, after a tough race when pushing it, Jack tends to get nauseous. It passes quickly and Jack will feel better again in about 10 minutes, but it is a sign that it was a long day and not to push it any longer. Jack knows this so he makes the decision to lodge at the nearest hotel he can find for the night. Once he gets into the hotel, he puts the bike away in the room, takes a quick shower and eats some Chinese take out he picked up from the Chinese restaurant from across the street. After eating the Chinese food, Jack hits the call button on his phone to call Isabella (The new property owner at Saddlebrook).

Jack: Hey Hun, how are you!

Isabella: Hey!! How was your race!

Jack: It was good ha-ha, I loved it! Thanks for remembering.

Jack: How were the horses today?

Isabella: I didn't go down to the barn today, I stayed at the house, read, and exercised on the cardio bike in the basement.

Jack: That sounds like an incredible day, I'm jealous babe!

Isabella: I saw you on tv I was live streaming the race!

Jack: Sweet! Yeah, I raced well today! Should make the top three championship for the season in my class if I keep on this same pace!

Isabella: Where are you headed right now?

Jack: I'm heading back to The Plains, VA to my house there, but I had to stop on the way home. I was too nauseous to make the whole drive back home after the race, stopped got some Chinese food by the hotel I am staying at for the night.

Isabella: Oh wow, are you feeling better at all?

Jack: Yeah, I feel incredible, I'm happy that I'm talking to you right now

Isabella: aww thank you, you're making me blush.

Jack: Will you be my girlfriend?

Isabella: Aww, I already am silly!

Jack: Really? I didn't know! I wanted to make sure that we are official.

Isabella: Yes silly! When was the last time you checked your Facebook? It says I'm in a relationship with you on there! It's mega official!

Jack: Oh! Yeah, I haven't logged into that app on my phone for probably a year and a half now.

Isabella: Yeah, you're my man Jack! Forever and always! I like the mood you're in right now! You haven't asked questions like these in a while.

Jack: What do you think about me asking you to marry me one of these days?

Isabella: (slight pause before answering) I think that would be a great thing Jack, I am looking forward to that day.

Jack: Awesome! I'm excited for that day as well! The GNCC season is almost halfway over too! Excited to spend quality time with you after the season ends.

Isabella: The manager has been running things perfect up here at Saddlebrook, the same manager that was running it before. What do you think of me coming to The Plains, VA house of yours and staying with you there? I love it here, but I miss you, Jack.

Jack: I didn't even think of that. Yeah, you would love it here. There's a small horse barn and a nice pasture at the house here. Oh! Oh! Oh Isabella! Can you remind me to tell you about the coffee shop here I like, you'll love it!
Isabella: Yeah, Jack I'll make sure to remind you.
The next week Isabella arrives in The Plains, Virginia with two of her horses. Isabella and Jack were ecstatic to see each other. The vibe of their entire relationship changed with that one phone call he made to Isabella that night after the Snow Show race in the room of his hotel while eating Chinese food. When Jack called Isabella, they kept a good steady healthy relationship but never talked about the rest of their life together, being serious, family and everything. Isabella went South to The Plains, Virginia to be closer to Jack and enjoy the nice landscape. While Jack was training for the GNCC race series to finish out the season. Isabella was able to link up with an Olympic Equestrian winning rider. Through this short season, Isabella and Jack not only got to learn more about one another, but they got to grow immensely as athletes as well. It has shown in both of their riding styles around the home

practice area and in the shows/races. It was healthy, the relationship worked, the perfect balance, understanding and remember, this didn't come over night. It took a long break in their relationship at one point and the time away letting both grow as individuals. Life brought them back together with a much better understanding of one another.

. . .

The following summer Isabella & Jack got married on top of a hilltop overlooking a beautiful Valley. It was an event to remember, a small wedding, nothing fancy, great food at the end, good drinks, and a great time to remember. Some big names in the equestrian industry came such as the Olympic equestrian rider, her husband, Georgina, her significant other, Jacks pro dirt bike friends, mothers, fathers, sisters, brothers, children, spouses, significant others, a few best friends, it ended up being around 100 people who came for the wedding. A photographer captured the moments of the wedding to be framed to hang up for the future. It was a great day to remember. A day to remember to go down in history for the family. Jack and Isabella. They stayed at The Plains, Virginia property for the rest of the summer and come that Fall, Jack and Isabella went south to Ocala to compete in the World Equestrian Winter series and Jack wanted to stay fresh by racing the Florida Trail Riders race series.

At the first horse show of the winter series, Jack was in the staff area for those helping the riders who were showing in the event. Jack was supporting Isabella and making sure everything was set and ready in case of a hard fall from pushing the jumping limits in this high competition show. While Isabella was loading up the horse for the show in the stall, Jack was in the staff area to go into staging before her performance. He was holding the door ready to open it when he saw her coming. Out of the corner of his eye, he sees a man waving at Jack to come up to see him. Jack is thinking, "what in the world?" There is no way Jack is about to leave his post. He is waiting for his wife to show in the Winter Series Grand Prix at the World Equestrian Center, this is every girls dream since she was a little girl if she's serious about horseback competition. There is no chance Jack is moving an inch, this man is Ludacris! Jack knows that the man waving at him is sitting in the VIP Seating at a table that costs $2,000 for the night to watch the show and no that does not even include food or drinks! Jack does notice that the guy and the woman who is with look familiar, but it doesn't matter. It's showing time. It is only round 1 of this 12-week winter series at the World Equestrian Center and the time is now for Isabella to throw down her skill level to see how she lines up. You never know how well your training is paying off until you get to the moment where it is time to compete. You go into the competition with a blank, clear, and controlled mind, the points are the last thing that you can think about. You need to relax and focus on each movement to perfect the routine. When it is over, you forget everything, relax, have a drink of water and when it is time, you go and look at the score. Jack forgets about the odd man waving at him like crazy to come to the VIP seating tables where he is sitting. Jack is staffing the post awaiting his beautiful wife to come riding through into the show, as she approaches. Jack opens the door and gives her the nod of good luck you're going to do great. Isabella is in competition and the atmosphere is still as the crowd stays silent. As Jack is watching Isabella in her glory. A voice from behind Jack says:

Random Voice: Hey Jack! (Talking inappropriately loudly)

Jack turns around and it is the weird guy who was waving at Jack from the VIP seating table, Jack starts to recognize him. It is his old friend the Waste Guy who stays in Ocala, the guy's company who bought Jack's old garbage company years ago. The same guy who it is rumored took Jack's ex-girlfriend who helped him create Saddlebrook from day one. With trying to figure out what is going on, a flood of emotions and just utter speechlessness from just the entire situation Jack is in right now. While analyzing the situation, Jack notices this man is out of shape and has gained roughly 20 extra pounds over the last couple of years.

Waste Guy: You look great my man!

Jack: I don't think you're allowed back here without a pass around your neck.

Waste Guy: ahhhh, it's okay if they kick me out, they kick me out! Well brother, my reason is to come over here is that my staff tells me you haven't been cashing the checks from the company after the buyout, have you not been getting them?

Jack (Jack looking at the show while Isabella his wife is showing but keeping a peripheral vision on the man right next to him to make sure he doesn't make any weird movements or gestures as Jack knows already, he is untrustworthy): (With a stern demeanor) Didn't think it would be right to cash any checks coming from you.

Waste Guy: Why is that?

Jack: Word has it, that you got with Isabella from Saddlebrook aka my ex-girlfriend who helped me build that property

Waste Guy: Yeah, so what? She said she likes me better.

Jack: That is a line you shouldn't cross. I want nothing to do with you and no money will be accepted from you.

Waste Guy: Oh, stop being a baby, you'll find somebody else, don't worry buddy.

Jack: I already did. Thanks for the suggestion though.

Waste Guy: Yeah right, who?

Jack: The woman everyone is looking at right now showing is my wife. Thanks for what you did, you did me a favor getting that other girl out of my life. I'll see you around. Be careful with the one you're dating.

Jack waits until he hears a couple more footsteps and turns to watch as the Waste Guy walks back out of his life again and hopefully for good this time. That man casts a cloud of envy around him, where the grass is never green, and he always wants what's on the other side. Jack watches as he walks back to the VIP table.

Isabella 100% noticed the interaction that Jack was having while she was showing. Let's hope that it didn't distract her from her focus during her show. Time will tell soon when the results are posted. Jack gets the signal that she is nearing completion and is getting ready with his hand on the gates latch to open it as she and the horse pass through at the end. After the course, Isabella doesn't care about what the results are from her competition. The first thing she says to Jack is after dismounting her horse.

Isabella: Who was that man talking to you? I saw him waving at you from the VIP Table before he went down to talk to you.

Jack: Want to talk about it later? I want today to be about you.

Isabella: Jack who was he? He didn't have a badge on to be back there.

Jack: That is the guy Isabella from Saddlebrook left about I don't know five years ago now to move in with, not talking to any of us again. He was asking why I didn't cash the checks coming from his company to my old company?

Isabella: He thinks it's appropriate to talk to you?

Jack: Yeah, that's what I was thinking! I don't think he is all there in the head.

Isabella: Why haven't you cashed the checks from his company?

Jack: Just him and my ex's whole as a person makes me want to throw up, just plain disgusting. I think that nothing good would come from depositing and spending any money that came from that couple. I mean that girl literally abandoned her horse at Saddlebrook and never once asked about it nor talked to Judy the elderly woman. Judy thought she was her friend. Just sickening who they are as people.

Isabella: If it was me, I would have called security to have him taken out of that area.

Jack: Yeah, that's what I was thinking too, I didn't even recognize him either, he must have gained 15-maybe 30 pounds since I saw him last!

Isabella: How do you feel about all of that? He coming to talk to you?

Jack: Oh honestly, I was just worried about screwing up your routine when you were out showing. I didn't want you to get thrown off focus!

Isabella: No, no, I'm a professional, I've learned to mask my emotions when it's game time! Did it bring up any odd feelings him talking to you?

Jack: I felt relieved! I am glad he took that bad woman out of my life that was I was dating! I want to barf just thinking about her, ew it's just so gross all together. That girl literally abandoned everyone at Saddlebrook, Judy, and not to mention her own horse! Like what kind of psychopath can just leave a horse like that. Absolutely disgusting!

Isabella: (Isabella laughs, smiling at Jack) You are funny. Thanks for coming today with me, I know my stress has got to wear off on you today as well.

Jack: Wouldn't have missed it for the world, you did great today

Isabella: Thanks Jack (Isabella leans in to give him a hug)

The married couple Isabella and Jack had a great first week at the World Equestrian Center for round 1 out of 12 for the start of the winter series. Isabella scored in the place that she would like to get on average for each competition, so it looks like it was a good decision for them to head south for the winter to compete!

Next on deck is Jack's first winter Hare scramble at the Florida Trail Riders (FTR) race of the season called Hogwaller in northern Florida. The days prior to the race Jack develops a bad cold, coughing, nasal drippage, low energy, head fog, body aches and a bad fever. Jack knows that the winter series is a short season only consisting of 12 races if that – due to hurricane weather. A few races were pushed to later dates and sometimes that ends up getting them cancelled due to insurance issues getting the property certified again by AMA sanctions, property owners have prior plans/property is already in use around that time of year for farming or other events… Etc.

Jack knows he must stick it out and do the race. Jack and Isabella drive to the Hogwaller compound where the race is being held. Instead of coming to the race the night before, they decided to day trip it from Ocala to Palatka, Florida where the Hogwaller race is. It is a short about an hour drive to the race. Jack gets to the race around 8am, he's pre-registered, all he must do is walk up to the sign up to scan his helmet and he is all set to race. Once he gets to the race, Jack parks next to his competitors who are also racing today, and they came with their wives as well. Jack tries to conserve energy before the race by not exerting as much energy by socializing too much. These races are a little different as they allow a practice lap before the race if you can get out there before 9:30am. Jack puts his practice gear on and gets out there to practice the track before the race at 1pm. Upon starting his practice lap, he feels completely off balance and everyone else is going much, much faster at a different pace. Jack is coughing, about to throw up the entire lap, fatigue sets in fast in his body and he knows the race at 1pm is going to be a rough two-hour race to get through. Jack finishes up the course practice lap, he doesn't notice anything out of the ordinary for the track, no real technical sections, no huge jumps with gaps, only part of course he thinks could pose some sort of difficulty to his skill level is the real deep sand in a few sections. Up North where he is used to riding with the CATRA NETRA Race Team Club, they don't have sand like that. The closest thing to it close by would be the Southwick Motocross track, but it isn't close to it. Southwick track is more of a loamy type of sand, Hogwaller is more of a fine silt deep sand. Jack gets back to the truck and pulls up to where Isabella is. Isabella waits till no one is around and asks Jack what he thinks of the course. Jack responds to Isabella:

Jack: It isn't bad, not bad at all

Isabella: How were the competitors doing out there?

Jack: (starts gagging about to throw up, holds it in, no vomit comes out and then starts blowing his nose as it is running from the cold he has) (Laughing while responding to Isabella) The competitors today are doing much better than me to be honest, I felt slow out there today, and my head is just in a fog. Usually, I can understand what is coming up next in my head on the course, but my mind was just real slow. I couldn't think fast enough to ride my normal race speed.

Isabella: You going to race still you think?

Jack: Yeah, its same thing, I just need to get mid pack. So, if I ride well, don't crash too many times, two competitors will DNF from bad crashes and blown-up bikes. I just must be faster than a couple others to get mid pack for this race. I think it is doable, there's a drop of two races too at the end of the year, so whatever races I race the worst at will get thrown out from the championship points. Most guys can't finish the whole season racing dirt bike, mainly due to injuries. Right now, for me, just show up every race and try my hardest. If I feel too bad during race, I'll pull off and call it a day.

Isabella: that sounds like a good plan!

Jack: (Jack laughing while saying this) You want to wake me up like at noon?

Isabella: An hour before your race?

Jack (Laughing) yeah, I think that is the best bet for this one! Rest up before

. . .

Isabella goes inside the truck that had the AC blowing while Jack is sound to sleep.

Isabella to Jack: (Nudging him to wake up) wakey wakey!

Jack opens his eyes.

Isabella: How are you feeling?

Jack: Good. It's race time.

Jack turns off the truck and gets out, opens up the back door behind the driver's seat and get his gear on

Within 2 minutes: Jack says to Isabella:

Jack: You ready?

Isabella: Holy crap! You're ready to race?

Jack: Game face baby, you getting on the back of the bike with me to the starting line or you making the walk?

Isabella: Hold up, hold up I'm not ready!!!

Isabella jumps up with excitement, grabs her umbrella and her cowgirl hat to keep the sun out of her face at the start.

Isabella: Lets go!! (As she hops on the back of Jack's bike putting her arms around his waist)

Jack grabs the race fuel gas container from the back of the truck and holds it in front of him on the dirt bike at the same time.

Jack drives the dirt bike to the pits where halfway through the race, he'll come in to fuel up the bike when it gets low on race fuel. Jack pulls over putting the bike to a stop and turns it off by the pit stop area.

Jack says to Isabella: Where do you think we should put the gas can?

Isabella: Where do you think?

Jack: Over there by that blue tent is good

Isabella: Okie (Isabella runs over and puts the gas can there)

Jack: The pit stop is all you! So, after the start go over to the pits and when I come in hand it to me, the fate of this race rests on you! (Jack is joking, he knows someone will help him in the pits with the fuel, but wanted to see what Isabella's reaction would be)

Isabella: OH my gosh! JACKKKKKK, that's a lot of pressure!

Jack: I'm just kidding, someone will be there to help you don't worry

Isabella hops back on the back of Jack's dirt bike to ride to the starting line. Once they get to the starting line, Jack finds a good place to line up to put his dirt bike for the race.

Isabella takes out the race umbrella the riders use in Florida to shade the racers from the sun for the half an hour before the start of the race as they wait on the line for the race to start.

Isabella and Jack are at the starting line, waiting down the clock for the race to start. This is the hardest part of the race, just waiting for it to start. Adrenaline and excitement are elevating the heart rate.

Engines are running, revving high to keep them warm ready to race. The announcer comes on the megaphone.

Announcer: Please shut your engines off and prepare for the national anthem.

These races have 400 riders lined up ready to race the course at the same time. It is staggered by different skill level of classes. The first row to go is the AA pro line, these riders are typically sponsored and ride dirt bikes for a living. The race consists of 12 rows. After the AA pro line that is row 1, each row back is a different skill level. Row 12 all the way in the back could be a beginner rider who has never raced before, this makes the race interesting because an hour into the race, the AA pro line will lap the row 12 during the race. The pros come up on the beginner riders really quick and often lead to crashes when a row 12 rider can't pick a side of the trail to be on.

Announcer: SHUT YOUR ENGINES OFF OR YOU WILL BE DISQUALIFIED.

Everyone is doing a hand signal over their head to shut off your dirt bike's engine and the ones in the back keep revving their engines.

Announcer: Staff, please escort those riders from the property.

Florida Trail Rider's staff come onto the starting grid and hit the kill switch button on the racers who did not shut their dirt bikes off like everyone else.

Announcer: If you can't listen to the rules, you're not safe to be on this course.

The riders in the back who didn't shut off their engines are not happy that they are told to leave the property due to not listening. The national anthem starts over the loudspeaker as all the engines are off now. While the national anthem is playing there is stillness in the air. Peace, calm, and everyone knows it's race time. Just like the World Equestrian Center in Ocala, Florida. This weekend anyone who is serious about dirt biking is at this FTR Hogwaller race, keeping fresh on their skill level in the off-season training and today they are competing to see where they will place in the results at the end of the day.

In this Florida Trail Riders series, the start is different unlike NETRA, unlike GNCC, there is a different type of start. The racer stands 10 feet in front of the bike and when the gun shoots in the air, the racer runs to their bike where their family member holds their dirt bike for them.

Jack is on the starting line, one minute from the start.

The announcer says 30 seconds.

Jack stands facing the dirt bike and Isabella is holding the dirt bike by the back fender.

The announcer says 10 seconds.

The gun blasts off, Jack runs towards the bike, as Jack gets close to the bike, his left hand grabs the left handle grip and as he grabs it. Isabella lets go of the dirt bike and backs away so when Jack throws his leg over the dirt bike to kick start it, she doesn't get kicked in the chest. Jack throws his leg over, the kick starter is already out, and he kicks the start, no good. Next kick, bike starts on second kick, and he is off.

After Jack is off and racing for the next two hours, she walks to the pit area waiting for

Jack to come in to fuel up his bike. Jack comes in for the pit stop, his friend takes over the refueling, relieving Isabella of the stress to have to do it by herself. Jack goes off to finish the last lap of the race, coming in through the finish line up to where Isabella was standing, pulling off to the side.

Isabella hands Jack an ice-cold water bottle to take a quick drink from after the race.

Isabella to Jack: How are you feeling???

Jack: I'm alive (laughing)

Isabella: Yeah, you are!

Jack: Do you know what place I got?

Isabella: Did you look at the board when coming in?

Jack: I did, but my vision was getting blurry on me, I couldn't read

Isabella: What do you want to do?

Jack: Hop on the back, will go back to the truck, and look up the results?

Isabella: Works for me!

Back at the truck once Jack gets out of his race gear and back into his casual clothes, he starts throwing up on the side of the truck on the ground. The feeling of sickness he has before the race comes back to him. He pulls out his cellphone and looks up the results for his class and he came in 4th place.

Jack: Came in fourth

Isabella: Wow that's incredible for how sick you were feeling before the race!

Jack: Yeah, it's a good starting point for the season too, you mind if I drive over to the showers here and I go rinse off? Hoping it might make me feel better.

Isabella: of course, I'm in no rush. Trophy for 4th place?

Jack: Nope just top three today I heard.

He drives the truck over to the showers which about a quarter mile away from where they parked, more towards the entrance of the property when they came in. Jack starts losing energy, his body fatiguing, and his fever that he had before comes back and is stronger.

Jack parks the truck, opens the door, stumbling to the shower with a towel over his shoulder and turns on the shower. The bathroom is a little run down, but still 100% usable, he turns the hot water on for the shower, and Jack is waiting for the shower water to start getting warm, but it doesn't seem to warm up. He can't wait any longer, it feels like being on the verge of death, his legs about to give out. He takes his clothes off and hangs them up on the shower door and gets in the cold shower. The close walls in the 4x4 shower seem to be closing in. Jack sits down in the shower, with his head leaning against the corner of the shower. Jack's vision starts going blurry, energy completely exerted from pushing during the race for two hours straight. Jack holds his head up with his hand resting his forehead in the palm of his hand while he's crunched up in the cold water that doesn't seem to be getting warmer. Jack closes his eyes and almost at once falls asleep. A few minutes later, he wakes up from overhearing moaning coming from one of the nearby shower stalls which sounds like a young couple having a good time. Jack opens his eyes, the cold water from the shower is hitting the top of his head and he makes himself stand up to rinse off with some soap to get the mud and sand off him. Gets out of the shower, puts his clothes on and heads over to the truck. Instead of going to the driver side, Jack goes to the passenger side of the truck to speak with Isabella:

Jack: Hey Hun, I love you. Thanks for coming today (almost crying while he is saying this to her)

Isabella: I love you too.

Jack: I don't trust myself to drive, I fell asleep in the shower the second I closed my eyes and I think I am hearing voices

Isabella: What are you hearing for voices?

Jack: I heard a young couple having sex in the shower a few stalls over from the one I was in, and the water never got warm, I couldn't tell if it was me or the showers just don't have hot water here

Isabella: Oh yeah, they were doing it! I could hear it from the truck, there was a family walking by, and we were laughing about it. If you want to take a nap, I can drive us home? It's only an hour, shouldn't be too bad for me to drive.

Jack: Yeah (Jack puts his hand on Isabella's shoulder), that would be good, thank you. Isabella gets out of the truck and goes around to the driver's seat. As soon as Jack enters the passenger seat of the truck, he puts his seat belt on and leans over on his side towards the passenger side mirror and closes his eyes. Falls fast asleep and the next time he opens his eyes, the truck is at a complete stop, and he is in the driveway of where Isabella and Jack are staying in Ocala, Florida for the wintertime.

A few weeks' time passes.

Jack and Isabella are staying in Ocala, Florida for this wintertime period, but there has been an issue going on around Jack's The Plains, Virginia property. It hasn't been an issue; it has been able to get worked out up until this point. Jack has been receiving phone calls from the property manager who is looking after the small farm he owns. Jack bought a small home on a few acres of land a few years ago in The Plains, Virginia. He built a small horse barn on the property. Across the street is a pasture that came up for lease and the price to lease the land right across the street was a great deal. Jack approached the property owner about leasing the land to raise cattle livestock. That is the part of The Plains, Virginia property that Jack has been drawn to deal with this past week. Jack now must fill in Isabella with what is going on, because he is going to have to head North to go there in person to try to reach a solution.

Jack to Isabella: I was wondering what you are thinking about the winter show World

Equestrian Center series, do you think you are doing all the shows?

Isabella: Yeah! I am hoping too, it looks like I should place pretty good overall for the whole series, how come? Why do you ask?

Jack: How often do you want to be training this week? You know if your Olympic equestrian friend is around The Plains right now?

Isabella: I can ask her, what is going on?

Jack: I have an issue with the cattle farm I have there, and I am concerned about what is going on.

Isabella: She doesn't answer the phone too much, I can ask my friend from Barre, Massachusetts. I think she rides with her up that way in the summertime, she might know her whereabouts. I am on the edge of burn out right now too from competing every weekend, time away from here might be a good thing!

Jack: Would you want to leave tomorrow morning or tonight and drive through the night? It's about an 11 maybe a 12 hour drive I'm thinking from here.

Isabella: You're scaring me a little, is this serious?

Jack: I am not sure to be honest Isabella. Everyone's interpretation of an event is different from their own perspective from what they have been through. But the manager there watching my cattle says it is cause for concern. One of the neighbors there is saying that he might poison our cattle if we don't adhere to his demands, and I don't know if there is a way around it.
Isabella: I never knew that you have cattle right now. Where do you keep them?
Jack: Right across the street from the house there, I lease the land from the owner, and I collaborate with the owner, he's the one who manages it. He and his wife are retired, but you know how it is, you always need something to keep you busy, so they have been nice and helping me out keeping an eye on things.
Isabella: Wow! That is a huge property, how many cows do we have there?
Jack: Luckily, we only have 150 head there right now. That's 150 cows (head is a farmer's term)
Isabella: Wow, how much money is that?
Jack: I'm not too sure what the plan is when they'll be ready, but I would say perhaps

$250,000. Going to depend on the market rate at the time. When started the cattle there, I was thinking of doing a lot more there, but I am glad to keep it on a small scale especially when one of the neighbors is threatening to poison them all.

Isabella: Wow, I am sorry you have been having to deal with all that.

Jack: It's okay, I am hoping to drive up there, spend a few days in town, go stop to get some coffee at the nice coffee shop and reach some sort of agreement with the complaining neighbor.

Isabella: Can't you just call the cops on them, and they'll deal with it?

Jack: I wish. Even if we have surveillance video footage of the neighbor trespassing and dropping poison to all the cattle, there is a slim chance the police will even arrest the guy. In these areas, unfortunately it is lawless territory.

Isabella: Well, what is he wanting then?

Jack: He wants money. He is saying that his best friend is on the zoning board and will shut down the farm if we don't pay him by making one phone call to his friend. I guess, the prior lessor it turns out he stopped renting the farm because he was sick of paying off this complaining neighbor.

Isabella: wow, which is incredibly unfair.

Jack: I agree Isabella, I agree. I am hoping for a peaceful resolution.

Isabella: I don't even need to pack, I'm ready at any time to go there. I have tons of clothes at that house. I think we should stop to get groceries on the way or in the morning tomorrow, we can go into town for food. I don't think that there's any food left.

Jack: Awesome, yeah that works, glad I get to be with you. Was hoping you'd be okay with doing the trip. We can aim to get back into town in the Ocala area for Thursday. So hopefully only there for a day or two, maybe three then come back to meditate and get in the zone for your next show coming up.

Isabella: It sounds like a fairy tale we live in right now Jack.

Jack: I know Hun, I'm glad I get to experience this world with you. I'm very grateful for the life we can live. 10 years ago, I would have never thought we would be where we are today right now. Thank you for being here.

Isabella: I agree, I love you, Jack.

Jack: I love you too Isabella

Isabella: Did you want to take the car or the truck tonight?

Jack: Truck I was hoping, might need truck up at the house up there, possibly leave truck there and fly back down here?

Isabella: Doesn't matter up to you.

Isabella and Jack start gathering their belongings in preparation for the travel through the night. Jack and Isabella put their suitcases in the back seat of the chevy pickup truck and got ready to make their way North to their house in The Plains, Virginia. The drive goes smoothly, from the start. In the middle of the night, Jack had a coffee to stay awake, Isabella fell asleep in the passenger seat. As Jack is driving, he notices the engine temperature starts to rise. This isn't alarming because the elevation is starting to change, going more uphill in some spots, but the temperature outside is getting cooler as they go north. Jack thinks it through, keeping an eye on the engine's temperature gauge and knows something is off. The engine's temperature shoots up to max, check engine light comes on, it starts blinking on and off, the dash warning sign reads Shut Off Engine Immediately. Jack finds the next safest place to pull over the truck, acting fast while traveling at 70 miles per hour. As he coasts onto the gravel side of the highway, when he slows down to under 25 miles per hour, he shifts the truck into neutral and is ready to shut it off to coast in a straight line to where he can park the truck safely. Jack has an idea what is going on with the truck he is driving, before doing anything further he decides to fill in Isabella with what is going on. He feels as if she would like to know now, rather than her waking up not knowing what is going on. Jack nudges Isabella's leg to gently wake her up.

Jack: (In a whispering voice) Hun, wake up

Isabella is slow to respond but wakes up.

Jack: Sorry to wake you, I just wanted to let you know, we might have to bundle up tonight

Isabella: What do you mean?

Jack: The truck's engine is overheating, so I had to turn it off, hoping I turned it off soon enough that it isn't blown up now.

Isabella: Is everything okay?

Jack: Worst case scenario will need a new engine, but it is most likely time for a new truck anyways. I got this truck used I don't know how many years ago now. Do you remember the black Porsche I had?

Isabella: Of course, that was your baby. You were so proud when you bought it.

Jack: Yeah (responding with a smile on his face), I traded that black Porsche for this truck when I first bought the Saddlebrook property. Patting the truck on the dashboard by the steering wheel, she's done me well and even made you come around again, maybe it wasn't me but because of this beautiful truck.

Isabella: haha

Jack: It's late, so we must be on the lookout because there can be bad people out at this time of night, it's low of 25 degrees where we are at tonight. I am going to pop the hood and look at the damage now while its fresh, if you can just go in the back seat, lock the doors and if anyone comes up on the truck call the police, don't interact with them.

Isabella: What?? What are you worried about?

Jack: Not worried about anything, I don't know the area here and what the crime rate is like, so figured tell you the game plan. If anything does happen, I'll stall, say I locked the key on accident in the truck, you call the police. It's just the way I think, always must have the next move planned, the backup and the survival plan!

Isabella: That must be why I feel safe around you, be safe. I'll keep my phone on me.

Jack goes outside of the truck using his phone as a flashlight to see in the dark. He locks the doors of the truck behind him when he exits it. The hood popped from when Jack was sitting in the driver's seat, he pulled the hatch to raise the hood to access inside it. Jack approaches the hood, slides his hand underneath to move the lever to fully release the hood to open it. As the hood opens, it releases a small cloud of smoke into the air from the overheating engine. The clouds are exaggerated to be more than it is due to the cold temperature which shows more heat in the air. When Jack's face was filled with smoke from the hood of the truck being opened. He backs up and as he waits, he moves his phone to shine the flashlight underneath. Jack leans down to inspect underneath the truck, he notices an obvious smell that he has smelled before in the past. He notices a puddling of orange liquid underneath the engine bay. The smoke emitting from the engine is gone now, Jack makes his way with his flashlight back to the engine bay. He sees what's going on, a radiator hose blew off he pushes it back into the part where it connects to stop the coolant from leaking underneath the truck. Jack closes the hood of the truck and knocks on the window of the driver's door. Isabella hits the unlock button to unlock the truck and Jack gets into the truck.

Isabella: I got blankets! Were good! How did the truck go?

Jack: (Laughing) haha, not too bad, I would say around 8am-10am tomorrow the parts car will be by from NAPA to bring us the parts we need. I have all the tools needed for it in my toolbox that's inside the bed of the truck.

Isabella: Wow! What do you think it is?

Jack: It looks like just a radiator hose came off; I have a feeling the thermostat went on the truck. It's about that time for it to go so guessing that's why it blew the hose off.

Isabella: Is it expensive you think?

Jack: My guess is around $100 in parts, hoping we're still on good terms with Napa so they bring it out to us for free. Hopefully the new owner of the trash company I sold didn't do NAPA bogus by not paying their bill. For parts, going to need a new radiator hose, two clamps, coolant, and a thermostat. Should be around $100 maybe a little more, so I wouldn't say that's expensive at all for working on a truck! The job should take about 10 minutes.

Isabella: How did you learn all of this?

Jack: I apologize if this offends you, I just can't remember it being so long ago. I believe I met you about 5 years into my trash company. So, you may not have been around me during this period of my life, but starting that company was no easy task. Started with one old beat-up pick-up truck and I was going around to all the neighbors on my street taking their trash to the town dump for them almost every load was overloading that truck! It was just me alone, I was running real old equipment with constant breakdowns. It was tough keeping everything going, I learned to be my own mechanic and after some time I got good at it. Some skills stay with you forever! It was very tough though, I remember thinking about giving up and calling it a day, but I was making such good money at the time. It wasn't until about 3 maybe 4 years when the company really took off. It's hard to remember because it was so long ago, but I do remember that a large company believed in me to manage their property's waste. I signed a large contract and I outperformed. I did more than was needed from me, I did a great job, and I was given another large contract. The company grew to where towns were calling my company to manage their trash for them. After that, it wasn't just me, we had a group of people at work to get it all done. It became quite a business.

Isabella: Do you regret selling the company?

Jack: (jack takes a pause before answering to think about his answer to Isabella's question) No, it was the good decision to make. I wouldn't be snuggling you on the side of the road in a broken-down old truck if I still owned that company. (Laughing, smiling at Isabella) I wouldn't trade my life right now for anything in the world. Each moment I appreciate, and I am so grateful.

Isabella: When we first met, if you would ask me what our lives would be like 10 years later, I would have never guessed this. It is every girl's dream to be doing what I am right now. Do you remember I would never leave my

barn in Brewster, NY when I first met you?
Do you remember that?

Jack: (Laughing) yeah oh I remember; I spent many hours at that barn with you. But me too, I almost never left my work in New York City. The only time I would get out of that area was to go to Brewster to see you! Now we are all over and financially more sound.

As Isabella and Jack are talking, huddled underneath the blanket in the truck making sure they are both staying warm, the sun starts to rise bringing light to the surroundings. As the sun rises, it starts to show that they are parked on an elevated part of the road allowing them to overlook into the surroundings for a long distance creating a surreal feeling. Jack pulls out his phone and calls the nearest Napa, he gives the operator the business he used to own in NYC to see if it pulls up anything in NAPA's national database.

The auto parts store nearby called Napa says it'll be about an hour until the parts arrive. Isabella and Jack sit tight underneath the blanket and Isabella takes out some nutri-grain bars and bottled water that she packed.

She leans over to Jack and says in a funny voice.

Isabella: SnAcKs?? (In the funniest most hilarious tone of voice)

Jack starts busting out laughing.

Jack: Yeah, I'll take some SnAcKs! You're going to make a good mother!

Isabella: Oh, is that right?

Jack: Yeah, you're hilarious!! All the kids love you in your lesson program. By the way, how is your business up at Saddlebrook going with you being away? I have been meaning to ask about it.

Isabella: Don't try to dilly dally around the subject! You just said you wanted to have kids!

Jack: I said you would make a good mother!

Isabella: Yeah, but with who! You're my husband Jack!

Jack: (Responding with a smile) I guess you would be baby making with me.

Isabella: We've never talked about this; do you want kids?

Jack: yeah of course if you want kids.

Isabella: Yeah, I do, so are we going to have a kid now? Or do you think we should think about it?

Jack: No need to think about it, I think we know everything about one another, granted we've been together for over ten years now? Yeah, let's try for a kid!

Isabella: Okay after this show season, but it probably won't happen right away, and Ocala winter shows are already halfway done so yeah! That makes sense, awesome! (Cheering of excitement, realizing that she is going to be a mother soon) Saddlebrook is going well I heard up there, the kids send me the horse pictures at least once a day and I love it. Very excited to get back up to that area this Spring. It is slow right now there, being the winter and all, we aren't missing much. Everyone is huddled underneath the heat lights in the indoor arena wearing jackets and warm clothing. It is a little rough up there to keep training in the wintertime, very grateful we get to go South in the winters now. Half of Saddlebrook is down here anyways too that's also why it's slow there.

Jack: Yeah, I bet they all miss you! They look up to you. I've noticed a huge change in how you are since you started your lesson program there, it's neat to see. Makes me a little nervous, because I must be a good example too for the little ones looking up to us!

Isabella: Oh stop (laughing) all those kids at the dirt bike races are always coming up to you asking about your dirt bike, they look up to you too!

Jack: Yeah, you're right!! They always ask me what I do for work, and I never know what to answer them.

Isabella: Well, what do you say when they ask you!

Jack: I usually say something like I started a waste management company at a young age that I ended up selling the business and now I live off my wife's equestrian business! (Laughing)

Isabella: Oh my gosh, you don't say that! Jack!!! You are a sponsored rider, why don't you talk about your sponsors!

Jack: Yeah, I probably should! I thought it was a funny answer that they weren't expecting, so I guess that's why I said it.

Isabella: Oh, that is too funny, do you tell them about my business?

Jack: Usually the kids ask me how I place and what type of races I do. So, we usually end up talking about dirt bikes. I think that one of the similarities about our sport is age doesn't matter. There are riders from 6 years old all the way up to 75 years old and the age doesn't really determine our skill level, I got beat by a 65-year-old in a race last year! That was crazy.

Isabella: Wow that's motivating that they can keep up at that age!

Jack: Yeah, riding keeps us young and in shape for sure! Hey Isabella, I have been meaning to talk to you about something that has been on my mind.

Isabella is about to respond, and a small white car pulls up to Jack and Isabella on the side of the road. Jack rolls down the window and the driver asks if they are the ones who ordered the parts.

Jack responds with yeah that's us!

Jack gets out of the car to talk to the driver and get the parts to fix the truck to get them back on the road!

Napa driver: here's your parts sir!

Jack: Thank you!

Napa driver: Do you ever talk to the new owner of your old company?

Jack: Once about 6 weeks ago I believe, not on good terms with him at this point. He took my ex-girlfriend from me, and it looked like he gained about 20 pounds.

Napa driver: wow now that is not cool, well he's not on good terms with us either.

Jack: What did he do to you?

Napa driver: Your old company hasn't paid us for brake pads, rotors, oil filters and oil for the trucks, bill is approaching 6 months old in the range of $4,000. It's not a big deal, but if the new owner doesn't have the money, he should at least try to work out a payment plan or something to get us back on track.

Jack: You hear anything else going on about the company? It's good to know, because my name is still somewhat tied to that company in the sense that I started it.

Napa driver: Haven't heard much about it, I can keep my ear open for you if you'd like.

Jack: Yeah, I would appreciate that very much, is it okay if I pay the $4,000 bill to settle the balance owed on the account and then you close it out?

Napa driver: Yeah, that would be nice, I can't take payment. I'm just a driver but here is the phone number for the parts counter. He can take the payment. (The driver hands Jack the business card for the store and then starts to unload the parts onto the back of Jack's truck in the pickup bed.)

Jack: Thanks again for delivering the parts especially with the balance due on the account The driver gets in the car and drives away after giving Jack a head nod. Jack takes the business card he just got out of his pocket to start calling the parts store. Jack places his phone against his ear and then uses his shoulder to balance the phone against his head allowing him to use both hands to work on his truck. While on the phone, Jack takes the new thermostat out of the box to inspect to make sure it isn't damaged. Jack takes out his wrench set which he uses to go and loosen up the radiator hose from the thermostat. As he is taking off the radiator hose from the thermostat and inspecting to make sure everything is safe to put back together, he looks for other components that may be damaged.

Jack (What Isabella is hearing while Jack is working on the truck and talking on the phone at the same time): Yeah, yeah, yeah, I agree with you guys its crazy. Yeah, I don't think you ever talked to her or met her. Yeah! She just up and left, I didn't hear from her for like 2 months so figured she was just done with me and yeah. The kids at the farm were telling me she left for the new owner who bought that company. I was worried if she was still alive, but the little investigators at the farm had their friends down in Florida take pictures of them kissing when out at an event! yeah hahaha! ohhhh, get this she just left her horse at the farm and never cared about it, yeah, they both are psychopaths! Crazy! Anyways, are you ready for the card number? Jack is holding his phone in with his shoulder against his ear, two zip ties in the corner of his mouth being held with his teeth, a 10mm ratchet in his right hand and his debit card in his left hand.

Jack: You ready for the numbers? (He starts reading them off still talking very clearly and competently while there are zip ties hanging from his mouth working on the truck at the same time.)

A few minutes more pass on the phone and some chit chat going back and forth, then he goes back to the back of the truck to grab the container of new coolant to fill it up. As he is walking back to the front of the truck, he stops by the driver's door and opens it to say hi to Isabella for a second.

Jack: Hey baby, we should be good to go in a jiffy! About five more minutes.

Jack shuts the door, goes to the front of the truck again, opens the coolant reservoir cap and starts filling up the reservoir with the much-needed coolant for the engine to run and not overheat. Jack leaves the coolant cap off, puts the container on a flat surface and then goes inside the truck again to start it. The truck fires right up, Jack goes to the front of the truck to watch it to make sure the level is staying at the best level as the system bleeds out the excess air. Jack looks underneath the truck and holds steady to watch for leaks for about 30 seconds. He doesn't see any leaks coming from underneath the truck. Jack makes sure the new hose was tightened, double checks the thermostat housing bolts are secured and looks to see the coolant level is in the correct position for what the temperature of the engine is at. The project is completed now while he was talking on the phone. This project meets Jack's expectations and approval requirements! He checks off a job well done, puts the coolant reservoir cap back on and closes the hood of the truck making sure it latches completely. Jack gets back into the truck and says to Isabella, "Good to go!"

The two resume their journey heading North, making the first stop at the nearest gas station exit, for a restroom break, top off truck with fuel, check over the truck one more time, grab some snacks, a coffee and then they continue their way back to The Plains, Virginia.

Isabella: Did you pay that guy's car parts bill for your old company?

Jack: Yup, I did

Isabella: How much was it?

Jack: A Little over $4,000. $4,451.19 to be exact.

Isabella: Jack Hun, why did you do that? You know we can't cut it too close this time of year, the companies are slow in the wintertime. That leaves us probably down to about $44,000 in our checking account right now. That must last us until April around springtime. If we cut it too close that might have to go into our savings account, I might have to go back up to Saddlebrook to collect the boarding rent to up our personal checking.

Jack: The Napa parts store is close to my old supervisor up at the old waste business of mine in NYC. I figured the $4,500 price tag to cover the bill would be completely beneficial to us to keep an eye on that company.

Isabella: How does throwing $4,500 into thin air for a bill you don't even owe benefit us??

Jack: Everyone talks, and I can guarantee you, now they're on our side. I have a feeling that the new owner might have a few other outstanding bills he owes. If word spreads around that area that the old owner is paying for the new owner's past due balances, I can guarantee that they will start reaching out to me about these issues to get resolved.

Isabella: So, you want to pay more of his bills that he doesn't pay?

Jack: I am not sure what I would do, but something strange happens when you create something that if someone else screws it up, sometimes the universe will bring it back to you to fix. I also want to hear about the status of the company to see what its business is like; I like to hear how competitors run their business. I still can't believe he would pay that much for that table and food at the World Equestrian Center, remember? That one time when he came up and talked to me when you were showing?

Isabella: Oh yeah, I remember! So now you want to get your old company back and move back to New York City?

Jack: No wayyyy! I am working a different angle!

Isabella: Please don't tell me you want to make him look bad to get back with your ex who left you?

Jack: Ew no way, she's disgusting. No way, but if I can finesse my way back into the company or that industry with little to no work to gain back the company. I know someone who would like to own it and 100% deserves it.

Isabella: Who?

Jack: My old foreman, he can run that company like no other, he has a family for himself now, we've been working with each other for I can't remember for how long, but I am going to work this moment forward getting that company back to give to that man. My non-compete contract with him is over and it is perfectly legal for me to do so. If you can keep your ears open or help me in any way, get it back from him, I would love to

work together on the idea. It still irks me to this day since he came up to me thinking it was okay to talk while you were showing at the World Equestrian Center that day.
Isabella: I'm in, I don't think they are setting a very good example and it is sad what she did to Judy at Saddlebrook. That amazing woman Judy was so hurt by Isabella betraying the horse and the Saddlebrook Family. But Jack, I just need you to promise me anything over a couple grand purchase or expenses that come in to talk to me about spending it? At least just for this winter season while business is slow, I am concerned about cutting our checking account too close, something unexpected could come up like a major horse vet bill or one of us getting injured in competition.
Jack: Yeah, that is fine! I can do that.
Isabella and Jack pull into their property in The Plains, Virginia and unload their suitcases they packed, put the blankets they used in the truck to keep warm and head inside the house to sit down to relax after a long drive.
Isabella: Ohhhh No!!!!! (Sheer terror in her voice like her foot got cut off on accident or something devastating happened)
Jack: What? What's wrong?

Isabella: We forgot to stop and get groceries!!!! Ughh!!

Jack: (Laughing) Oh my gosh, I thought you were about to die or something! Hold on, we can order groceries on our phone, and they'll deliver them to us!

Isabella: Really? Do they do that now? I don't want fast food; I must eat healthy; I mean food from the grocery store.

Jack: Yeah! You put in what you want, and a person goes grocery shopping for you, and they deliver it to our house! It is a $5 delivery fee on top of the food, it would cost us more than $5 in fuel to take the truck there to get it ourselves.

Isabella: Score! That works!

Jack selects the grocery items from the app on his phone that he would like brought to the house, then he hands the phone to Isabella, she chooses what she would like from the grocery store and then submits the order for the delivery.

Jack says to Isabella: Remember when we were in the truck and I said I wanted to talk to you about something, then the parts arrived to fix the truck? I couldn't finish telling you what was on my mind.

Isabella: Yes! Tell me, I completely forgot about that.

Jack: Ever since the guy came up to me while you were showing in Ocala at the World Equestrian Center, I am not sure what happened. But the ex-girlfriend of mine, the one that is dating that odd man who we just paid his $4,500 NAPA car parts bill, she has been trying to reach me. I didn't think anything of it, I figured she forgot about me and seeing me with you made her curious to see what I was up to. She followed me on Instagram and liked one of my pictures. I took it as a friendly gesture, but then about another week later she added me on Facebook. I was going to talk to you about it but wasn't too sure how I felt about being her friend on Facebook, because I leave that just for close friends and family to add me on. So, I was going to think about it for a couple of weeks. Anyways, the other day she called me out of the blue. I believe, I have a new phone number since I was with her, so not sure how she got it, maybe from her boyfriend/husband the waste guy. But I didn't know it was her calling and I answered the phone.

Isabella: What did she say on the phone?

Jack: She just asked if it was me, apologized for how she left Saddlebrook and everyone behind, asked about her horse, she asked me about you. I didn't know how to take it or what her intentions were. I'm okay with being friends with her, but I am not sure because it might be a liability. I just don't trust her and please don't think I have any intention of leaving you for another woman, I am completely happy in our relationship.
Isabella: What did you say to her?
Jack: I was pretty put on the spot in the moment, I said don't apologize to me, apologize to the people you left behind. I said to her that I wasn't sure what happened to your horse, probably got sold or donated to someone whose always wanted a horse because it was abandoned property. Then I said that I'm married to my wife and that I should get off the phone. The only thing I really said is if she is concerned about her horse, I said that she should call Saddlebrook staff. They can say what details are allowed to be released after looking at privacy laws about the matter.
While Jack was telling the details of his ex-girlfriend who left him to his Wife, his phone

rang. Jack answers the phone: Isabella is overhearing the conversation and at once knows it is a serious interaction as Jack's posture changes and he gets out of his chair to stand up.

Right now, Jack isn't laid back on the phone with his shoulder pressing the phone to his ear, he is holding his phone to his ear and only concentrating on the conversation.

Jack on the phone, which Isabella is listening to too: Yup, Yeah, we made it back into town, little later than expected, we had a breakdown. What is he saying? What time? Okay. How much money? $10,000 dollars. What happens if we don't pay him? It can't be that bad. Did It go up? How does he want to get paid? Is this the same as earlier he was getting paid? Oh of course. Can you postpone the meeting till tomorrow, I don't want to meet them in the dark. We can do early morning. Who are you coming with? No, you can't go alone, you come to my house before going there, we must do this right. Can you let me know if you can't make it in the morning, just don't show up there by yourself, please, this is extortion and we need to treat it that way, please. Ok Talk to you soon.

Jack hangs up the phone and moves toward the wall, looking down, putting his hand on the wall trying to think through the entire conversation he just had. Jack takes out his phone to make another phone call.

Jack on the phone, Isabella listening to the conversation in the background: Hey my man, how you been? Yeah, about the same. I just had a question and wanted to let you know that my wife and I have something in the works that'll hopefully benefit you in the future. Can you keep your ear open, we just paid the NAPA bill for your business there, no not my business its your business there. Yeah, your new boss didn't pay one of the bills, see if there's more bills outstanding, you and I will work with those creditors. Yeah, yeah, yeah! Exactly, yup, slowly but surely. Nope I don't want that company back, Isabella and I have enough business right now. You'll be the new owner if we can make that happen. No, we aren't buying it back, we'll push him out. Do you have that company's phone number for the security firm we used before? No nothing crazy is going on, just dotting my I's, and crossing my T's. ensuring safety and accountability, which is all. Okay thank you, let me know if hear anything about past due bills. Talk soon.

Jack gets off the phone with his old supervisor and looks more confident, his mood changes slightly. He looks at Isabella thinking that he is glad that she is overhearing the conversations to know what is going on. He makes one more phone call to the phone number he got from his old supervisor.

Jack: (Isabella overhearing him talking while on the phone again) Hey, my name is Jack I am looking to hire private security in The Plains, Virginia area for tomorrow morning. Yeah, we used your company at one of your branches in New York City area years ago, not sure if you have a record. Yeah, we are supposed to be there for dawn tomorrow to meet someone we must pay. Yes, they should be armed. Yeah, there is no cell coverage there, so one person on your team will have to have a radio and the other team member will have to sit where there is cell coverage in case, we need to make a phone call out. Yes, we will need two vehicles as well. I am not sure who we are meeting, and it is in an area that I am not familiar with. I know nothing about the local politics in the town. Yeah, that is fine for a price, which is very reasonable for finding someone nearby here and on such short notice. Do you want my debit card numbers now? Okay that is fine, I will have debit card in the morning for you tomorrow when your staff gets here. (Jack starts reading off his house address for the company to meet them tomorrow). Yes, this is my cell phone number. You can text the confirmation for the appointment to this number. Okay thanks, see you tomorrow.

Jack gets off the phone and relaxes, takes a deep breath, sits down in the chair back at the table he was sitting at and starts crying. Isabella puts her arm around Jack and doesn't say anything knowing that there are just no words to describe this situation. This is what is happening now, to the couple, and no one can relate to this issue. No cops can help them in this situation until a proven crime is committed where there is strong evidence. In this situation, politics is not on their side and the local community will not help.

Jack looks at Isabella.

Jack (Tears in his eyes): I don't like this position. I don't like what this feels like. I have no choice but to pay him off.

Isabella: $10,000?

Jack: Yeah, we must pay him $10,000 out of our account. In cash

Isabella: What happens if we don't pay him?

Jack: Nothing will happen to you and me, we can move the cattle to a different property and just be stuck paying what the land lease was. But the property owner who we lease the land from will be arrested and the town will take his land from him.

Isabella: What? This doesn't make since, why would he get arrested?

Jack: What happens is if we don't pay him the $10,000 that he has been getting paid once a year, he will call the town to make a complaint of some sort of zoning violation. His friend is the zoning agent in town and what will happen is the zoning agent will come and arrest the owner if the "zoning violation" is not "fixed" immediately. I called a couple buddies I do know, and they asked around. I guess we are on the side of this town that borders the next town over and they aren't for agriculture and farms. I can see why the town would be able to push out this farm and it would cost me a lot to move all my cattle. For us we keep the landowner out of jail, and it is just the cheapest choice to pay the $10,000 at this moment in time. Unfortunately (Jack is looking down while trying to explain this to Isabella)

Isabella: Yeah, I don't believe that one bit.

Jack: Yeah, I said the same thing, but then I pulled a background check on the property, and the property owner has been arrested once by the "Code Enforcement Agency" in this town. So, he is not lying. He paid the guy the money and the charges were dropped, but he was held in jail, and it is still a public record to this day that it happened. On top of that, I researched zoning violation case laws about this matter, and this is a common thing in the farming industry unfortunately. There aren't many if any, law firms that help farmers. I even talked to the USDA, the federal farming agency, about this and they said it is a civil right violation of the town and to report it to the Department of Justice. But there aren't many, if any, I can find in the state of Virginia of the Department of Justice stepping in when the town and the town's attorney sues a property owner.

Isabella: Okay so he gets arrested, but out on bail, how does he lose the property?

Jack: Yeah, that's the thing, they are very sneaky. The local town puts it into the court system to sue for a "zoning violation." They can add as many zoning violations as they can come up with, sometimes I have read that they say it is a zoning violation even if it also says it is allowed for the property. Let's say the town issues 14 zoning violations and they will announce that the charge for each zoning violation is $100 a day for each one. 14 zoning violations x $100 = $1,400 and if the land is only worth $400,000. The town will try to foreclose on the property after 285 days.

Isabella: They can't do that!

Jack: They can, and they have unfortunately, there is an overstep in the government right now when it comes to agriculture, they don't want it. They never have, they want postage sized yards, brand new cars, lots of houses on ¼ acre properties for the most tax dollars to come in for revenue for the town. This town is mostly rural and country, but not paying this guy the $10,000 I believe would be a 75% chance of the property owner getting arrested.

Isabella: What do you think we should do Jack?

Jack looking down towards the ground, moves to look up at the ceiling and then looks at Isabella.

Jack: I spent about 50-man hours trying to decide on this matter over the course of the last few weeks. What made up my mind is when I looked at the website called casetext.com and searched in the court case keywords zoning violations farming. Just looking through what the town can consider a "zoning violation". They are unaccounted for, and it is one of the saddest things I have seen. Unfortunately, I think with your permission, we will pay the $12,000 it is going to cost tomorrow. $10,000 to the person who is threatening to report the property and $2,000 for private security as we are dealing with a criminal here. I really would like your honest input.

Isabella: Take the money out of the horse show and dirt bike race fund for the winter?

Jack: We might have too eventually, but the cattle feed budget we can use the money from that and perhaps grass feed the cattle more, could also sell off some of the cattle to a neighboring farmer to compensate the loss. It

is smarter to use the cattle business checking account to pay for the cattle farm expenses.
Isabella: Thanks for talking to me about this.
Jack and Isabella start to wind down for the night. Not much talking happens as there is anxiousness in the air and both of them know that tomorrow awaits a big day.
They fall asleep holding each other's hands and time to wake up comes early before the sun comes up the next day. Isabella stays lying in bed, Jack gets up and out of bed to freshen up before a visitor comes to the door followed by the hired security. Jack makes his way to the bathroom, starts brushing his teeth, everything he does is normal, but it seems as if each moment is slowly going by. Jack starts the shower to warm up as he goes back to brush his teeth in front of the mirror in the bathroom. Jack finishes brushing his teeth, rinses off his toothbrush, swishes a mouth full of water in his mouth to spit out the toothpaste. He walks into the shower and gets in to rinse off. Jack hears his phone start to ring. He quickly reaches out of the shower, grabs his towel, and then wipes his hand so that he doesn't get the screen on his phone wet, he answers:

Jack: Hello

Man on the phone: Hey, just pulled into the driveway.

Jack: Come inside, I'll be at the front door, our ride is about ten minutes away

Jack hangs up the phone, quickly rinses the shampoo out of his hair and soaps his body real quick rinsing off. Gets out of the shower, dries off with a towel, walks over puts briefs on and then his athletic shorts. He walks over to the front door barefoot and shirtless, opens the door, it's the property owner of the land he leases.

Jack to property owner: come in.

The cattle farm property owner walks in, and Jack says:

Jack: If you want to wait in the kitchen, I'm going to go to my bedroom to put clothes on. There is a fresh pot of coffee if you want some and you can have anything in the fridge or on the counter for breakfast if you're hungry too.

Property owner: I appreciate it, but the wife made a good breakfast for me

Jack walks into this bedroom, closing the door behind him and taps on Isabella to wake her up. She wakes up.

Jack to Isabella: Baby, I just wanted to let you know I hope you have a good day (then he leans in and kisses her on the lips)

Jack walks to the closet to finish putting on clothes, jeans, work boots and a sweatshirt.

Jack grabs the briefcase that has the cash in it for the meeting. Jack is all dressed now, says goodbye to Isabella again as she lays back down in the bedroom. Jack walks to the kitchen

Jack says to property owner of the farmland where his cattle is: Well, I got the money (places the briefcase on the counter), how do you feel about this meeting?

Property owner: I was trying to put it off and hope they would forget it, didn't happen. Seems about average, believe we haven't done the meeting in probably 3 years. Before you, the property was vacant for about two years not bringing in any rent.

Jack: Do you think the security coming with us is overkill?

Property owner: I do, it's not needed.

Jack: Your probably right, if we had cell coverage there, I wouldn't have called security. I'm not from around The Plains, Virginia area. The word I have heard in these parts is that everyone is pro farming and livestock, but I guess when it comes down to it, is all it takes is one bad neighbor.

Property owner: It's better safe than sorry though to bring security! You could be right, it's all about trusting your gut and hey for me I get a free ride there in style, so I don't care either way!

The two black tinted SUV's come into Jack's driveway, Jack and the property owner start walking out of the house. Walking toward the vehicles to the meeting to pay the $10,000 farming fee to the neighbor who is threatening to call his friend to issue a zoning violation on Jack's cattle farm. If Jack doesn't pay this neighbor, the owner of the land that Jack rents this land from will end up in jail and the property to be held up in litigation for the next five years.

In attempt to buy another year of keeping the cattle farm on the landlord's property going, Jack leaves Isabella to go with the property owner down the street to pay the $10,000 extortion farming fee. Isabella watches from the bedroom where she was pretending to sleep as the two get into the SUV. They get into the SUV that's in the back, leaving the front SUV more for looks.

Once the two guys pull out of the driveway, Isabella walks to the front door to get a better angle to see them leaving the property for a little bit longer. Isabella watches as they leave, each moment goes slower and slower, mixed emotions, changing quickly, feelings, adrenaline up and her heart rate is pounding. It is probably something minor, Jack is always extra precautious and always making sure he is one step ahead in case anything unexpected happens. Isabella feels safe alone in the house set back from the road. However, the sense of danger is in the air, ever since Jack drove away with the property owner from across the street. Is it a set up to lure away the man of the household to leave Isabella all alone in the house for a break in to take her to extort more money out of Jack? There are no neighbors who would be able to even hear her scream nearby. Her mind runs with thoughts of what could happen. Isabella does know that Jack over the years has tended to hide problems that are going on so that she doesn't stress about it. In recent years, Jack has been more open with Isabella when something is troubling him, his business, their relationship, anything really, but it took them a long time to get to that. Isabella's mind is still flooded with what ifs, is this the mafia or an organized crime club in this area that Jack is dealing with? What extent of illegal and criminal activity are they capable of? Isabella puts her jeans on, a work jacket, boots and then she walks to the gun closet. She grabs the hunting shotgun and makes sure it cocks then loads correctly, checks for shotgun shell ammo, put two in the chamber, places four shells in her side purse. She puts a pistol holder on her hip, loads the pistol, puts it in the holster on her hip, opens the drawer to the side of her bed and pulls out her folding cutting knife. Isabella walks around the inside of the house, checks to make sure each window is shut, makes sure each door is locked. She closes the curtains because if they are open, it shows too much inside of the house to give away Isabella's position in case there is a situation. Isabella proceeds to the second floor of the house where she has two views of the property to front and the back of the house. To the front she can see the driveway and, in the back, can see behind the house. It allows an entrance to an intruder without her seeing ahead of time if the intruder approaching to the sides of the house. Isabella writes a note in her cell phone to ask Jack to install security cameras around the house for the future. It is very rural, and criminals play differently in the country, there aren't many people around and the criminals will wait till the house is empty to break in to steal belongings.

Isabella stays upstairs of the house awaiting Jack to get back from his drive and meeting, about an hour passes and Isabella sees the two SUVs pull into the driveway, once Isabella sees its Jack in the vehicle in the back, she walks downstairs and unloads the guns, puts them back where they were, puts the knife back in the drawer. She goes and unlocks the front door, then pulls the curtains back to where they were when Jack left the house. Isabella watches Jack come to the front door of the house and as he gets closer, she opens the front door to let him in. He walks expressionless, Isabella can't tell what mood he is in.

Isabella: Everything okay?

Jack: (Not looking at Isabella, but looking out the front door toward the end of the driveway to across the street where the cattle of his stays at) It is okay

Isabella: (wondering what: It is okay means) Where did the old man go?

Jack: (Still looking out the front door toward the cattle farm) we dropped him off at his house first

Isabella: What was it like there?

Jack: I have no words for what happened, but I don't think I want to be around these parts much longer. Raise these cattle, one run, finish this group of them that is it… Would you be disappointed if I put this place up for sale?

Isabella: Why Jack? What happened?

Jack: I don't do business like this, not even in New York City when I ran a trash company. If I was going to pay someone, a neighbor, a business, a competitor, I would always get something in return that would benefit me as well. That is business even with extortion, this however… This is just plain corrupt. City official says pay me $10,000 or there throwing an old man in jail? That is just the start, next time they are going to push even more. I don't think we have a future here in this town (looking down while saying this), I could be wrong, but maybe you have a better feeling about this area? I heard great things up north about this area, but I am not sure about this now, after today.

Isabella: I wrote down a note when you left today, I was awake. I watched you and him leave driving down the driveway. Once you left, I grabbed the shotgun, pistol, and a knife. I locked all the doors and checked that it was secured. I haven't done or felt that way in quite some time Jack. I did not have a good feeling when you left, there was something in the air. I went upstairs to look out for intruders entering the property. I could only see the front and back of the house from there, I was going to ask you tonight at dinner if you could install cameras. I don't think you should be here alone by yourself and if you are, maybe, you can install cameras so at least I can help watch the property and you to make sure your okay when I'm not here.

Jack: Yeah Isabella, I don't want to be around this area anymore either. Going to finish out the cattle here, perhaps sell some of them off early and list the property for sale this coming summer when the housing market goes up in value because of peak season. It's just real sad,

I think this is a turning point in our lives Isabella. Throughout the years we have accumulated wealth and for you and me, it's normal to us. To people who just meet us they don't know all the work that we have done through the last ten-twenty years, we don't even make much money to be honest. It seems to be rare if we even make a profit in what we do. If we do make a profit, what sets us aside is that we put the profits aside or reinvest it in ourselves and just over the course of years we have become wealthy. Our cars aren't flashy, our money is mostly in our properties and our businesses. But I think moving forward, we need to watch out for our family, each other and tighten down on our security, close our social circle a little unfortunately and reevaluate who is on our side in life to help us grow.

Isabella: It is a lot to think about and we don't want to make a mistake, but that man who was able to access us at World Equestrian Center the other day, that man is irritational, has done us wrong before and is untrustworthy. Jack, if you add it together, we are worth about $5 million - $10 million on any given day between business values, properties, and our miscellaneous assets. I think we could be under a threat at any time. I know this sounds bad, but in other countries I could see someone killing over $10,000. I know crime is more regulated in the Unites States, but I could still see someone killing in an attempt to get $100,000.

Jack: You are right one hundred percent Hun. I hate to say it, there is no real solution on how to protect us more. Just to be careful I guess, maybe it is just the times everyone is going through that we are feeling this way, I think it should pass. For now, this is what we are dealing with and tomorrow it may be different.

Isabella: how long until you want to go back to Ocala, Florida area?

Jack: Oh, I am ready any moment!

Isabella: You want to go home tonight? I have nothing going on. I checked in with the manager up at Saddlebrook property already for the day, she just said they were running low on hay stock, I already placed the order for more hay. So, I'm caught up on everything, responded back to parent's lesson emails, but the manager has been taking good care of it, so I haven't had to do too much in that department.

Jack: Yeah! I'm down to leave tonight! (Laughing while responding) another trip through the night? Sounds adventurous!

Isabella: Yeah, its nice not having any traffic and maybe we'll break down again, so we get to cuddle again!

Jack: Yeah, that doesn't sound like a bad time! Let me check in with the insurance company, I am going to up the insurance limits on this Virginia property and the cattle business across the street in case anything goes wrong while away. What time do you want to leave you think? I am going to check in on the truck little bit too, just make sure we don't have to pick up any parts to fix her up a little more.

Isabella: I'm ready whenever you are.

Jack: Do you want to leave around 4pm? It's still early in the day, I'll call the insurance agent while looking through the truck, shouldn't take more than an hour or two. If we leave around 4pm we could stop at a Valvoline oil change place to have them do an oil change and check the truck too, then after that we could stop at a restaurant to sit down and get eat food!

Isabella: Sweet, can I find a place for us to stop at? Please please please! Are you picky what I pick??

Jack: (Jack starts laughing, Isabella is so funny, the difference between a woman and a man as to what they look forward too in life is much different!) Yeah! Anything works, just let me know what you think I should wear so I fit in when we get there!

Isabella: I got you! Yay, I'm excited!

Isabella and Jack packed up their house and belongings that they had at The Plains, Virginia property and started their way towards Ocala, Florida. They make it safely, taking their time through the nighttime to make it there the following morning. Stopping to enjoy their time together, the night drive allows for less traffic, a clear roadway, less drama, faster travel speeds and it is nice to be awake when no one else is. Sometimes the hard work is done when no one else is awake. Sometimes the most precious moments in life are not at extravagant events, but traveling through the night, running on coffee to stay awake and wearing sweatpants & PJs to be comfy in the car ride there!

. . .

Isabella and Jack make it safely back to Ocala from their brief The Plains, Virginia visit to settle a business development that occurred. The two settled back into Ocala to finish their winter goals.

. . .

Isabella and Jack finish their horse show and racing season in the winter to complete their goal of both competing for the winter to advance their skills. The season started off great and joyfully, but slowly went into a dark period of their relationship. Before, a dark period would work against them, but this time, it strengthens their relationship and brings them closer together. The bond and trust between them have grown, confidence has remained. They are moving forward in life. As their relationship stays strong, it seems like every other force that could come against them is. They are struggling to make their way in life right now. Their skills are fresh, but they do not have any race or show plans after the winter, it seems like their career is at a standstill. It isn't like they are doing bad in life, it isn't like anything too drastic has really changed to hurt or harm them, but the mood has shifted.

The momentum moving them forward and their surroundings that has boosted their energy in a positive and supportive way seems not to be there anymore. The direction of their lives has changed course. Just overnight, it seems like a darkness fell over them, ever since Jack got in the Black SUV to pay off the $10,000 bribe, it seems as if they have been stuck in a fog. The outside forces that have been coming against them have put the couple on the defensive side which has been an odd feeling. Perhaps the couple's personal connections can feel the defense mechanism that has automatically kicked in since the SUV payment day.

As the couple near the spring season, the house that Jack & Isabella rented in Ocala for the winter season, the lease is coming up for the month and they are to go elsewhere. Isabella and Jack decided to go back to the Saddlebrook property at the end of the month to come up with a plan to move forward in their life. They agree to go North at the end of the month to the Saratoga Springs area, without stopping to stay at The Plains, Virginia on the way there.

The taste of that entire town (The Plains, Virginia) puts a gross taste in their mouth where it makes them nauseous even thinking about it. It is just such a weird thing that has shifted the couple's entire mindset. Owning land and real estate over time has always been one of the greatest ways to success, retirement, investment, and long-term benefits. But one neighbor has changed their entire perspective and the odd thing that happened is word must have spread that Jack and Isabella paid the bribe to keep their cattle farm in business. It seems as if people talked about it or just the universe has put Jack & Isabella into a system where people can feel what happened to them in that town. While Isabella & Jack went back to Ocala, Florida, people started coming up to the couple and talking to them about issues that neighbors have started about their own properties.

Now, it isn't just Isabella and Jack who have had a major concerning issue about one of their properties, but they have heard dozens of stories of people who have approached them about issues they have had on their own properties. It has put the couple in a much different position in their life, not knowing what all this new information about all these agricultural issues surrounding this industry they have been in for years now. It seems to be putting fear in the couple. Moving forward they are not sure they even want to own any real estate anymore, as for how much of a liability it can be as a property owner. Unsure if it has always been like this or if there has been a modification to the real estate industry which could happen. Real estate is a business, and the business market is evolving and one of the quickest changing things. This real estate thing Isabella and Jack have been questioning almost everyday whether they should keep or sell all of their real estate holdings. The properties that the couple owns right now at this giving time is the house in The Plains Virginia, the Saddlebrook property near Saratoga Springs and the residential rentals near the Saddlebrook property which Jack bought for his retirement when he sold his waste management company from the New York City. Jack did already sell his apartment that he had in the city and the last thing related to real estate that they have in holdings is Jack's cattle across the street from the house in Virginia. Isabella does own a fleet of 12 horses personally at the Saddlebrook property, some sale horses/some lesson horses/then her own horse. Liquidating, dial back, regrouping to plan and execute the next step is what Isabella and Jack are planning to do it seems. They haven't exactly said this to one another, but they both are getting the same emotion that this is a necessity as all the information that has come into their inner circle has created self-development for each of them. This new information has changed their mindset and it is hard to comprehend in such a short time with a lot going on around them. They are taking time to settle down, after a long winter competing to decide for the next direction for their lives. As Isabella and Jack go North back to Saddlebrook, they look forward to getting back in the swing of things.

Jack hasn't been back to the Saddlebrook property in quite a while now. As he pulls into the driveway in his truck, he has Isabella in the passenger seat of the truck. As they pull into the driveway, Jack goes slow at the entrance and parks to the side of the gate. Jack looks at Isabella as he brings the truck to a stop and puts it into park.

Jack: Did I ever tell you about the property when I first bought this place?

Isabella: No, I heard stories from the grape vine where I was training but not actually what it was like, just rumors.

Jack: Do you remember that Black Porsche I had?

Isabella: Yes of course

Jack: Well, when I first bought this property, the driveway was so uneven I could barely even get the little car onto the property, I tried to make it as far as I could into the property taking this driveway, but the farthest I could get was where we are parked now. Each day I would come here to work when I first bought this place, I would park the Porsche right here and walk up to the cabin up top.

Isabella: That is a very long walk.

Jack: It is about a 5,000' long walk on the driveway to the top and I believe it is a 500-foot elevation difference from where we are parked here at the bottom to the top of the property. The reason why I remember is because of how good of shape I got in from walking up and down this property so much.

Isabella: What made you buy this property?
Jack: It was so long ago, but I wanted to just ride my dirt bike here and I wanted to try to build a log cabin here out of the lumber. (Laughing when trying to explain his reasoning) I bought it knowing it was only land. I found out that the property was a horse equestrian property years ago only after I bought it here. It seems like buying this property brought its own customers and community the second I bought it. It put me into an entirely different world creating new connections and relationships with everyone up here. I walked to the top to find out there was already a cabin at the top. I was kind of mad about it because I wanted to make my own from scratch. I realized it was a blessing that the cabin was already there because I have no experience when it comes to building and it would have come out terrible. I don't know if you remember my ex, whom we saw down in Ocala, but she saved my life up here.
Isabella: Really? Yeah, I know who you are talking about, but how did she save your life?
Jack: When I first bought the property, I was going to demolish the house that's at the top, but the locals didn't seem to want that, and

the house started to grow on me. At first, I would stay at the hotel nearby each night, but after a couple weeks I was too tired to drive to the hotel, the fifteen-minute drive at the end of the day. Most nights after working on the cabin, I would just fall asleep in the living room on the old furniture that the cabin came with. The condition of the house now is nowhere close to what it was when I bought it. There were a lot of structural issues in it that had to be tended too, but it all took time to make fixes. One night, when I was sleeping one of the support beams fell from the ceiling and it pinned me underneath it. I was stuck underneath the beam, halfway through the floorboard my body was crushed against for a few days. I was in and out of consciousness, was losing my mind and I came to terms with my life that I was going to die underneath the beam that fell. There was no electricity yet in the cabin, I remember that when the sun went down, I would lose all the light in the living room, except for one night there was almost a full moon which kept it lite enough to see the surroundings around me. At night, when the sun went down, it would get dark quick. Before all the construction we did on the property to grow it, it was just the cabin that was close to being dilapidated. The nature and the wildlife were very active here. It took a long time for us to overcome the wildlife here, as the animals outnumbered the humans.

 At night, when the sun went down the coyotes would come out. You first heard a howl, and then across the property or across the valley after a few minutes another coyote would howl back. Sometimes, it seemed as if they were just checking in to see if there was any company in the area, so they didn't feel so alone in their nightly adventures. On some nights, it seemed like the howl would be to summon to each other to meet up, as when the howl happened not only one would return the greeting but many from different angles and from miles. When there was more action, you could hear the echoes and the repeats bringing together this animal community of coyotes. I could hear the different tones in the howls, sometimes it may have been a territorial thing, where they were fighting over areas, perhaps coyotes were fighting over a female, or they were each suppose to stay within their own area to find their own food to eat. It seemed like they communicated to achieve an even playing field for all of them. The most interesting night, I heard the oddest howling, more of a yipping, yip, yip noise. I remember, just plain silence and then a whining screech of death from a large animal, which lasted about 10 seconds and then went completely silent. The screech stopped quickly, and it must have been a coyote communicating to the neighboring territories that a good kill was gotten. It was yipping with joy, and the neighboring coyotes came quickly. It seemed like it was a ritual or something. I remember that I tried to remain as calm and silent as possible because there was power in the group that they had, and I didn't want them to know my presence. The coyotes surrounded the house, I think the coyote that got the kill might have been a young coyote and it was its first good kill. All the other coyotes seemed to be howling and celebrating the kill, it was like there was a coyote party celebrating this young coyote in becoming an adult. Either kind of a coyote initiation ritual to adulthood or perhaps the valley was hungry, and they were rejoicing for the size of the kill that fed a lot of them for the night, so they weren't hungry any longer. After days of being stuck in the floorboards pinned by the fallen beam, I remember the sun coming up over the horizon waking me up in the morning and a little bit of time passed. My time dimensions in my head were way off. I was losing track of my natural clock in my mind. I know it was still morning as the sun was still in the view of the window, I could see out of and not above the house. I heard someone driving up the driveway, I don't think that at this point anyone else besides me has driven up the driveway. I heard someone driving up the driveway and I had a glimpse of hope. I heard footsteps minutes later, on the front porch of the house and I yelled for my life. Luckily, they heard me, I asked for them to come inside. She came inside and looked at me in this vulnerable position. I requested her to grab the car jack out of my truck and she put the jack underneath the beam freeing me from being trapped against the floor of the cabin. I know she isn't looked upon favorably right now because of what she did, but many years ago when I first met her, she was my angel.

That was my ex-Isabella who saved my life. It was a lonely place here, it was empty, there were no people. Her and I started this place, looking around we have maybe 100 people coming in and out of the property on any given day. We brought light to this place and made it successful. We carried out a task that most people would not even dream of doing. Just looking back up this driveway, it reminds me of every day of the work put into this property. It is a great feeling. I'm not sure about moving forward with the plan for this property, but its yours now and whatever you feel is fit for it, I am sure you'll make a great decision. (Looking over toward Isabella as he stops talking)

(Jack ends his story that he was telling Isabella about the property)

Now this is probably not something you should talk to your significant other about. It is never a good idea to bring up an ex-significant other, but in all honesty sometimes the past is meant to be remembered, to learn from it.

Isabella and Jack have just made the trip from Ocala Florida to the Saddlebrook property, located by Saratoga Springs, NY and are still sitting in the same spot where Jack started telling the story of when he first bought the property. Before continuing up the driveway, Jack looks over at Isabella once again.

Jack: Sorry I told you that much information about that story. I haven't remembered that about this property in a long time.

Isabella: It's okay, I like hearing about this place. This place has helped a lot of people through a hard time in their life. It gave people motivation, a place of peace and brought families close together.

Jack smiles and looks away toward the driveway. He starts up the truck and shifts it into drive to go up the driveway. As they get near to the top of the property, a couple kids run up to the truck running along with the truck driving slowly as they get to the house.

Kids: Isabella!!!!!!!!

Isabella leans down to say hi to the kids, with a few tears of joy as being greeted by the younger horse riders who missed her. It was such a touching moment, Isabella looks at Jack to see if he is seeing the precious moment.

Isabella: Hi!!!!!! How have you been? Been riding horse?

Kids: YESSSS! How was Florida Isabella! I saw videos of your competition; I hope I can be just like you one day!

Isabella: I missed you all so much, it was a great time, but I couldn't stay away from you guys!

Kids: Here Here Here!!! Can I show you what I can do now??

Isabella: How about tomorrow? Jack and I still must unpack.

Kids: (All as a whole respond) AAAAAWWWWWW

Isabella looks over at Jack.

Jack: I'll unpack! Go check it out Isabella!

Kids: YAYYYYYY (As they run away toward the barn where they keep their horse) (Isabella follows the kids running) (The kids are yelling) ISABELLLAA HURRRYYYYYYY

Kids: Look you see how pretty his hair is! I have been standing on this stool and can groom my horse all by myself now! Oh my gosh Isabella!!!

Isabella: What! What!

Kids: Check this out, I taught the horse this awesome trick!

The kid somehow taught the horse to put its head down, and the kid straddles the horse's head, and the horse knows exactly when to lift its head up. As the horse lifts its head up, the kid is lifted onto the horses back. The kid moves across the horse to the seated saddle position.

Kid: Done! Isn't that awesome! I taught him how to do that by using carrots!

Isabella: Wow now that is crazy, I have never seen that one before!

Isabella sits in the barn for a couple hours, sitting and listening to all the stories, injuries, falls, new relationships, the kids, new teachers at school, their sports, the football games at their schools, the new horses, the barn drama. As the night starts slowing down at the barn, the sun starts to go down. Isabella says goodbye for the night and that she will be back tomorrow to see everyone. Isabella walks into the house and Jack is sitting on the couch with his laptop on his lap.

Jack looks up to Isabella as she walks in the front door: Hey You, how is it being back?

Isabella: I love it (laughing) its like we are home Jack.

Jack: Yeah, they love you here

Isabella: What are you up to?

Jack: I am supposed to be going through emails from what was missed on the road and go through paying the bills, but I am looking through photo albums from the wintertime. Oh! Do you want to come over here and see them? There are great ones of you.

Isabella walks to the fridge to get a bottle of water and then leans against the chair that Jack is sitting in to look over his shoulder at the laptop.

Jack: I meant to ask you, are you cool with me staying with you up here? It is your property here.

Isabella: Yessss please! I never want too not be with you. I love you being here wherever I am Hun!

Jack: I think I might stick around these parts for a little bit

Isabella: Yay!!! Thank youuuu! Want to come down to the barn with me tomorrow am?

Jack: ha-ha (laughing) yeah, I'll go, as long as I don't make you nervous there (winking at Isabella when saying this)

Isabella: Oh, please I can compete in front of thousands, I'm sure I can handle the pressure of riding by you

Jack: Just messing with you!

. . .

Jack and Isabella enjoy the next few months together at Saddlebrook with the team there and have a great time together. While Jack was at the Saddlebrook property, he and Isabella listed the house for sale in Virginia with a local realtor there. It is a beautiful property and at once had showings with interest for purchase. In the course of the next week, they received a good offer for the property. They accepted the offer. It is time for them to clean out the house, selling what is there for furniture, throwing it away, moving it to Saddlebrook or putting it away in storage. Ever since the time when Jack and the neighbor who watches his cow farm had to go pay someone $10,000 so they wouldn't arrest the neighbor. They ended up not liking the property anymore. It was sad that it happened, Jack and Isabella in the back of their minds both knew that the man who got the money out of them will be back again soon asking for more money. The event ruined their perspective on the area, and they no longer want to be affiliated with owning a property in that town. Jack did consult Isabella on her moving plans for the property, they concluded that Jack would go away for a week to stay at the house in The Plains, Virginia to pack up for the sale. They decided to rent one big U-Haul box truck to put all the furniture they wanted to bring to Saddlebrook. The rest of the unwanted belongings in Virginia, Jack rented a thirty yard dumpster from a local garbage company to throw it all away. Jack heads South toward the property to spend the week there packing everything up. When Jack gets to the property of theirs in Virginia, there isn't too much he wants to keep. Remembering back why he bought the property; it was to spend some time away from Saddlebrook and to be more centrally located for the GNCC national dirt bike racing series that he was competing in. Jack looking through the property to clean it up for it to be sold, he realizes that it is basically a bachelor pad as he doesn't need to take any of it home. Most of the furniture in the house is cheaply made and he didn't spend too much time on any fancy interior designs for the house. Jack realizes that it doesn't really matter how much he cleans up the house anyways, because the sale price will be the same. This means that either way Jack and

Isabella will be getting paid the same amount. Jack moves a little faster when packing up the place now that he realizes that it really doesn't matter at all. Material possessions don't matter to Jack anymore as the only thing he cares about is Isabella. She is the only thing in his life that gives him peace. Jack is almost finished packing, he hears his phone ringing and checks the screen of his phone, it's Isabella who is calling:

Isabella: Jack, they are here taking the horses.

Jack: What do you mean? Who are they?

Isabella: The town zoning agent again, the police department and some out of state horse haulers – His tag on the back isn't from New York, he's running a flag of convenience for trailers, a Maine License plate on the back.

Jack: Where are they taking the horses?

Isabella: I'm not sure, they are telling me they are going to arrest me if I don't load the horses on the trailer for them.

Jack: Is there anyone there with you?

Isabella: No, I'm the only adult and 3 children are here, the manager is off already for the day.

Jack: What do you think we should do? Can you make sure to remember the license plate of the horse trailer?

Jack: There not telling you where there going or anything?

Jack over hearing Isabella yelling in the background with the tone of survival instinct in her demeanor: HEY! You don't dare touch our horses; you can't do that.

Voice in the background: little lady we can do whatever we want here, step down or you will find out.

Jack listens to the noises of what sounds like Isabella's phone being knocked out of her hand and falling to the ground.

The phone line gets disconnected, Jack's thoughts are running wild, bringing flashbacks of his lowest points of his life and survival instincts. In one 30 second phone conversation, Jack knows his life may never be the same if those horses are hurt or not returned. Emotions of helplessness cast a shadow of gloom over Jack, and nothing can undue what was just done at the Saddlebrook Farm.

Owners have the right to protect their property, but in today's day and age constitutional rights and farmers rights are rarely considered. Even when filing a civil rights violation done to a property owner by a local zoning agent or the police department, very rarely will the Department of Justice even respond back to the request for consideration to listen to a property owner's argument.

Jack knows for a fact what is being done at Saddlebrook at this moment has been swept under the rug and not done according to the adequate legal process which consists of multiple hearings, witnesses. A two-year case builds up and then ruled in favor of the local zoning agents by a judge of the civil courts. Saddlebrook has been sent two letters from the town that Saddlebrook is in and Saddlebrook's lawyer responded with case law nuisance laws about this matter in the state of New York. Quoted paragraphs allowing the operation of their property according to zoning by laws. Not to mention the property has been grandfathered in because the property was doing the same thing in business before the town was even incorporated as a legal entity.

Five minutes have passed since Isabella called Jack about the trespassing by the Town

Zoning Agent, Police Department, and the horse hauler. Jack tries calling Isabella again, hoping she is free and away from whomever was harassing her. The phone call Jack makes to Isabella to try to contact her for further information goes straight to voicemail. Jack sits there staring in midair trying to think everything through, but the only concern on Jack's mind is the woman he loves Isabella and his soon to be born child Isabella is carrying. A few moments pass, Jack stuck in awe, frozen in time, and dumbfounded. The shadow of gloom over him grows immensely, a feeling of hope being taken from his body aging Jack by 25 years in a matter of seconds. Unable to move, stuck and feeling every ache, groan, injury that Jack has been ignoring for the past 15 years. Jack's phone rings from an unknown number, the only thing he knows is a New York City area code.

Jack gathers himself, bringing him back to the reality that he is here and realizes a feeling that he has never thought of is that if Isabella isn't here in life with him, he must still go on and function somehow. Trying to remain calm and collected. He answers the phone to the New York City number that is calling.

Jack: Hello, this is Jack.

Georgina: Jack, have you heard anything from Isabella? This is her friend Georgina.

Jack: When was the last time you talked to her? It has been about 23 minutes now since she called, her phone goes to voicemail right now.

Georgina: I just got a text message, there was no cell service when she messaged me, the message said she needed my help asap there, and then it looked like the message cut out and she just pressed send to me.

Jack: The Zoning agent, Police Department and a horse hauler came and took horses from the property in front of all the kids there saying there is a zoning violation, I have no idea what to do. She wrote down the license plate number for the hauler, it's a Maine Trailer plate there running as a flag of convenience. I got in my truck, I'm heading up that way now since she called, the gps says I'm about 6 hours out. I would call someone there on site, but Isabella was the only adult there at the time she said. I don't have any of the contact files for her business, it's probably in tack room office. Have you ever dealt with something like this in your family?

Georgina: I'll try to get the plate number checked and let you know what I find out. Hopefully Isabella is okay.

Jack: Thank you, my phone is on, let me know.

The drive to the Saddlebrook property is one of the hardest drives Jack has ever made. It is going by very slow, and his mind is constantly replaying the chain of events on how he could of acted differently to change the outcome that is occurring at the moment. Jack is perplexed as he did everything by the book, how you are supposed to act. Got a letter from town about the property, he made the minor change requested by the town. Jack had his lawyer respond formally to the town. Jack was assured by his lawyer that it was a very minor issue. It doesn't make sense at all that anyone has the authority to trespass on private property and take another man's horse. Jack's phone rings from a restricted phone number:

Jack answers phone: Hello, this is Jack.

Unknown: Jack, it is Isabella

Jack: Isabella, is everything okay?

Isabella: They arrested me for interfering.

Jack: What police department? Do you know? You're not in the wrong on that, I would have reacted probably ten times worse than you. Are you good Hun?

Isabella: Yeah, I'm fine, I believe I was charged with misdemeanors, they are taking me to the Saratoga Springs police station. Can you write this down? Do you have a pen and paper on you?

Jack: What is it?

Isabella: Plate number from the horse trailer that took three horses from Saddlebrook.

Jack: Ready for it

Isabella: 7-7-3-0 TD

Jack: Got it

Isabella: truck has a dot number on the side write this down.

Jack: Ready, go for it

Isabella: 4-4-1-9-9-5-0-0

Jack: Got it, good. We're going to get the horses don't worry. I am on the way up that way so doesn't worry everything is going to be okay, take a deep breath. Your friend Georgina is helping us as well. She didn't have cell coverage when you texted her and was concerned when you didn't get back to her. I am going to give her the numbers, she has someone to look them up. Is there anything else you can remember about the interaction that I should write down?

Isabella: I don't think what they did was legal. They wouldn't answer any of my questions and I am not sure if it's a competitor behind this, but this can't be right.

Jack: I agree too, the zoning violation that they are referring to was corrected and fixed months ago, almost 6 months now. I asked the lawyer if he received a response from the town's attorney about the letter, they sent a long time ago. He got confirmation that it is all cleared up and resolved.

Isabella: Not sure what is going on.

Jack: I'm not sure either. Are you okay in there? Is it cold?

Isabella: It's just me here, it isn't too bad. Thanks for asking.

Jack: Okay, you should be out in no time, I'm going to forward the numbers for the plate and DOT number. I just don't want anything happening to your horses. Bail should be posted hopefully within the hour, and I can get you an uber away from there if you want to call me. Do you need to stay on the phone with me? Or is it okay if I get off the phone to start making those phone calls?

Isabella: yeah, go, go, go thank you Hun!

Jack: Miss you.

. . .

Jack calls his old supervisor from the business he used to have.

Jack: Hey!

Supervisor: Hey boss! Long time no talk!

Jack: Sorry to bug you but remember when that new hire got a dui in one of our trucks at work on a Monday at 1pm and totaled two other vehicles.

Supervisor: Well of course! You and I are the ones who had to fix putting his truck back together!

Jack: Remember, we went and bailed him out of jail, do you remember what business we used to post the bond?

Supervisor: Who got arrested?

Jack: Isabella!

Supervisor: I thought she left you for the guy who bought your company, my new boss?

Jack: Yeah, she did! But I got back with my Ex before that one, her name is Isabella too!

Supervisor: Interesting, I want to hear this story when you get it settled. Can I text you the bond businesses number?

Jack: Yes please! And lunch when I'm in the city next? (New York City)

Supervisor: Of course, boss! Text coming your way now, be safe out there Jack!

The next call Jack makes is back to Georgina.

Jack: Hey Georgina!

Georgina: Whatcha got for me? Any news?

Jack: Isabella was arrested for interfering there saying she should be bailed and out of jail soon.

Georgina: Wow, did you get the plate numbers?

Jack: Yes! License Plate: Maine – 7 – 7 – 3 – 0 – T D

Jack: We got a DOT number too if you want it might bring up something

Georgina: Go for it, I'm ready for DOT.

Jack: its 8 digits. 4-4-1-9-9-5-0-0

Georgina: Keep your phone on you, be back in five minutes.

The phone rings again in five minutes.

Jack answers the phone.

Jack: Hey, how are you?

Georgina: Good

Georgina: The tag on the truck isn't coming back as anything. My agent tells me that this type of person will register a trailer under a corporation with no officers that are real and then dissolve the company once the truck is registered. So, we are not getting anything back the trailer tag.

Jack: Okay.

Georgina: However, luckily the DOT is more regulated for truckers then the actual registrations are. The DOT numbers that you have given me come back registered to a farm in Texas right on the border of Mexico.

Jack: What does this mean?

Georgina: We ran the properties owned by the registered farm trucking company that the DOT numbers come up as. The property brings up some old cases of animal abuse, specifically horses. Jack, I do not think you have high probability of getting those horses back. It doesn't look good.

Jack: Georgina, I'm not into horses. I ride dirt bikes. What do you mean animal abuse?

Georgina: The types of places that receive those complaints that they have gotten are usually commercial. In other countries, horses are shipped to slaughter for their meat. It sounds like that's whose hands the horses are in right now.

Jack: So there in Texas?

Georgina: No not exactly, what it means is the horses were called in to get moved, but you got an illegal shipper who the town overlooked the paperwork, as they do not have the legal authority to run a plate number on a vehicle. Right now, the horses are most likely at these people's property near by where they are waiting to have enough horses to fill a horse hauling tractor trailer. They'll either go to Canada or Mexico or shipped in container overseas. Where they go is dependent on the going rate for the meat at the given time.

Jack: The horses are going to be eaten? How in the world do I break the news to Isabella about this?

Georgina: I can tell her.

Jack: What should we do about it? How do we find them?

Georgina: I would call the town, have your attorney call the town and try to figure out where they are now before they leave the state. They can be very tricky people and they can switch hauling trailers, different license plates, switch trucks as well, different drivers. It is a major business.

Jack: Okay, I'll call the lawyer and call the town. Thanks for the information.

Georgina: Sorry I had to be the bearer of this news Jack.

Jack: Your help is appreciated.

. . .

Jack calls the police department of Saratoga Springs

Jack: Hello, how are you. My name is Jack, and I am calling you on a recorded phone line. I am one of the owners of Saddlebrook. Your department was previously at our property where you took horses off our property and arrested one of the owners it sounds like.

Dispatcher: How may I help you?

Jack: My lawyer is going to be pulling the police report and all if any call logs or notes for this incident, but do you have any information on where the animals are going as they are not ours. It is a commercial horse boarding facility, and the owners are very concerned of where their horses are going.

Dispatcher: All we can give you is the phone number to the shipper who picked up the call when we put it in to the towing company.

The dispatcher tells the phone number to Jack, he writes it down and then calls it at once. Jack calls the towing company that the police department called to move the horses: Hey, how are you? Are you the towing company that hauled the horses away from Saddlebrook?

Tow guy: No, we do not haul horses, we've never gotten a call like this before. The town put us on the spot saying they would cancel our entire towing contract if we couldn't find them a horse shipper today for the job to move horses.

Tow guy: We went to a horse hauling bid post website and then called for three different bids, I gave the middle bid to the police officer whom we were in contact with. The police department put in the order himself for the town, we are not insured to haul animals or any type of livestock at this time. Would you like the phone number that I gave to the officer?

Jack: Yes of course

Tow guy: I didn't give you this number, and if I must testify under oath, this conversation did not exist you got it?

Jack: noted.

Tow guy: And for whatever it matters, if I had known you or had your phone number I would of called you ahead of time to give you a heads up, but our hands are tied. There isn't much towing up this way and that town is 70% of our entire business revenue right now. The towing company representative reads off the horse hauling company that the towing company gave to the police department. Jack makes the call to the horse hauling company. The phone rings and goes straight to voicemail. Perhaps the driver is on the other line. Or what if the phone is just a burner phone and it was turned off?

Jack calls the towing company back again, because the phone number must not have been right

Jack: Hello, can you double check the phone number you gave me for the horse hauler?

Towing guy: yeah, do you want to read it back to me?

Jack reads the phone number back to him.

Towing guy: yup, that's the right phone number

Jack: well, it goes straight to voicemail. Do you want to try calling them yourself?

Towing guy: hold on, stay on the phone.

Towing guy holds his cell phone and dials the number on the ad he gave the police department to call for the towing of the horses. The phone call also goes straight to voicemail. The towing guy puts his cell phone back in his pocket and picks up the cordless shop phone in the towing company's office. Towing guy: It went straight to voicemail for me as well. I tried calling the number from my cell phone. Do you want to try calling the police department again so they can try to figure it out? We're not the ones who did the tow, all we gave was a phone number off a website that we found to the police department. The police department would be responsible to make sure they were properly insured and to do their own due diligence on hiring the company.

Jack: Thanks for trying.

Jack works while driving trying to find the horses for Isabella after what happened up at Saddlebrook. He tries calling the police department, his lawyer, Georgina, the towing company, the phone number that he was given for the horse hauler, and he is coming up short with no answers. It is as if the horses have vanished without a trace, lost in faulty paperwork fallen through the cracks. Jack doesn't know what to say, doesn't want to say too much or too little. This will have a very large effect on morale on not only the love of his life Isabella, but all the other children and families involved in Saddlebrook.

Saddlebrook is no longer a safe haven to enjoy life and escape from the everyday rat race that everyone is in. A place where people can come to forget about their problems for a short moment.

Jack is finally arriving back at Saddlebrook where Isabella is now.

Jack first words talking to Isabella seeing her for the first time since his return from The Plains Virginia and the Saddlebrook theft of horses.

Jack comes up to Isabella and hugs her.

Jack: You look great today

Isabella: Thank you, but I know you're lying. I have been crying all day today.

Jack: You always look perfect to me Hun.

Isabella: I haven't heard anything about the horses, I'm guessing it isn't good.

Jack: I wanted to talk to you about it, but I am not sure how to communicate what I have learned, I also don't have an update on the horses as well.

Isabella: Georgina filled me in on her perspective what she thinks may have happened.

Jack: What do you think of everything that has happened?

Isabella: (Jack and Isabella are now seated on a bench that overlooks the outdoor riding practice arena where once was joyful to ride in every evening afterwork. Isabella looking down to the ground at her feet, she lifts her head staring straight into the arena) We are never going to see the horses that they took ever again.

Isabella: They took a 12-year-old girls' horse that she bought with her own money, her first horse. They took Judy and your ex-girlfriend's horse, and they took my horse that I've had since he was a colt. (A young male horse)

Jack: Oh gosh. Have you told them yet? Your horse you placed at Land Rover Kentucky with, right?

Isabella: Yeah, that is the horse they stole from me. I haven't told anyone, but everyone already knows. The 12-year-old, I haven't heard from her, but I am assuming she is devastated and feeling the same way I am.

Isabella: I am not sure if Judy has heard anything, because your ex-Isabella isn't in the loop up here anymore, no one will talk to her here and everyone has her blocked on social media because of what she did to you.

Jack: When do you want to let Judy know?

Isabella: I was going to call her around 5pm tonight, would you want to be the one to talk to her about it? She seemed to always have a connection with you, she doesn't talk to me very much.

Jack: Yeah, I will go over to Judy's and talk to her. Are you doing okay though Isabella?

Isabella: I don't know what life is anymore. Someone came here and stole from us, and they are saying they are allowed too. I just don't know anymore about anything. I have been on the phone today to find a new barn that has enough open board to take the horses in. I've ruined my name in the horse industry and no one will ever board their horse with me ever again. I must break the lease of ours on Saddlebrook Jack, I hope you won't leave me.

Jack: I would never leave you. We are in this together and you have blessed my life beyond understanding. I don't care about things Isabella, I lost touch with material objects many years ago. All I want in my life is to be surrounded by people I love, and I can't imagine going through life without you.
Isabella leans over and places her head on Jack's shoulder.
Jack: You are holding it together. I don't know how you are either. The only thing I wanted to say is that the kids here who are young and growing up, are always going to remember this. What happened here right now. It's important that we handle it correctly as this could be a very traumatizing experience for them.
Isabella: Yeah, they look up to us, so they are going to see how we are reacting first. I am hoping to have all the horses moved out of here tomorrow morning.

. . .

(A few days pass, the Saddlebrook property has been quiet ever since the horses moved out of the property the next day. Isabella has been in her bedroom since the night of the robbery when the three horses were taken from the property)

Jack: Do you need my help with anything?

Isabella: I was going to put in a new gate at the beginning of the driveway with a key code to come in and out. We are still not sure who is behind who has been reporting our property to the town for their issue with the horses that were here.

Jack: I can do that for you Hun, we will make this place secure. I talked to my parents, and they said we can stay with them until we figure out what to do next. What do you think? I'm open to staying with your parents too but figured it should be coming from you to ask them.

Jack notices that Isabella hasn't checked her phone in a few days and that it isn't even in the same room as her. It's been left in the kitchen on the counter by the fridge, left uncharged, it has died now. The phone was ringing with missed calls, text messages and miscellaneous communications from friends and family. Isabella has been in the bedroom for the last couple of days lying down, looking out the window to the outside. She hasn't eaten anything since she went to lay down.

Isabella: I haven't seen our parents in a long time. It has probably been a few years since we went to visit them. (Isabella turns away from the window very slowly for the first time in a couple of days) How long do you want to see them for? (Looking at Jack while responding)

Jack: There is no timeline for anything like this Hun, I think getting back to our roots, seeing our family would be one of the best things for us. I don't care how long we are with them for! I think it'll be nice to see everyone!

Isabella: Jack (looking at him), do you think they'll ever find our horses? I feel so bad that I couldn't protect them, I had no control, I couldn't do anything.

Jack: I think they'll find them!

The chance of finding these animals is slim to none unfortunately. The company that took the horses are professionals in their industry and do it for a living, finding horses to send to slaughter. For them to admit that they took the horses and then return them to Isabella and the riders at Saddlebrook. It would open them up to major legal consequences and the thieves would never do that. The last chance of Isabella getting the horses back is if they are adopted by an organization that specializes in saving horses from the slaughterhouse.

Isabella: (reiterating everything she just previously said) I tried everything I could Jack. I tried everything I could.

Jack: It's okay, you did great Hun. You did great. (walking closer to Isabella, sitting down on the bed next to her. Jack lays down and puts his hand around her as he cuddles up next to her) Tomorrow we can start packing to head out of here if you'd like.

The young couple continue to lay next to each other for the next coming hours in silence. Both look out the window until the sun starts to go down and once it becomes dark, they remain in bed until the next morning as the sun comes up.

Jack walks to the kitchen to get a glass of water for Isabella and a banana. He brings it to the bedroom to give to Isabella for when Jack wakes her up. Jack sits on the edge of the bed on the other side of her from where he was cuddling up next to her when they slept. Jack nudges her shoulder to wake her up.

Jack: Hey baby, it's a new day. Wake up baby.

Isabella opens up her eyes and looks up at Jack, her eyes empty of hope and her body slow moving. This is the first time Jack has ever seen Isabella's body moving so slowly.
Jack: (Jack looks away but leaving his arm on her side, rubbing her slightly on the side of her waist) Baby, I need you
Isabella: (Looks up toward Jack but doesn't say anything)
Jack: I know we are going through a lot, but I just can't have you letting go babe. We are going to get through this, but we just need to get out of the house Hun. This house isn't going to help us staying here with the memories of what happened.
Jack notices that Isabella's eyes have a little bit of light shine through them. He thinks this is his chance to try to shed just a glimpse of motivation into her.
Jack: Be right back, I'm going to go check the mail quick
Jack power walks out of the bedroom with excitement that Isabella is being responsive right now. He walks to the kitchen and grabs Isabella's phone to put it on the charger. He leaves the phone on the charger to charge just enough to get a few battery percentages to stay

on. Jack leaves through the front door to buy some time so Isabella doesn't think he is lying to her. He slowly takes the drive down to the bottom of the driveway to get the mail and then drives back up to the house to return to Isabella, walking through the front door of the house. As he goes through the front door, he tip toes to where the cell phone is charging and sees that it has come back on and is showing 7% battery life now. Jack knows this is not enough as it'll be depleted real quick the second it is unplugged from the wall charger. Jack goes slowly to the bedroom with the mail still in his hand so if Isabella looks over, she'll know that he just went to the mailbox. Jack says to Isabella:

Jack (To Isabella): Hey babe! (A little bit of pep in his tone now, with more energy behind him with his quickly devised plan to try to motivate Isabella again) Do you want a coffee? I was going to make one quick for myself. Do you still like it the same as before? Coffee, two creams, two sugars? I could mix in a shot of baileys alcohol in it too.

Isabella: Yeah, I'll take one.

Jack: (So excited with excitement now, Isabella is actually talking again, this is huge, he is on a roll, let's see if he can keep the energy up and makes sure to not touch on any sensitive subjects) Awesome! Coming right up!

Jack knows that suspense will be on his side right now. Jack knows that Isabella likes this coffee, and he hasn't made it for her in months, Jack knows for a fact that Isabella is very turned on right now that he remembers what her favorite coffee is when she's on vacation. Jack knows that she will most likely be focused on receiving the coffee for the next 10-15 minutes, so he goes as slow as possible to make the coffee being made lasting the maximum amount of time to let the phone charge. Jack's plan is to bring Isabella's phone into her bedroom where she is lying down and when she sees the notifications from all her friends and family who love her it'll motivate her to start talking to them again.

Jack finishes up making the coffee and unplugs Isabella's phone from the charger and proceeds toward the bedroom door, as he cracks open the door slowly. He notices through the crack that Isabella is out of bed and standing up. He watches through the crack of the door as she is standing next to the closet. Her body is weak compared to at her peak, still very athletic, but Jack has never seen her moving without a pep in her step, with lack of motivation and low energy. As jack is about to open the door, his mind starts to wander, and he can't tell who she is anymore. Everything he knew about Isabella had changed during the last couple of days, her as an entire person is entirely different. Jack is unsure what to think of this. Playing defensively, as perhaps Isabella's taste in man could have changed completely as well. Perhaps now Isabella has an instinctual need of a more protective type male partner now, Jack is questioning himself. He wasn't able to protect his wife when she was in need, he let everyone at Saddlebrook down.

He plans to play defense here and let her lead the conversation. Jack walks slowly toward Isabella who is near the closet with the cup of hot coffee in his hand. Jack forgot to bring Isabella's phone into the room as he was so thrown off by seeing her standing and walking around. Jack gets close to Isabella, and she turns around towards him as he gets closer to her. Jack reaches out to hand Isabella the coffee. As his arm is half extended, Jack makes eye contact with Isabella to see if she is going to accept the coffee. Isabella has a much different look in her eyes and a much different demeanor in her voice as she says.

Isabella: Coffee on the nightstand.

Jack looks puzzled at first but doesn't say anything. Jack stood there for 2 seconds as he had no idea what she was about to say. Jack about to move towards the nightstand, before he could lift his right foot to move his right foot forward to start the walk, Isabella then says:

Isabella: Now. (Not yelling, but a stern order as if Jack is a new hire stable help being ordered to muck stalls for the first time with no experience.)

Jack moves as fast as he can, he has never been ordered by Isabella to do anything in their entire relationship together. He gets to the nightstand by the side of the bed and puts the coffee down without spilling any. Jack stands still not knowing what he is supposed to do after, waiting and hoping Isabella will lead this conversation as this is unchartered territories here.

Jack, still looking down at the coffee, begins to look up and starts to turn around to look back at Isabella. Before he can turn his body just a little bit, Isabella says to Jack.

Isabella: Don't turn around. Look away from me. Take off all your clothes Jack.

Jack still standing there. Jack takes too long to start undressing the same as he did with the coffee demand. (Jack's mind isn't used to this and it is a lot to comprehend)

Isabella: Take off all your clothes and give them to me. Now (the order is sterner and louder than before)

Jack hurries to undress and starts to turn around to look at Isabella. Before he is turned around, Isabella says:

Isabella: No keep facing the wall, don't look at me. I will tell you what to do next when all your clothes are off.

Jack takes off his clothes and is holding them in his hand, not making another move or saying anything.

Isabella: give me your clothes now.

Jack hands over his clothes to Isabella. She starts to walk out of the bedroom holding Jack's clothes, closing the bedroom door behind her with Jack locked inside the bedroom naked. Isabella thinks to herself that she hopes that there are no clothes for him to put on in there. She wants him to stay as he is. She locks the bedroom door with Jack inside the bedroom.

Isabella makes her way to the kitchen and grabs the bottle of Bailey's Alcohol that Jack had out on the counter and opens the lid. Isabella takes a big gulp of the bailey's alcohol as she hasn't drank it like that since she was in college. Isabella proceeds to check her phone on the counter. She sees missed calls from family, friends, people she hasn't talked to in years that read about her in the newspaper. Isabella responds to one message from an old equestrian friend who she doesn't trust and usually tries not to answer her phone calls or text messages. The only reason Isabella makes some contact with her is due to professional reasons in her horse-riding career as they are both sponsored by one of the same companies and attend some of the same shows. So, Isabella keeps the contact with her, mostly in case Isabella forgets something when competing on the road. She can lean on her riding friend for an extra piece of horse tack or something she may need related to the equestrian industry. Isabella has the slight suspicion that this friend has had feelings for

Isabella's husband Jack. This friend of Isabella's, she tends to only come around to talk when Jack is there. When Jack isn't around, this woman is no where to be found, but when Jack comes around to see Isabella or is accompanying Isabella at a show, this woman will suddenly try to be best friends with Isabella and smiling being an entirely different person. Isabella hasn't eaten or drank barely any water or food in the past few days, the one large gulp of Bailey's Alcohol gets Isabella beyond tipsy almost to being drunk. Isabella sees a missed call from this so called "friend", and Isabella decides this should be the person that she should call out of all the people who have tried to reach out to contact her.

Isabella hits the button to call back this missed call from the person who has been drooling over Jack in plain sight. Literally, in front of Isabella at every horse show and event that Jack accompanies Isabella too.

The phone starts to ring as she makes the outbound phone call.

The woman who has the hots for Jack answers the phone.

Isabella: Hey girlfriend! I just saw your missed call, how have you been?!!!

Isabella holds her phone to her ear and starts walking toward the bedroom door, she opens the door and sees Jack underneath the blankets. Isabella walks over to the bed where jack is laying underneath the blankets and stands next to the bed side and takes her right hand to grab the blanket while she maintains a clear conversation on the phone, her left hand is holding the phone to her ear. Isabella holds the blanket tighter and starts walking back toward the closet bringing the blanket with her, so that Jack has nothing to cover up with. As Jack is laying on the bed naked, Isabella is standing near the closet on the phone talking to her "friend" and is looking at Jack dead straight in the eyes.

This is the phone call conversation that Isabella is having while she looks at Jack laying there naked.

Isabella (Into the phone to the woman who has been trying to get with Jack at all the horse shows when she runs into Isabella, and he is there): Oh yeah! I'm not sure when the next time I am competing down there in Florida. I'm up in Upstate New York right now.

Jack's Admirer who is on the phone with Isabella right now: Is Jack there with you in Upstate, New York or did he stay down here? Isabella walks toward the bed and sits on the edge of the bed close to Jack. Isabella places her hand on Jack's crotch, not moving her hand on his private parts but just leaving it placed there to tease him.

Isabella to the person on the phone: Oh yeah, Jack is up here with me right now.

Jack's admirer: Oh, that's so awesome! You two are the perfect couple! I can't wait to see you guys again.

Isabella feels that Jack has been teased successfully and she moves her hand away from his private parts.

Isabella: Yeah, I love Jack so much, he is so hot, I can't wait to see him naked again.

Jack's admirer: (Silence over the phone as she doesn't know what to say next)

Isabella: (laughing) I'm so sorry, I shouldn't of said that I was just thinking out loud.

Isabella smiles at Jack and moves her hand back to Jack's private parts to tease him.

Isabella's friend starts talking again about her next show she is excited for.

Jack's admirer (to Isabelle over the phone): Oh no your right, he is a good-looking man! I have never seen him naked though.

Isabella: (laughing in response) Yeah, the things I am going to do with him tonight.

(Isabella winks at Jack while she says this over the phone)

Jack's admirer: I wish it was me doing that to him.

Isabella: (laughing) yeah, he has a lot of admirers, I'm so glad that he is my husband. I am going to go downstairs to do the laundry now! Do you want me to call you before the next show I am thinking of doing?

Jack's admirer: Yes Please!

Isabella: Okay! Nice talking to you! Be safe out there!

Isabella hangs up the phone and stands up away from the bed. Isabella goes to where she puts Jack's clothes and walks back to over by Jack and Isabella says to Jack.

Isabella: Get out of bed.

Jack stands up besides the bed.

Isabella throws Jack back his clothes that he was wearing before she told him to take off everything.

Isabella says to Jack: Put your clothes back on.

Isabella looks at Jacks body as he puts his briefs on.

Isabella: Now put your pants back on.

Isabella smiles as Jack is left teased.

Isabella walks back over toward Jack and kisses him and says I love you.

Isabella: (Completely changes her mood back to submissive and innocent) Is it okay if I drink the coffee you made me now baby?

Jack: Yeah definitely

Isabella: I can't wait to sleep next to you tonight, Jack, is it okay if we start packing in the meantime and then tomorrow morning we go stay at my parents' house?

Jack: Yeah, that sounds amazing babe. How much should we pack? How long are we staying away you think?

Isabella: Pack everything you need, and we'll come get the rest if we sell the place.

Jack: Do you think we will ever be coming back here again?

Isabella: After what happened, no horse boarding facility can ever happen here again babe. It would be our fault if the same thing that happened here happened to the next horse boarders. I don't think our insurance company would cover the same issue again, leaving us open to a lot of liability.

Jack: Okay babe, yeah whatever you think works for me! I think you have a valid point too with the insurance.

As the couple move from the Saddlebrook property, Jack is driving the truck from the property, he looks in the rearview mirror when coming down the driveway. He is thinking to himself that he is questioning his sanity with everything that is going on. He remains calm, collected, and quiet. Inside Jack's mind, he is thinking about what just happened yesterday with Isabella. Was that just a one-time thing or is everything in the bedroom going to be like when she had him stuck in the bedroom naked with no clothes? Jack is questioning what really happened at the property with the town when he wasn't there, and Jack is wondering what the aftereffects long term for the loss of Isabella's best friend are. (Her horse)

In the following weeks and months after leaving Saddlebrook, the property's shape begins to change so quickly with the property being vacant. With it being located so far out in a rural area, it seems the wildlife takes over much quicker then if it was in the city. The animals, bears, deer, birds start coming out more and more at night. The coyotes start coming back at night. The trimmed manicured lawn with every edge cut maintained on a weekly basis starts to grow out, taking shape of a wild field. The bottom of the fences can no longer be seen, and the sides of the structures started to grow mold and moss on the side where sunlight doesn't shine on it. Jack and Isabella decide to let nature take over the property and to leave it in despair to make a statement. They felt that it wouldn't be a good idea to put money into a town that treats their residents so poorly. As the couple were visiting Isabella's parents for the next couple of months, one of the families reached out to Isabella regarding the stolen horses from the property. It was a very sensitive subject for all of them as Isabella had one of her horses stolen and sold for slaughter as well. The family that approached Isabella: Family: Hey Isabella, we have contacted an attorney to sue the town and police department for damages for what happened. We are hoping that you will join the lawsuit because we feel it would help us achieve a stronger case to help us win.

This was an email that was in Isabella's emails from when she was asleep for a couple of days after the incident. When Isabella and Jack got to their parent's home, they responded with: Isabella: We will stand by you guys one hundred percent. Please include us in this lawsuit to be one of the parties suing them with you. Thank you for reaching out.

Isabella has seen the lawsuits that Jack has been through in his career and is familiar with what an actual trial entail. Sometimes a court case can be closed and settled within 2 months, sometimes it takes them five years. When Isabella accepts being on this family's side to help them in this case, 9 out of 10 people in life would decline to do this. Isabella and Jack are basically saying we back you and we are going to help you no matter what it takes or what the outcome in the lawsuit might be. This is an admirable thing and not many people these days would do such a thing to help someone out.

As the court case transforms, certain things are brought to light about the situation. It turns out that the Saddlebrook Farm was storing manure piles too close to the neighboring property. It also turned out that the town was wrong as well for not approaching enforcement of a zoning violation in the right matter. As they were both, semi at fault, what really led to the lawsuit being filed is the fact that animal rights activists' groups joined the lawsuit when they heard of horses being sold and when the local police department arrested Isabella for trying to defend their animals. These local activist groups got the surrounding fire departments and police departments to protest at the town hall. This was a huge thing for the community, Isabella didn't know it was going on at the time. She was in bed, unable to move from grieving lying down. Jack got a message on his phone about what was going on, but he didn't look into it too much and was mostly focused on his wife's mental state of mind. The incident at Saddlebrook made national news as for the Civil Rights Violation that occurred. A federal lawyer came in to take over the case for Saddlebrook and the families moving it from the state of New York civil system in the national court system on a Federal Level. When the federal lawyer joined the lawsuit, the lawyer did its pro-bono (meaning for free) for the families of Saddlebrook. Another key benefit of moving this lawsuit to the federal level is that the local municipality could barely afford to hire a lawyer to represent them in this matter, let alone the recurring court fees to the lawyer and filing fees to keep their representation. This change to the federal court put a lot of pressure on the local municipality to reach a settlement quick so it wouldn't have to cause the town to go bankrupt or to take out a loan/ municipal bond to pay the ongoing legal fees. The Saddlebrook case ultimately got each family involved, including Isabella, over a million-dollar settlement for each of them, because of everything that went wrong. It is important that every system has the proper checks and balances.

The families each did different things with their settlement money. It was kind of an unspoken thing in the equestrian industry what each of them did with their settlement. Most of the families mostly lived modest lives, were already decently wealthy middle-class individuals and used the money to better their futures. Mainly to do things like pay off their house, put the money in savings, pay off debts and to set themselves up for success. Jack and Isabella's household were debt free already before they got their million-dollar settlement. They don't have the highest income at the Saddlebrook Farm, but they have a very passive income. They are in the positive's income wise each month putting a little more away towards savings.

Isabella and Jack didn't touch the Saddlebrook settlement money, but this conversation changed what they did with the money.

Jack to Isabella: Hey baby

Isabella: Hey, how are you?

Jack: Good, in love with you <3

Isabella: (Laughing) ha-ha thank you babe.

Jack: I was wondering what to do with our settlement from the case, what did you want to do with it?

Isabella: Savings? What did you want to do for work without Saddlebrook?

Jack: I mean I don't like paying taxes, we could donate it to a good cause, and it should offset our taxes from the donation write off for the next 5-10 years?

Isabella: Hmmm, yeah taxes are no fun! What organization were you thinking?

Jack: I was thinking of the organization called Farmer's Rights, it's a 501c3. They lobby to protect farmers and their rights. Basically, what we went through at Saddlebrook was because there was no one protecting farmers and their rights, so I was just thinking it would be a good fit.

Isabella: Do you think we should invest the money instead?

Jack: I mean it is only a million dollars, I think that it would affect our name as individuals more in a positive way than if we were to just put the money into real estate. I think if we donated this money, it could make a national name for us. I think our last name could potentially go down in history to be remembered forever. Not only that but it'll always be remembered for what we stand for in the equestrian and dirt biking industry.

Isabella: Would it be okay if I slept on it for the night to think about it?

Jack: Yeah of course! I haven't reached out to them or anything, take as long as you want to decide.

Isabella: If you really want me to decide to donate the money, I think you should prove it in the bedroom tonight.

Jack: (laughing) okay babe I will see what I can do!

The next day Isabella and Jack decided to donate their settlement money from the Saddlebrook case to a national farming rights organization. Before making the donation, they made sure to check with their lawyer and accountant to make sure that it puts them in a great financial position for the coming years of their lives. Their lawyer called the organization to ask them what they would need to bring to make the donation, if they preferred online with an ACH payment, a check or cash in person. The organization was really surprised about this donation and stated that they have never received a donation that large before. The organization asked if they could take Jack and Isabella out to dinner to discuss it more. Jack's lawyer set up the meeting at Lake George, New York at a little restaurant on the lake there.

. . .

Isabella is excited to dress up in a cute dress, she straightens her hair, curls her eyelashes, and puts on her cowgirl boots. Jack puts on a button-down long sleeve shirt and jeans with some nice shoes. It is a couple hour drive from Isabella's parents house, but this is one of their favorite spots to vacation and the time of year is perfect to enjoy the view. The couple plan to stay in Lake George for the weekend to enjoy their time there. They are enjoying their time at their parent's and Jack's parent-in-laws house, but it is tough being back home for so long. It seems when you get back to your parent's place, you tend to fall back into the children and parenting roles. Isabella and Jack are very grateful to be able to relax and unwind with less responsibility. They have both been on their own for many years now. Isabella and Jack have both been responsible for teams of people, complex businesses and maintaining large properties. That alone is a lot of pressure and responsibility that weighs on you. Sometimes being free in life is what lets you live. Being free to do what you want helps in your sport; when you're competing, you must clear your mind entirely to focus on the moment at hand right there in front of you.

Anyways, Jack and Isabella are excited about the dinner at the Lake George restaurant with the farmer's rights non-profit they are donating too! As they are walking up to the restaurant, they see the people they are meeting, a man, and his wife. Jack noticed that they were looking at them as they were approaching where they said for them to meet, and Jack said to the man:

Jack: Hey! Are you meeting Jack and Isabella here by chance?

The man: Yes! Nice to meet you. This is my wife!

Isabella shakes his wife's hand.

Jack: This is my wife Isabella

The man: Awesome! Do you guys want to get a table?

Jack: Yeah!

The man and his wife wave to the waitress doing the seating at the restaurant for the evening. The four of them walk toward the table through the filled tables of people eating in the restaurant to the back of the room to the deck that over looks the lake. The temperature is perfect, not too cold, and not too warm. As they sit down the man from the farmer's rights group starts to talk:

The man: How was the drive? Are you guys hungry! Do you like it here? It's an amazing view!

Jack: (Looking over at Isabella quick before responding) Yeah, we love it here! We haven't been here in I don't know, maybe four years. Yeah, ha-ha we figured we wanted to save our appetite for dinner tonight, so we are hungry. It wasn't too bad of a drive for us, perhaps 2 and half hours to get into town here.

The man: Awesome! Glad to hear. I read about you guys online! Quite an impressive resume. Pro dirt biking and professional horse riding?

Isabella: (giggles a little)

Jack: Yeah! We try to compete when our schedules allow!

The man: So a professional dirt biker and equestrian, I am just curious where you have $1 million to donate to a charity? Sorry to ask you, but I am very curious.

Jack: Oh sure! It is a valid question! This money was won in a lawsuit from a settlement. It had to do with our civil rights being violated on one of our farming properties. We don't really need the extra money, well it wouldn't hurt, but I think your organization would be much better appreciative of the money. Your organization would also be able to help others by putting this money to work to develop a strong team to help stand by farmers to allow them to continue what they do.

The man: Wow neat! So, do professional dirt biking and horse riding really pay that good that you don't need a million dollars?

Jack: Oh it pays alright, our main source of income comes from other things

The man: What else have you guys done in the past?

Jack: (Looks at Isabella) Isabella has been running a very successful horse training facility now for over 8 years and I made most of my money from a waste management company I owned for about 10 years when I was younger. Now, I pretty much live off Isabella's successful business.

The man: Wow, now that is a neat life! Yeah, did you hear about why I started this nonprofit to help farmers?

Jack: No, why did you start it?

The man: My father owned a farm when I was a little boy, and it was in our family. The local town took the farm from my family, they said they were allowed to take it due to "zoning violations" but once they took it from my father, the town sold it to be developed. They parceled off the land, selling it in tiny quarter acre lots to build homes on. It left my father devastated. My father is gone now, and I have always remembered that. He wasn't good with paperwork and realtors, he was a farmer, so I made this organization to help families keep their farms from being taken away from them.

Jack: Yeah, tell me about it, seems like that is all towns want is to take landowners rights and their land away from them.

The man: I assume that you have the same mission as I still do. I read about what happened at the Saddlebrook property. That is one of the saddest things I have heard.

Jack: Yeah, took us a while to even leave the house after that one, it's crazy how lawless it is, and unregulated small-town politics can be. I just started realizing that in recent years.

The man: Yeah, tell me about it. We have many great lawyers who can really utilize this donation to help improve the business industry for farmers. And these lawyers support what we are doing, they charge us way below the going rate for their time. Jack, this donation is going to make a change and help a lot of things in the farming industry. Don't tell anyone, but this is the largest donation my organization has received, we will put this money to good use. If you'd like to be involved as well, you're welcome to join the board of directors' meetings. If your ideas are accepted by the other board members, I am sure we could have a seat at the board for you as well.

Jack: Thank you, I am glad the money will be helping others

The man from the farming rights organization stands up to shake Jack's hand.

The man: (With a sincere smile on his face) Thank you Jack, we are going to let you two be, if you're okay with that?

Jack: Yeah, yeah that's great! Do you know when and where I can check the board meetings when they are?

The man: Yeah, tomorrow we'll send you an email with this year's board meetings! I hope to see you there.

Jack: Yeah! Thank you, guys, nice to meet you.

Isabella: (Saying goodbye to the man's wife) nice meeting you!!

As the couple walk away from the table, Jack and Isabella start talking. They notice that the couple go to the cashier to cash out the dinner and it looks like The Man just paid for the bill for their table for the night.

Jack says to Isabella: That guy has a presence for sure, something about him. I could tell they are going to do some serious things with this money.

Isabella sitting to the outside of the table closest to the water, she leans close to Jack putting her head on his shoulder and holding his left arm with her left hand from across her body.

Isabella: I hope he does Jack (In a sincere tone) I hope he does. (Saying this as she watches the fire in the lantern on the table flicker from the flames and the boats in the background on the lake)

Jack: He's going to, you think they wouldn't mind if I did go to those meeting, he was talking about? It would be interesting to see what is going on, I don't have much to do anyways, my cattle down in Virginia are pretty much all sold off and you run your business top notch all by yourself.

Isabella: I'm not sure, but I mean he did seem like they would appreciate you being on their team.

Isabella leans back toward her chair to be able to look at Jack.

Isabella: He could have been just being nice though, maybe go to a meeting and see what it feels like when you are there?

Jack: Yeah, that's a good idea!

Isabella: Where do you think the meetings are at?

Jack: Oh, that's a good question (laughing), I think they might have flown here to see us tonight to be honest. I would say they probably have a different meeting in a different state around the country once a month, because it is a national organization.

Isabella: makes sense, different territories for their different farms that they are helping.

Jack: Yeah, wonder what the schedule will look like! I would like to go to at least one of the meetings coming up.

Isabella: I would go!

Jack: Sweet! Awesome, it's nice having you come with me.

The rest of the night Isabella and Jack decided no to discuss work anymore, as this weekend they are in vacation mode. The two are so success and career orientated that, it's like when they don't have to work, they don't know what to talk about. The conversation resorts to talking like 12-year-olds. Isabella was talking about what her horse was doing the other day.

Isabella: Jackkkkkk, my horse was so bad! (laughing) it snuck in to get hay and then rolled on the hay bale to scratch an itch.

Jack loves to listen to these equestrian stories, because for a glimpse of time, nothing else matters. This moment in time, no problems they are going through matters. Nothing they have been through together matters, nothing that will happen in the future matters. The only thing that matters in this moment is how nice the evening is and that they are both here tonight to be with one another.

Jack talks about his dirt bike and how he feels like he has been out of shape because he hasn't been doing all the races this season.

Jack: look at this! Look at this hun! (He is saying this quietly to Isabella to not create a scene) (Jack points to his belly) when I was racing all last winter, I swear! I swear! I'm not lying, I had an 8 pack on these abs!

Isabella: (Laughing) I wasn't saying you were lying ha-ha.

Jack: I think I got to race dirt bike more, ughhh I just feel so gross! Blah blah blah, it'll get me in better shape again!

Isabella: Ohhhh another race series? When are you thinking!

Jack: hmmmmm, any ideas? Different country?

Isabella: hmmmm, Europe? Haha I don't know, did you like Florida the winter we were there competing?

Jack: yeah, was fun! We have friends down there too.

Isabella: Do Florida for the winter coming up again? I'm not competing yet, but soon I'll get back to it, I'll go to watch your races though!! I love going to those.

Jack: Sweet! Yeah, I'll start training soon and riding more, winter Florida race series! I'm pumped!

Isabella: (Leans into Jacks shoulder and holds his arm again, looking towards the water again over the lantern's flame) Yeah, it's going to be great baby

Jack puts his arm around Isabella rubbing her back.

Jack: What time are you waking up tomorrow you think?

Isabella: I have no plans, what about you?

Jack: Hmmm 6am!! Coffee and do you want to go to this hotel we can walk to in the morning? They rent Kayaks for $10 for 3 hours. There's a cool place I can show you on the kayak! There are cup holders in the kayak for our coffee too!

Isabella: Yeah, I'm in! What time is it now? Oh yeah, it's still early, we should be awake by then.

Jack: We can also sleep in a little too. We could just go when we wake up haha , I didn't mean to make it sound like we have to wake up exactly at 6am. Coffee sounds so good though

Isabella: I can't wait Hun.

. . .

The next morning, Jack wakes up to Isabella, she brought him coffee in bed with a burst of energy.

Isabella to Jack: Hey!! Do you still want to go kayaking??

Jack rolls over to his side and responds to Isabella.

Jack: haha (laughing) I didn't think you wanted too, but yeah, it'll be awesome out there

Isabella: Yeah, I was in an odd mood last night, was just a lot on my mind. I miss my horse. But that didn't have to do with the kayaking, I'm super pumped! I already put my bathing suit on under my clothes and put on sunscreen, I was wide awake at 4am today!
Jack just starts busting out laughing.
Jack: Haha, this is awesome, ugh, (Jack looks to the side of the bedroom where he can see his reflection in the mirror) Oh gosh, I am not ready to go out yet, I look like I got hit by a freight train!, ughhh as he moves to get out of bed (reaching out with a smile to Isabella for the coffee to sip on) gosh I do not look ready to start my day, is it cool if I shower real quick?
Isabella: Yeah! Is it okay if I sit in the bathroom while you shower to talk to you?
Jack: Yeah, for sure! (Jack doesn't mind but he is a little out of it still being early in the morning, he is also wondering if there is anything specific that they have to talk about) Jack walks to the shower turns it on and gets in, Jack leaves his coffee on the back of the toilet that is flat, it's within reaching distance of the shower.

Isabella: Hey! What did you think of last night's dinner?

Jack: (As he is reaching out of the shower to grab his coffee to take a drink of it) Oh, the food last night, I did like the chicken wings I got, kind of wish I got the fish though because it was on the lake so it would have probably been good there. I also wish I had a cocktail to drink too last night, but I just had a glass of water, trying to get in shape a little more for the next race season coming up. What did you think of your food at last night's dinner?

Isabella: I meant the conversation with the couple we went out to eat with. And my food was good, I can't remember what I ordered, think I did a glass of water too with the meal, I was eyeing the dessert pie though. It looked good!

Jack: Oh, the conversation, how did the conversation go? Hmmmmm. (Thinking to himself) I can't really remember what we talked about. How did you think it went? I mean it was just like them thanking us for the donation I think, they were nice I thought.

Isabella: Remember they invited you to the board meetings of the organization?

Jack: Oh yeah! Did you look to see the board member meetings for those? I thought that was nice of them to include us inviting us to go to those meetings! Means they like us!

Isabella: Jackkkkkk you should pay attention when you talk to people! They were saying they were going to send an email to us for the schedule, they'll probably send us an email on Monday I'm guessing when they get back in the office for the week.

Jack: Oh yeah, I'm hoping one of the meetings is in Montana, it looks so beautiful there! We could go to Montana to see what it is like and then go to the meeting. Would you come with me?

Isabella: Yes! I know a good photographer there actually. Do you want to do a couple's photo shoot there with the mountains in the background? Our anniversary is coming up soon too! It would be a perfect picture for our anniversary couple photos. We are getting old!

Jack: Sweet, I can wear my cowboy boots! So, all in favor of Montana soon whether a meeting is there or not? Have you ever been there?

Isabella: I have never been there; I am totally down to go! Looks pretty too.

Jack: Gosh, I love this warm water (Talking about the shower), ugh well time to turn it off. (Jack turns off the shower, grabs the towel to start drying off and stepping out of the shower)

Isabella goes on to talk about her friends, what they are up to and how everyone from the Old Saddlebrook property is doing and where everyone went off too. Everyone really went to many different places, some pursued dreams in different states, some moved to the neighboring barn nearby. But no barn compared to Saddlebrook and Isabella stays in touch with many people who visited their old barn.

Jack goes into the bedroom to the closet to figure out what to wear for the day, Isabella follows Jack and is now sitting on the bed while he goes through his clothes that he brought with him for the trip.

Jack: What do you think I should wear for the day? Hmmm. We already got our coffee so no more coffee, oh do we need to stop for breakfast. Do you think we'll stop for lunch too after kayaking? Hey Isabella, what do you think I should wear today?

Isabella: I mean this is what I am wearing, what do you think? Flip flops, swimsuit, and a t shirt?

Jack: Yeah, that sounds like a simple enough outfit for the day! Beach outfit I like that.

Jack puts on his swimsuit, finds his flipflops and a t shirt to wear. Jack checks to make sure he has everything that he needs for the day.

Jack says to Isabella:

Jack: Are you ready to leave? I finished my coffee already; I think I have everything.

Isabella: Yeah! (Isabella stands up and walks swiftly towards the door) Where are we going! I'm excited to find out this secret place of yours

Jack: Alright cool, yeah, we can walk or drive there either or

Isabella: Oh, can we drive! Let's take the long way so we can see what this city is like too.

They both get into Jack's truck, the drive is only a half mile away, it's walking distance. Instead of going straight there, Jack continues to drive North on Lake Shore Drive which turns into more of a rural area but follows along Lake George, it's a beautiful drive and as they drive North, Isabella gets a beautiful view from outside her passenger side window.

Once they go about twenty minutes North, Jack turns around to go to his secret kayak place that rents Kayaks cheap!

Jack: I used to come up here once or twice a summer to race dirt bike in the NETRA Hare Scramble series and I remember this one race was about an hour from here. I would stay at the Lake Crest Inn; a nice little hotel and I would sneak my dirt bike into my hotel room so it wouldn't get stolen from the back of my truck when I was sleeping.

As they pull into the parking lot, you can see how each hotel has its own entrance and it overlooks Lake George in the background.

Isabella: I don't see any kayaks here.

Jack: Yeah, that's what's awesome about it, they hide them so the tourists don't come here, I hope they still do it, they hide the kayaks and the paddleboards under the porch by the water.

Jack says to Isabella:

Jack: Be right back, I'm just going to walk in, I doubt they remember me, but I'm not trying to act like a tourist. I think the owners here are from a different country too, they go back to their home countries during the off season and then come back during the busy season, at least that's what they were telling me a couple years ago. They were pretty nice to me; they definitely saw me bringing in my dirt bike inside the hotel room and they didn't say a word to me about it. Some places get mad about that.

Jack leaves the truck and shuts the door of the truck behind him, he walks into the Lake Crest Inn that he used to go to.

Jack approaches the front desk and says to the staff member:

Jack: Hey good morning, guys, I haven't been in here in a little bit, but I was wondering if you were still renting kayaks by chance. I remember, I used to always rent them here from you guys.

Front desk of hotel: (looks both ways, side to side before responding) don't tell anyone, it's usually just for the guests. We are getting $10 for 4 hours for each of them.

Jack: Awesome, how do you want payment?

Front desk of hotel: $20 cash and $20 cash for deposit, when you bring back the kayaks and life jackets, you get your $20 back, we hold onto a picture of your ID while you're using them.

Jack: Awesome no problem, here's my ID if you want to take a picture and $40

The front desk at the hotel scans the photo ID driver's license of Jack and writes him a receipt for the kayak rental. He reaches behind the counter for two life jackets and hands them over to Jack with two ores for the kayaks.

Front Desk of hotel: Now is the time, it'll start in about 15 minutes to give you guys some time to get ready and out there. Then due back in about 4 hours, if keep it longer then four hours we charge another $20 (your deposit)

Jack: Awesome yeah, no problem! Will check in once we get back with them.

Jack walks back to his truck where Isabella is with the two life jackets, the kayak rental paperwork and the ores for the kayaks. Jack goes around the truck to the passenger door where Isabella is sitting and says to Isabella as her window is down in the truck:

Jack: We got four hours! We are ready to Kayak!

Isabella: Awesome!

Isabella gets out of the truck and follows Jack to where they get the kayaks at. They walk to the back of the property closest to the lake and walk down the staircase to the water. When they get to the water they turn around and the kayaks are underneath the back deck.

Jack pulls out two kayaks and places them half in the water and half on the land so that its ready to get in and push off to start the kayaking.

Jack signals for Isabella to get in her kayak so that he can push her off. Isabella tip toes in the water, getting used to the temperature of the water, making sure it isn't too cold and smiles as she balances the kayak as she steps onto it to sit down. She puts the life jacket on the seat to sit on while kayaking. Jack hands her the ore for the kayak and then pushes the kayak toward the open water. Once Isabella is off and started to kayak, Jack pushes his kayak off the beach shoreline and hopes in it, balancing it so it doesn't flip over. Jack uses the ore of the kayak to go to where Isabella is about 100 feet toward the middle of the lake. Jack pulls up to the side of Isabella's kayak to see how she is doing.

Jack to Isabella: How's it going?

Isabella: It's so beautiful out today, I saw a fish in the water too.

Jack: Do you want to see the beach I used to kayak up too when I used to come here?

Isabella: Sure

Jack takes the lead, maintaining a decent pace, having Isabella following behind his kayak. The beach is close by, on a kayak it will take them 10-15 minutes. Isabella and Jack stop about every fifty feet to relax and take in the scenery. The various properties along the shoreline each have their own very distinct character which Isabella and Jack talk about. The couple (Isabella and Jack) come near the beach that Jack wanted to show Isabella on their kayaks. Jack speeds the kayak up by rowing faster with the Ore in his hands as he approaches the shoreline. The kayak approaches the shoreline and moves up on the beach keeping it firm on the sand to not drift off again. The beach is very busy, Jack and Isabella are the only two who came to the beach with Kayaks and the rest of the beach goers are tourists wondering where they kayaked from. Jack gets off his Kayak and turns around for Isabella to drift onto the beach. He's ready for her to get closer to the shore so that he can pull her kayak up on the beach. Isabella and her Kayak drift up to the beach and Jack pulls them all the way up so that she can get out of the Kayak easily.

Jack reaches his hand out to Isabella for her to hold to help her get out of the Kayak. Jack says to Isabella:

Jack: Follow me

Jack walks to the back of the beach so all the tourists and their family aren't staring at them anymore.

Jack whispers to Isabella: This beach has been locked for some reason, so everyone goes around this gate on the far side over there, follow me.

Jack walks the fence line to the end of it where there is a path everyone walks behind to get to the beach.

Isabella asks Jack: Why does everyone sneak onto the beach?

Jack: I think it has been closed officially by the local town here since the covid pandemic and it never actually opened again. It's like an unspoken thing here I guess, the town says the beach isn't open, but everyone still comes here. They don't enforce kicking anyone out. Guess some things just work themselves out.

Isabella: oh okay, where are we going?

Jack: (Laughing) to the bathroom, I guess it is "shunned upon" to pee in the lake these days!

Isabella: haha, okay

Jack: it's nice to be back on land too

Isabella: we've only been on the kayaks for twenty minutes!

Jack: Potato, Tomato!

Isabella: haha (Laughing) that makes no sense, but okay!

Jack: alright we are here, be right back! I must use the restroom quickly.

Jack goes into the restroom to go pee; he comes back out after a few minutes and smiles at Isabella who's standing outside the restroom facilities.

Jack to Isabella: hey, do you want to check out the events and schedule for the area?

Isabella doesn't respond but gives the facial expression that she was interested in what they are.

Jack to Isabella: There's a little bulletin here that people post the events coming up.

Jack moves over to the bulletin, and they stand reading the upcoming event fliers coming up in the Lake George area.

Jack and Isabella enjoy their time on this beach that they paddled to on their kayaks. As they stopped to use the restroom and looked around at what was happening in the Lake George area. They walked around on the beach that is in the Downtown area of Lake George. The couple Isabella and Jack, after a short walk, they make their way back to the kayaks and get on them to make their way back to the Lake Crest Inn. The time they have been at Lake George for their Farmer's Rights meeting and their short weekend getaway is ending and as they get back to the lakeside property called the Lake Crest Inn of Lake George, they both start to realize that the weekend is coming to a close. They don't say it to each other, but they both know that Monday is quickly approaching. Isabella and Jack enjoy the last remaining hours of their weekend vacation and they don't talk about work or about anything that is going on in their life right now. But as they are back at the front porch of their hotel overlooking the lake in front of them. They sit as a young couple and in this one moment in life, it is peaceful. No matter what is going on in life, no one can take this moment away from them. The peace, the nature, the community, and the feeling of being where they are right now today is a good feeling. No words are spoken, but it is appreciated that they can relax with a free mind. They sit enjoying the view while reminiscing of the years they have been together and everything they have been through.